PRAISE FOR

News of the Spirit

"Lively . . . wise and wry tales." —*The Seattle Times*

"Some of her best work . . . 'Southern Cross' and 'News of the Spirit' are magic . . . These stories . . . glitter with insight and a sharp personal vision."

—*The Raleigh News & Observer*

"Lee Smith is a writer's writer, a teller of tales for tale tellers to admire and envy." —*Houston Chronicle*

"A thoroughly enjoyable and moving reading experience."
—*Milwaukee Journal Sentinel*

"Lee Smith has a great way of stepping aside as a writer and slipping into the skin of her characters . . . [She] doesn't so much write stories as tell stories—and darn good ones at that."
—*Jane*

NEWS
of the
SPIRIT

Lee Smith

BERKLEY BOOKS, NEW YORK

THE BERKLEY PUBLISHING GROUP
Published by the Penguin Group
Penguin Group (USA) Inc.
375 Hudson Street, New York, New York 10014, USA
Penguin Group (Canada), 90 Eglinton Avenue East, Suite 700, Toronto, Ontario M4P 2Y3, Canada
(a division of Pearson Penguin Canada Inc.) • Penguin Books Ltd., 80 Strand, London WC2R 0RL,
England • Penguin Group Ireland, 25 St. Stephen's Green, Dublin 2, Ireland (a division of Penguin
Books Ltd.) • Penguin Group (Australia), 250 Camberwell Road, Camberwell, Victoria 3124, Australia
(a division of Pearson Australia Group Pty. Ltd.) • Penguin Books India Pvt. Ltd., 11 Community
Centre, Panchsheel Park. New Delhi—110 017, India • Penguin Group (NZ), 67 Apollo Drive,
Rosedale, Auckland 0632, New Zealand (a division of Pearson New Zealand Ltd.) • Penguin Books
(South Africa) (Pty.) Ltd., 24 Sturdee Avenue, Rosebank, Johannesburg 2196, South Africa

Penguin Books Ltd., Registered Offices: 80 Strand, London WC2R 0RL, England

This is a work of fiction. Names, characters, places, and incidents either are the product of the author's
imagination or are used fictitiously, and any resemblance to actual persons, living or dead, business
establishments, events, or locales is entirely coincidental. The publisher does not have any control over
and does not assume any responsibility for author or third-party websites or their content.

The author acknowledges permission from Hal Leonard Corporation to reprint lyrics from "Tragedy,"
words and music by Gerald H. Nelson and Fred B. Burch. Copyright © 1958 (Renewed) Wren Music Co.
All rights reserved. Used by permission of Hal Leonard Corporation.

Five of the stories in this volume, some in slightly different form, first appeared in the following magazines,
to whose editors the author offers thanks: "The Bubba Stories" and "Live Bottomless" in *The Southern
Review*; "Blue Wedding" in *Southwest Review*; "The Southern Cross" (as "Native Daughter") in *The Oxford
American*; and "The Happy Memories Club" in *The Atlantic Monthly*. "News of the Spirit" (as "We Don't
Love with Our Teeth") was published in a limited edition by Chinook Press, Portland, Oregon, in 1994.

PUBLISHING HISTORY
G. P. Putnam's Sons hardcover edition / September 1997
Ballantine trade paperback edition / September 1998
Berkley trade paperback edition / July 2012

Berkley trade paperback ISBN: 978-0-425-24768-6

The Library of Congress has cataloged the G. P. Putnam's Sons hardcover edition as follows:

Smith, Lee, 1944–
News of the spirit / Lee Smith.
p. cm.
Contents: The Bubba stories—Blue wedding—Live bottomless—The southern cross—The happy
memories club—News of the spirit.
ISBN 0-399-14281-9
1. Southern States—Fiction. 2. Social life and customs—Fiction. I. Title.
PS3569.M5376 N48 1997
813/.54
97011660

PRINTED IN THE UNITED STATES OF AMERICA

10 9 8 7 6 5 4 3 2 1

Many thanks to Liz Lear for Key West information for "Live Bottomless"; to Alan Archibald for his expertise in Spanish; to Peggy Ellis for help in manuscript preparation; to Anna Jardine for her copyediting; to Liz Darhansoff for her longtime guidance and support; and most of all to Hal for his love and good advice. On individual stories, I appreciate the editing of C. Michael Curtis, Dave Smith, Bob Durand, Marc Smirnoff, and Willard Spiegelman.

The title "News of the Spirit" comes from a phrase used in a talk years ago by the wonderful writer and teacher George Garrett. I copied it down, and have always remembered it.

For Faith Sale,
my great friend and editor

CONTENTS

The

BUBBA STORIES

Even now when I think of my brother Bubba, he appears instantly just as he was then, rising up before me in the very flesh, grinning that one-sided grin, pushing his cowlick out of his tawny eyes, thumbs hooked in the loops of his wheat jeans, Bass Weejuns held together with electrical tape, leaning against his green MGB. Lawrence Leland Christian III—Bubba—in the days of his glory, Dartmouth College, ca. 1965. Brilliant, Phi Beta Kappa his junior year. The essence of cool. The essence not only of cool but of *bad*, for Bubba was a legendary wild man in those days; and while certain facts in his legend varied, this constant remained: Bubba would do anything. *Anything.*

I was a little bit in love with him myself.

I made Bubba up in the spring of 1963 in order to increase my popularity with my girlfriends at a small women's college in Virginia. I was a little bit in love with them, too. But at first I was ill at ease among them: a thistle in the rose garden, a mule at the racetrack, Cinderella at the fancy dress ball. Take your pick—I was into images then. More than anything else in the world, I wanted to be a writer. I didn't want to *learn to write*, of course. I just wanted to *be a writer*, and I often pictured myself poised at the foggy edge of a cliff someplace in the south of France, wearing a cape, drawing furiously on a long cigarette, hollow-cheeked and haunted, trying to make up my mind between two men. Both of them wanted me desperately.

But in fact I was Charlene Christian, a chunky size twelve, plucked up from a peanut farm near South Hill, Virginia, and set down in those exquisite halls through the intervention of my senior English teacher, Mrs. Bella Hood, the judge's wife, who had graduated from the school herself. I had a full scholarship. I would be the first person in my whole family ever to graduate from college, unless you counted my aunt Dee, who got her certificate from beauty college in Richmond. I was not going to count Aunt Dee. I was not even going to *mention* her in later years, or anybody else in my family. I intended to grow beyond them. I intended to become a famous hollow-cheeked author, with mysterious origins.

• • •

BUT THIS IS THE TRUTH. I GREW UP IN MCKENNEY, Virginia, which consisted of nothing more than a crossroads with my father's store in the middle of it. I used to climb onto the tin roof of our house and turn slowly all around, scanning the horizon, looking for . . . what? I found nothing of any interest, just flat brown peanut fields that stretched in every direction as far as I could see, with a farmhouse here and there. I knew who lived in every house. I knew everything about them and about their families, what kind of car they drove and where they went to church, and they knew everything about us.

Not that there was much to know. My father, Hassell Christian, would give you the shirt off his back, and everybody knew it. At the store, he'd extend credit indefinitely to people down on their luck, and he let some families live in his tenant houses for free. Our own house adjoined the store.

My mother's younger brother Sam, who lived with us, was what they then called a Mongoloid. Some of the kids at school referred to him as a "Mongolian idiot." Now the preferred term is "Down's syndrome." My uncle Sam was sweet, small, and no trouble at all. I played cards with him endlessly, every summer of my childhood—Go Fish, rummy, Old Maid, hearts, blackjack. Sam loved cards and sunshine and his cat, Blackie. He liked to sit on a quilt in the sun, playing cards with me. He liked to sit on the front porch with Blackie and watch the cars go by. He loved it when I told him stories.

My mother, who was high-strung, was always fussing around after Sam, making him pick up paper napkins and turn off the TV and put his shoes in a line. My mother had three separate nervous breakdowns before I went away to college. My father always said we had to "treat her with kid gloves." When I think about it now, I am surprised that my mother was able to hold herself together long enough to conceive a child at all, or come to term. After me, there were two miscarriages, and then, I was told, they "quit trying." I was never sure what this meant, exactly. But certainly I could never imagine my parents having a sexual relationship in the first place—he was too fat and gruff, she was too fluttery and crazy. The whole idea was gross.

Whenever my mother had a nervous breakdown, my grandmother, Memaw, would come over from next door to stay with Sam full-time, and I would be sent to South Hill to stay with my aunt Dee and my cousins. I loved my Aunt Dee, who was as different from Mama as day from night. Aunt Dee wore her yellow hair in a beehive and smoked Pall Mall cigarettes. After work she'd come in the door, kick off her shoes, put a record on the record player, and dance all over the living room to "Ooh-Poo-Pa-Doo." She said it "got the kinks out." She taught us all to do the shag, even little Melinda.

I was always sorry when my dad appeared in his truck, ready to take me back home.

When I think of home now, the image that comes most clearly to mind is my whole family lined up in the flickering darkness of our living room, watching TV. We never missed *The Ed Sullivan Show, Bonanza, The Andy Griffith Show*, or *Candid Camera*—Sam's favorite. Sam used to laugh and laugh when they'd say, "Smile! You're on *Candid Camera*!" It was the only time my family ever did anything together. I can just see us now in the light from that black-and-white Zenith: me, Sam, and Memaw on the couch, Daddy and Mama in the recliner and the antique wing chair, respectively, facing the television. We always turned off the lights and sat quietly, and didn't eat anything.

No wonder I got a boyfriend with a car as soon as possible, to get out of there. Don Fetterman had a soft brown crew cut and wide brown eyes, and reminded me, in the nicest possible way, of the cows that he and his family raised. Don was president of the 4-H Club and the Glee Club. I was vice-president of the Glee Club (how we met). We were both picked "Most Likely to Succeed."

We rubbed our bodies together at innumerable dances in the high school gym while they played our song—"The Twelfth of Never"—but we never, never went all the way. Don wouldn't. He believed we should save ourselves for marriage. I, on the other hand, having read by this time a great many novels, was just dying to lose my virginity so that I would mysteriously begin to "live," so that my life would finally *start*. I knew for sure that I would never become a great writer until I could rid myself of this awful burden. But Don Fetterman stuck to his guns, refusing to cooperate. Instead, for graduation, he gave me a pearl "pre-engagement" ring, which I knew for a fact had cost $139 at Snow's Jewelers in South Hill, where I worked after school and on weekends. This was a lot of money for Don Fetterman to spend.

Although I didn't love him, by then he thought I did; and after I got the ring, I didn't have the nerve to tell him the truth. So I kept it, and kissed Don good-bye for hours and hours the night before he went off to join the Marines. My tears were real at this point, but after he left I relegated him firmly to the past. Ditto my whole family. Once I got to college, I was determined to become a new person.

LUCKILY MY FRESHMAN ROOMMATE TURNED OUT TO BE a kind of prototype, the very epitome of a popular girl. The surprise was that she was nice, too. Dixie Claiborne came from Memphis, where she was to make her debut that Christmas at the Swan Ball. She had long, perfect blond hair, innumerable cashmere sweater sets, and real pearls. She had lots of friends already, other girls who had gone to St. Cecilia's with her. (It seemed to me a good two-thirds of the girls at school had gone to St. Something-or-other.) They had a happy ease in the world and a strangely uniform appearance, which I immediately began to copy—spending my whole first semester's money, saved up from my job at the jeweler's, on several A-line skirts, McMullen blouses, and a pair of red Pappagallo shoes. Dixie had about a thousand cable-knit sweaters, which she was happy to lend me.

In addition to the right clothes, she came equipped with the right boyfriend, already a sophomore at Washington and Lee University, the boys' school just over the mountain. His name was Trey (William Hill Dunn III). Trey would be so glad, Dixie said, smiling, to get all of us dates for the Phi Gam mixer. "All of us" meant our entire suite—Dixie and me in the front room overlooking the old quadrangle with its massive willow oaks, Melissa and Donnie across the hall, and Lily in the single just beyond our study room.

TREY FIXED US UP WITH SEVERAL PHI GAMS APIECE, but nothing really clicked; and in November, Melissa, Donnie, Lily, and I signed up to go to a freshman mixer at UVA. As our bus approached the university's famous serpentine wall, we went into a flurry of teasing our hair and checking our makeup. Looking into my compact, I stuck out my lips in a way I'd been practicing. I had a pimple near my nose, but I'd turned it into a beauty spot with eyebrow pencil. I hoped to look like Sandra Dee.

Freshman year, everybody went to mixers, where

freshman boys, as uncomfortable as we were, stood nervously about in the social rooms of their fraternity houses, wearing navy-blue blazers, ties, and chinos. Nobody really knew how to date in this rigid system so unlike high school—and certainly so unlike prep school, where many of these boys had been locked away for the past four years. If they could have gotten their own dates, they would have. But they couldn't. They didn't know anybody, either. They pulled at their ties and looked at the floor. They seemed to me generally gorgeous, completely unlike Don Fetterman with his feathery crew cut and his 4-H jacket, now at Camp LeJeune. But I still wrote to Don, informative, stilted notes about my classes and the weather. His letters in return were lively and real, full of military life ("the food sucks") and vague sweet plans for our future—a future that did not exist, as far as I was concerned, and yet these letters gave me a secret thrill. My role as Don Fetterman's girl was the most exciting I'd had yet, and I couldn't quite bring myself to give it up, even as I attempted to transform myself into another person altogether.

"Okay," the upperclassman-in-charge announced casually, and the St. Anthony's Hall pledges wandered over in our direction.

"Hey," the cutest one said to a girl.

"Hey," she said back.

The routine never varied. In a matter of minutes, the four most aggressive guys would walk off with the four prettiest girls, and the rest of us would panic. On this occasion the social room at St. Anthony's Hall was cleared in a matter of minutes, and I was left with a tall, gangly, bucktoothed boy whose face was as pocked as the moon. Still, he had a shabby elegance I already recognized. He was from Mississippi.

"What do you want to do?" he asked me.

I had not expected to be consulted. I glanced around the social room, which looked like a war zone. I didn't know where my friends were.

"What do *you* want to do?" I asked.

His name (his *first* name) was Rutherford. He grinned at me. "Let's get drunk," he said, and my heart leaped up as I realized that my burden might be lifted in this way. We walked across the beautiful old campus to an open court where three or four fraternities had a combo going, wild-eyed electrified Negroes going through all kinds of gyrations on the bandstand. It was Doug Clark and the Hot Nuts. The music was so loud, the beat so strong, that you couldn't listen to it and stand still. The Hot Nuts were singing an interminable song; everybody seemed to know the chorus, which went, "Nuts, hot nuts, get 'em from the peanut man. Nuts, hot nuts, get 'em any way you can." We started dancing. I always worried about this—all I'd ever done before college, in the way of dancing, was the shag with my aunt Dee and a long, formless *clutch* with Don Fetterman, but with Rutherford it didn't matter.

People made a circle around us and started clapping.

Nobody looked at me. All eyes were on Rutherford, whose dancing reminded me of the way chickens back home flopped around after Daddy cut their heads off. At first I was embarrassed. But then I caught on—Rutherford was a real *character*. I kept up with him the best I could, and then I got tickled and started laughing so hard I could barely dance. *This is fun*, I realized suddenly. This is what I'm *supposed* to be doing. This is college.

About an hour later we heard the news, which was delivered to us by a tweed-jacketed professor who walked onstage, bringing the music to a ragged, grinding halt. He grabbed the microphone. "Ladies and gentlemen," he said thickly—and I remember thinking how odd this form of address seemed—"ladies and gentlemen, the President has been shot."

The whole scene started to churn, as if we were in a kaleidoscope—the blue day, the green grass, the stately columned buildings. People were running and sobbing. Rutherford's hand under my elbow steered me back to his fraternity house, where everyone was clustered around several TVs, talking too loud. All the weekend festivities were canceled. We were to return to school immediately. Rutherford seemed relieved by this prospect, having fallen silent—perhaps because he'd quit drinking, or because conversation alone wasn't worth the effort it took if nothing else (sex) might be forthcoming. He gave me a perfunctory kiss on the cheek and turned to go.

I was about to board the bus when somebody grabbed me, hard, from behind. I whirled around. It was Lily, red-cheeked and glassy-eyed, her blond hair springing out wildly above her blue sweater. Her hot-pink lipstick was smeared; her pretty, pointed face looked vivid and alive. A dark-haired boy stood close behind her, his arm around her waist.

"Listen," Lily hissed at me. "Sign me in, will you?"

"What?" I had heard her, but I couldn't believe it.

"Sign me in." Lily squeezed my shoulder. I could smell her perfume. Then she was gone.

I sat in a rear seat by myself and cried all the way back to school.

I CAUGHT ON FAST THAT AS FAR AS COLLEGE BOYS WERE concerned, girls fell into either the Whore or the Saint category. Girls knew that if they gave in and *did it*, then boys wouldn't respect them, and word would get around, and they would never get a husband. The whole point of college was to get a husband.

I had not known anything about this system before I arrived there. It put a serious obstacle in my path toward becoming a great writer.

Lily, who clearly had given up her burden long since, fell into the Whore category. But the odd thing about it was that she didn't seem to mind, and she swore she didn't want a husband, anyway. "Honey, a husband is the *last* thing on my list!" she'd say, giggling. Lily was the smartest one of us, even though she went to great lengths to hide this fact.

Later, in 1966, she and the head of the philosophy department, Dr. Wiener, would stage the only demonstration ever held on our campus, walking slowly around the blooming quadrangle carrying signs that read "Get out of Vietnam," while the rest of us, well oiled and sunning on the rooftops, clutched our bikini tops and peered down curiously at the two of them.

If Lily was the smartest, Melissa was the dumbest, the nicest, and the least interested in school. Melissa came from Charleston, South Carolina, and spoke so slowly that I was always tempted to leap in and finish her sentences for her. All she wanted to do was marry her boyfriend, now at the University of South Carolina, and have babies. Donnie, Melissa's roommate, was a big, freckled, friendly girl from Texas. We didn't have any idea how rich she was until her mother flew up and bought a cabin at nearby Goshen Lake so "Donnie and her friends" would have a place to "relax."

By spring, Dixie was the only one of us who was actually pinned. It seemed to me that she was not only pinned but almost married, in a funny way, with tons and tons of children—Trey, her boyfriend; and me; and the other girls in our suite; and the other Phi Gams, Trey's fraternity brothers at Washington and Lee. Dixie had a notebook in which she made a list of things to do each day, and throughout the day she checked them off, one by one. She always got everything done. At the end of first semester, she had a 4.0 average; Trey had a 0.4. Dixie didn't mind. Totally, inexplicably, she loved him.

By then, most of the freshman girls who weren't going with somebody had several horror stories to tell about blind dates at UVA or W&L fraternities—about boys who "dropped trou," or threw up in their dates' purses. I had only one horror story, but I never told it, since the most horrible element in it was me.

THIS IS WHAT HAPPENED. IT WAS SPRING FLING AT THE Phi Gam house, and Trey had gotten me a date with a red-headed boy named Eddy Turner. I was getting desperate. I'd made a C in my first semester of creative writing, while Lily had made an A. Plus, I'd gained eight pounds. Both love and literature seemed to be slipping out of my sights. And I was drinking too much—we'd been drinking Yucca Flats, a horrible green punch made with grain alcohol in a washtub, all afternoon before I ended up in bed with Eddy Turner.

The bed was his, on the second floor of the Phi Gam house—not the most private setting for romance. I could scarcely see Eddy by the light from the street lamp coming in through the single high window. Faintly, below, I could hear music, and the house shook slightly with the dancing. I thought of Hemingway's famous description of sex from *For Whom the Bell Tolls*, which I'd typed out neatly on an index card: "The earth moved under the sleeping bag." The

whole Phi Gam house was moving under me. After wrestling
with my panty girdle for what seemed like hours, Eddy
tossed it in the corner and got on top of me. Drunk as I was,
I wanted him to. I wanted him to *do it*. But I didn't think it
would hurt so much, and suddenly I wished he would kiss
me or say something. He didn't. He was done and lying on
his back beside me when the door to the room burst open
and the light came on. I sat up, grasping for the sheet that I
couldn't find. My breasts are large, and they had always
embarrassed me. Until that night, Don Fetterman was the
only boy who had seen them. It was a whole group of Phi
Gams, roaming from room to room. Luckily I was blinded
by the light, so I couldn't tell exactly who they were.

"Smile!" they yelled. "You're on *Candid Camera*!" They
laughed hysterically, slammed the door, and were gone, leaving us in darkness once again. I sobbed into Eddy's pillow,
because what they said reminded me of Sam, whose face
would not leave my mind then for hours while I cried and
cried and cried and sobered up. I didn't tell Eddy what I was
crying about, nor did he ask. He sat in a chair and smoked
cigarettes while he waited for me to stop crying. Finally I
did. Eddy and I didn't date after that, but we were buddies
in the way I was buddies with the whole Phi Gam house due
to my status as Dixie's roommate. I was like a sister, giving
advice to the lovelorn, administering Cokes and aspirin on
Sunday mornings, typing papers.

It was not the role I'd had in mind, but it was better than

nothing, affording me at least a certain status among the girls at school; and the Phi Gams saw to it that I attended all the big parties, usually with somebody whose girlfriend couldn't make it. Often, when the weekend was winding down, I could be found in the Phi Gam basement alone, playing "Tragedy," my favorite song, over and over on the jukebox.

> *Blown by the wind,*
> *Kissed by the snow,*
> *All that's left*
> *Is the dark below.*
> *Gone from me,*
> *Oh, oh,*
> *Trag-e-dy.*

It always brought me to the edge of tears, because I had never known any tragedy myself, or love, or drama. *Wouldn't anything ever happen to me?*

Meanwhile, my friends' lives were like soap opera—Lily's period was two weeks late, which scared us all, and then Dixie went on the pill. Melissa and her boyfriend split up (she lost seven pounds, he slammed his hand into a wall) and then made up again.

Melissa was telling us about it, in her maddeningly slow way, one day when we were out at Donnie's lake cabin, sunning. "It's not the same, though," she said. "He just gets *too mad*. I don't know what it is—he scares me."

"Dump him," Lily said, applying baby oil with iodine in it, our suntan lotion of choice.

"But I *love* him," Melissa wailed. Lily snorted.

"Well . . ." Dixie began diplomatically, but suddenly I sat up.

"Maybe he's got a wild streak," I said. "Maybe he just can't control himself. That's always been Bubba's problem." The little lake before us took on a deeper, more intense hue. I noticed the rotting pier, the old fisherman up at the point, Lily's painted toenails. I noticed *everything*.

"Who's Bubba?" Donnie asked.

Dixie eyed me expectantly, thinking I meant one of the Phi Gams, since several of them had that nickname.

"My brother," I said. I took a deep breath.

"*What?* You never said you had a *brother*!" Dixie's pretty face looked really puzzled now.

Everybody sat up and stared at me.

"Well, I do," I said. "He's two years older than me, and he stayed with my father when my parents split up. So I've never lived with him. In fact, I don't know him real well at all. This is very painful for me to talk about. We were insepa-rable when we were little," I added, hearing my song in the back of my mind. *Oh, oh . . . trag-e-dy!*

"Oh, Charlene, I'm so sorry! I had no idea!" Dixie was hugging me, slick hot skin and all.

I started crying. "He was a real problem child," I said,

"and now he's just so wild. I don't know what's going to become of him."

"How long has it been since you've seen him?" Melissa asked.

"About two years," I said. "Our parents won't have anything at all to do with each other. They *hate* each other, especially since Mama remarried. They won't let us get together, not even for a day. It's just awful."

"So how did you see him two years ago?" Lily asked. They had all drawn closer, clustering around me.

"He ran away from school," I said, "and came to my high school, and got me right out of class. I remember it was biology lab," I said. "I was dissecting a frog."

"Then what?"

"We spent the day together," I said. "We got some food and went out to this quarry and ate, and just drove around. We talked and talked," I said. "And you know what? I felt just as close to him then as I did when we were babies. Just like all those years had never passed at all. It was great," I said.

"Then he went back to school? Or what?"

"No." I choked back a sob. "It was almost dark, and he was taking me back to my house, and then he was planning to head on down to Florida, he said, when all of a sudden these blue lights came up behind us, and it was the police."

"The *police?*" Dixie was getting very nervous. She was such a good girl.

"Well, it was a stolen car, of course," I explained. "They nailed him. If he hadn't stopped in to see me, he might have gotten away with it," I said, "if he'd just headed straight to Florida. But he came to see me. Mama and Daddy wouldn't even bail him out. They let him go straight to prison."

"Oh, Charlene, *no wonder* you never talk about your family!" Dixie was in tears now.

"But he was a model prisoner," I went on. I felt exhilarated. "They gave all the prisoners this test, and he scored the highest that anybody in the whole history of the prison had *ever* scored, so they let him take these special classes, and he did so well that he got out a whole year early, and now he's in college."

"Where?"

I thought fast. "Dartmouth," I said wildly. I knew it had to be a northern school, since Dixie and Melissa seemed to know everybody in the South. But neither of them, as far as I could recall, had ever mentioned Dartmouth.

"He's got a full scholarship," I added. "But he's so bad, I don't know if he'll be able to keep it or not." Donnie got up and went in and came back with cold Cokes for us all, and we stayed out at Goshen Lake until the sun set, and I told them about Bubba.

He was a KA, the wildest KA of them all. Last winter, I said, he got drunk and passed out in the snow on the way back to his fraternity house; by the time a janitor found him the following morning, his cheek was frozen solid to the road. It took two guys from maintenance, with torches, to melt the snow around Bubba's face and get him loose. And now the whole fraternity was on probation because of this really gross thing he'd made the pledges do. "What really gross thing?" they asked. "Oh, you don't want to know," I said. "You really don't."

"I *really do*." Lily pushed her sunburned face into mine. "Come on. After Trey, nothing could be that bad." Even Dixie grinned.

"Okay," I said, launching into a hazing episode that required the KA pledges to run up three flights of stairs, holding alum in their mouths. On each landing, they had to dodge past these two big football players. If they swallowed the alum during the struggle, well, alum makes you vomit immediately, so you can imagine. . . . They could imagine. But the worst part was that when one pledge wouldn't go past the second landing, the football players threw him down the stairs, and he broke his back.

"That's just disgusting," Donnie drawled. "Nobody would ever do that in Texas."

But on the other hand, I said quickly, Bubba was the most talented poet in the school, having won the Iris Nutley Leach Award for Poetry two years in a row. I pulled the name Iris Nutley Leach right out of the darkening air. I astonished myself. And girls were just crazy about Bubba, I added. In fact, this girl from Washington tried to kill herself after they broke up, and then she had to be institutionalized at

Sheppard Pratt in Baltimore. I knew all about Sheppard Pratt because my mother had gone there.

"But he doesn't have a girlfriend right now," I said. Everybody sighed, and a warm breeze came up over the pines and ruffled our little lake. By then, Bubba was as real to me as the Peanuts towel I sat on, as real as the warm gritty dirt between my toes.

During the next year or so, Bubba would knock up a girl and then nobly help her get an abortion (Donnie offered to contribute); he would make Phi Beta Kappa; he would be arrested for assault; he would wreck his MGB; he would start writing folk songs. My creativity knew no bounds when it came to Bubba, but I was a dismal failure in my first writing class, where my teacher, Mr. Lefcowicz, kept giving me B's and C's and telling me, "Write what you know."

I didn't want to write what I knew. I had no intention of writing a word about my own family, or those peanut fields. Who would want to read about *that*? I had wanted to write in order to *get away* from my own life. I couldn't give up that tormented woman on the cliff in the south of France. I intended to write about glamorous heroines with exciting lives. One of my first—and worst—stories involved a stewardess in Hawaii. I had never been to Hawaii, of course. At that time, I had never even been on a plane. The plot, which was very complicated, had something to do with international espionage. I remember how kindly my young teacher smiled at me when he handed my story back. He asked me to stay for a minute after class. "Charlene," he said, "I want you to write something true next time."

Instead, I decided to give up on plot and concentrate on theme, intending to pull some heartstrings. It was nearly Christmas, and this time we had to read our stories aloud to the whole group. But right before that class, Mr. Lefcowicz, who had already read our stories, pulled me aside and told me that I didn't have to read mine out loud if I didn't want to.

"Of course I want to," I said.

We took our seats.

My story took place in a large, unnamed city on Christmas Eve. In this story, a whole happy family was trimming the Christmas tree, singing carols, and drinking hot chocolate while it snowed outside. I think I had "softly falling flakes." Each person in the family was allowed to open one present—selected from the huge pile of gifts beneath the glittering tree—before bed. Then everyone went to sleep, and a "pregnant silence" descended. At three o'clock a fire broke out, and the whole house burned to the ground, and they all burned up, dying horrible deaths, which I described individually—conscious, as I read aloud, of some movement and sound among my listeners. But I didn't dare look up as I approached the story's ironic end: "When the fire trucks arrived, the only sign of life to be found was a blackened music box in the smoking ashes, softly playing 'Silent Night.'"

By the end of my story, one girl had put her head down on her desk; another was having a coughing fit. Mr. Lefcowicz was staring intently out the window at the wintry day, his back to us. Then he made a great show of looking at his watch. "Whoops! Class dismissed!" he cried, grabbing his bookbag. He rushed from the room like the White Rabbit, already late.

But I was not that stupid.

As I walked across the cold, wet quadrangle toward my dormitory, I understood perfectly well that my story was terrible, laughable. I wanted to die. The gray sky, the dripping, leafless trees, fit my mood perfectly, and I remembered Mr. Lefcowicz saying, in an earlier class, that we must never manipulate nature to express our characters' emotions. "Ha!" I muttered scornfully to the heavy sky.

The very next day, I joined the staff of the campus newspaper. I became its editor in the middle of my sophomore year—a job nobody else wanted, a job I really enjoyed. I had found a niche, a role, and although it was not what I had envisioned for myself, it was okay. Thus I became the following things: editor of the newspaper; member of Athena, the secret honor society; roommate of Dixie, the May Queen; friend of Phi Gams; and—especially—sister of Bubba, whose legend loomed ever larger. But I avoided both dates and creative writing classes for the next two years, finding Mr. Lefcowicz's stale advice, "Write what you know," more impossible with each visit home.

• • •

THE SUMMER BETWEEN MY SOPHOMORE AND JUNIOR years was the hardest. The first night I was home, I realized that something was wrong with Mama when I woke up to hear water splashing in the downstairs bathroom. I went to investigate. There she was, wearing a lacy pink peignoir and her old gardening shoes, scrubbing the green tub.

"Oh, hi, Charlene!" she said brightly, and went on scrubbing, humming tunelessly to herself. A mop and bucket stood in the corner. I said good night and went back to my bedroom, where I looked at the clock; it was three-thirty a.m.

The next day, Mama burst into tears when Sam spilled a glass of iced tea, and the day after that, Daddy took her over to Petersburg and put her in the hospital. Memaw came in to stay with Sam during the day while I worked at Snow's in South Hill, my old job.

I'd come home at suppertime each day to find Sam in his chair on the front porch, holding Blackie, waiting for me. He seemed to have gotten smaller somehow—and for the first time I realized that Sam, so much a part of my childhood, was not growing up along with me. In fact, he would *never* grow up, and I thought about that a lot on those summer evenings as I swung gently in the porch swing, back and forth through the sultry air, suspended.

In August, I went to Memphis for a week to visit Dixie, whose house turned out to be like Tara in *Gone With the*

Wind, only bigger, and whose mother turned out to drink sherry all day long. I came back to find Mama out of the hospital already, much improved by shock treatments, and another surprise—a baby-blue Chevrolet convertible, used but great-looking, in the driveway. My father handed me the keys.

"Here, honey," he said, and then he hugged me tight, smelling of sweat and tobacco. "We're so proud of you." He had traded a man a combine or something for the car.

So I drove back to school in style, and my junior year went smoothly until Donnie announced that her sister Susannah, now at Pine Mountain Junior College, was going to Dartmouth for Winter Carnival, to visit a boy she'd met that summer. Susannah just *couldn't wait* to look up Bubba.

Unfortunately this was not possible, as I got a phone call that very night saying that Bubba had been kicked out of school for leading a demonstration against the war. Lily, who had become much more political herself by that time, jumped up from her desk and grabbed my hand.

"Oh, no!" she shrieked. "He'll be drafted!" The alarm that filled our study room was palpable—as real as the mounting body count on TV—as we stared white-faced at each other.

"Whatever will he do now?" Donnie was wringing her hands.

"I don't know," I said desperately. "I just don't know." I went to my room—a single, this term—and thought about it. It was clear that he would have to do something, something to take him far, far away.

But Bubba's problem was soon to be superseded by Melissa's. She was pregnant, really pregnant, and in spite of all the arguments we could come up with, she wanted to get married and have the baby. She wanted to have lots of babies, and one day live in the big house on the Battery that her boyfriend would inherit, and this is exactly what she's done. Her life has been predictable and productive. So violent in his college days, Melissa's husband turned out to be a model of stability in later life. And their first child, Anna, kept him out of the draft.

As she got into her mother's car to leave, Melissa squeezed my hand and said, "Keep me posted about Bubba, and don't worry so much. I'm sure everything will work out all right."

It didn't.

Bubba burned his draft card not a month later and headed for Canada, where he lived in a commune. I didn't hear from him for a long time after that, tangled up as I was by then in my affair with Dr. Pierce.

DR. PIERCE WAS A FIERCE, BLEAK, MELANCHOLY MAN who looked like a bird of prey. Not surprisingly, he was a Beckett scholar. He taught the seminar in contemporary literature that I took in the spring of my junior year. We read Joseph Heller, Kurt Vonnegut, Flannery O'Connor, John Barth, and Thomas Pynchon, among others. Flannery O'Connor would become my favorite, and I would do my senior thesis on her work, feeling a secret and strong kinship, by then, with her dire view. But this was later, after my affair with Dr. Pierce was over.

At first I didn't know what to make of him. I hated his northern accent, his lugubrious, glistening dark eyes, his all-encompassing pessimism. He told us that contemporary literature was absurd because the world was absurd. He told us that the language in the books we were reading was weird and fractured because true communication is impossible in the world today. Dr. Pierce told us this in a sad, cynical tone full of infinite world-weariness, which I found both repellent and attractive.

I decided to go in and talk to him. I am still not sure why I did this—I was making good grades in his course, I understood everything. But one blustery, unsettling March afternoon I found myself sitting outside his office. He was a popular teacher, rumored to be always ready to listen to his students' problems. I don't know what I meant to talk to him about. The hour grew late. The hall grew dark. I smoked four or five cigarettes while other students, ahead of me, went in and out. Then Dr. Pierce came and stood in the doorway. He took off his glasses and rubbed his eyes. He looked tired, but not nearly as old as he did in class, where he always wore a tie. Now he wore jeans and a blue work shirt, and I could see the dark hair at his neck.

"Ah," he said in that way of his that rendered all his remarks oddly significant. "Ah! Miss Christian, is it not?"

He knew it was. I felt uncomfortable, like he was mocking me. He made a gesture; I preceded him into his office and sat down.

"Now," he said, staring at me. I looked out the window at the skittish, blowing day, at the girls who passed by on the sidewalk, giggling and trying to hold their skirts down. "*Miss Christian*," Dr. Pierce said. Maybe he'd said it before. I looked at him.

"I presume you had some reason for this visit," he said sardonically.

To my horror, I started crying. Not little ladylike sniffles, either, but huge groaning sobs. Dr. Pierce thrust a box of Kleenex in my direction, then sat drumming his fingers on his desk. I kept on crying. Finally I realized what he was drumming: the *William Tell* overture. I got tickled. Soon I was crying and laughing at the same time. I was still astonished at myself.

"Blow your nose," Dr. Pierce said.

I did.

"That's better," he said. It was. He got up and closed his office door, although there was no need to do so, since the hall outside was empty now. Dr. Pierce sat back down and leaned across his desk toward me. "What is it?" he asked.

But I still didn't know what it was. I said so, and apologized. "One thing, though," I said. "I'd like to complain about the choice of books on our reading list."

"Aha!" Dr. Pierce said. He leaned back in his chair and made his fingers into a tent. "You liked Eudora Welty," he said. This was true; I nodded. "You liked *Lie Down in Darkness*," he said. I nodded again.

"But I just *hate* this other stuff!" I burst out. "I just hated *The End of the Road*, I hated it! It's so depressing."

He nodded rapidly. "You think literature should make you feel good?" he asked.

"It used to," I said. Then I was crying again. I stood up. "I'm so sorry," I said.

Dr. Pierce stood up, too, and walked around his desk and came to stand close to me. The light in his office was soft, gray, furry. Dr. Pierce took both my hands in his. "Oh, Miss Christian," he said. "My very dear, very young Miss Christian, I know what you mean." And I could tell, by the pain and weariness in his voice, that this was true. I could see Dr. Pierce suddenly as a much younger man, as a boy, with a light in his eyes and a different feeling about the world. I reached up and put my hands in his curly hair and pulled his face down to mine and kissed him fiercely, in a way I had never kissed anybody. I couldn't imagine myself doing this, yet I did it naturally. Dr. Pierce kissed me back. We kissed for a long time while it grew completely dark outside, and then he locked the door and turned back to me. He

sighed deeply, almost a groan—a sound, I felt, of regret—
then unbuttoned my shirt. We made love on the rug on his
office floor. Immediately we were caught up in a kind of
fever that lasted for several months—times like these in his
office after hours, or in the backseat of my car parked by
Goshen Lake, or in cheap motels when I'd signed out to go
home.

Nobody suspected a thing. I was as good at keeping
secrets as I was at making up lies. Plus, I was a campus leader,
and Dr. Pierce was a married man.

He tried to end it that June. I was headed home, and he
was headed to New York, where he had a fellowship to do
research at the Morgan Library.

"Charlene—" Dr. Pierce said. We were in public, out on
the quadrangle right after graduation. His wife walked
down the hill at some distance behind us, with other faculty
wives. Dr. Pierce's voice was hoarse, the way it got when he
was in torment (which he so often was, which was one of
the most attractive things about him. Years later, I'd realize
this). "Let us make a clean break," he sort of mumbled.
"Right now. It cannot go on, and we both know it."

We had reached the parking lot in front of the chapel; the
sunlight reflected off the cars was dazzling.

Dr. Pierce stuck out his hand in an oddly formal gesture.
"Have a good summer, Charlene," he said, "and good-bye."

Dr. Pierce had chosen his moment well. He knew I
wouldn't make a scene in front of all these people. But I

refused to take his hand. I rushed off madly through the parked cars to my own and gunned it out of there and out to the lake, where I parked on the bluff above Donnie's cabin, in the exact spot where Dr. Pierce and I had been together so many times. I sat at the wheel and looked out at the lake, now full of children on a school outing. Their shrill screams and laughter drifted to me thinly, like the sounds of birds in the trees around my car. I leaned back on the seat and stared straight up at the sun through the trees—just at the top of the tent of green, where light filtered through in bursts like stars.

BUT I COULDN'T GIVE HIM UP, NOT YET, NOT EVER.

I resolved to surprise Dr. Pierce in New York, and that's exactly what I did, telling my parents I'd gone on a trip to Virginia Beach with friends. I got his summer address from the registrar's office. I drove up through Richmond and Washington, a seven-hour drive. It was crazy and even a dangerous thing to do, since I had never been to New York. But at last I ended up in front of the brownstone in the Village where Dr. Pierce and his wife were subletting an apartment. It was midafternoon and hot; I had not imagined New York to be so hot, hotter even than McKenney, Virginia. I was still in a fever, I think. I rang the doorbell, without even considering what I would do if his wife answered. But nobody answered. Nobody was home. Somehow, this possibility had not occurred to me. I felt exhausted. I leaned against the wall and then slid down it, until I was sitting on the floor in the vestibule. I pulled off my panty hose and stuffed them into my purse. They were too hot. I was too hot. I wore a kelly-green linen dress; I'd thought I needed to be all dressed up to go to New York.

I don't even remember falling asleep, but I was awakened by Dr. Pierce shaking my shoulder and saying my name.

Whatever can be said of Dr. Pierce, he was not a jerk. He told me firmly that our relationship was over, and just as firmly that I should not be going around New York City at night by myself, not in the shape I was in.

By the time his wife came home with groceries, I was lying on the studio bed, feeling a little better. He told her I was having a breakdown, which seemed suddenly true. Dr. Pierce and I looked at the news on TV while she made spaghetti. After dinner she lit a joint and handed it to me. It was the first time anybody had offered me marijuana. I shook my head. I thought I was crazy enough already. Dr. Pierce's wife was nice, though. She was pale, with long, long blond hair, which she had worn in a braid on campus, or twisted on top of her head. Now it fell over her shoulders like water. She was not much—certainly not ten years—older than I was, and I wondered if she, too, had been his student. But I was exhausted. I fell asleep on the studio bed in front of a fan that drowned out the sound of their voices as they cleaned up from dinner.

I woke up very early the next morning. I wrote the Pierces a thank-you note on an index card I found in Dr. Pierce's briefcase, and left it propped conspicuously against the toaster. The door to their bedroom was open, but I did not look in.

On the street, I was horrified to find that I had gotten a parking ticket and that my convertible top had been slashed—gratuitously, since there was nothing in the car to steal. This upset me more than anything else about my trip to New York, more than Dr. Pierce's rejection, or his renunciation, as I preferred to consider it—which is how I did consider it, often, during that summer at home while I had the rest of my nervous breakdown.

My parents were very kind. They thought it all had to do with Don Fetterman, who was missing in action in Vietnam, and maybe it did, sort of. I was "nervous," and cried a lot. Finally my aunt Dee got tired of me mooning around, as she called it. She frosted my hair and took me to Myrtle Beach, where it proved impossible to continue the nervous breakdown. The last night of the trip, Aunt Dee and I double-dated with some realtors she'd met by the pool.

Aunt Dee and I got back to McKenney just in time for me to pack and drive to school, where I was one of the seniors in charge of freshman orientation. Daddy had gotten the top fixed on my car; I was a blonde; and I'd lost twenty-five pounds.

• • •

THE CAMPUS SEEMED SMALLER TO ME AS I DROVE through the imposing gates. My footsteps echoed as I carried my bags up to the third floor of Old North, where Dixie and I would have the coveted "turret room." I was the first one back in the dorm, but as I hauled things in from my car, other seniors began arriving. We hugged and squealed, following a script as old as the college. At least three girls stopped in mid-hug to push me back, scrutinize me carefully, and exclaim that they wouldn't have recognized me. I didn't know what they meant.

Sweaty and exhausted after carrying everything up to the room, I decided to shower before dinner. I was standing naked in our room, toweling my hair dry, when the dinner bell rang. Its somber tone sounded elegiac to me in that moment. On impulse, I started rummaging around in one of my boxes, until I found the mirror I was looking for. I went to stand at the window while the last of the lingering chimes died on the August air.

I held the mirror out at arm's length and looked at myself. I had cheekbones. I had hipbones. I could see my ribs. My eyes were darker, larger in my face. My wild damp hair was as blond as Lily's.

Clearly, *something had finally happened to me.*

That weekend, Dixie, Donnie, Lily, and I went out to

Donnie's cabin to drink beer and catch up on the summer. We telephoned Melissa, now eight months pregnant, who claimed to be blissfully happy and said she was making curtains.

Lily snorted. She got up and put Simon and Garfunkel on the stereo, and got us each another beer. Donnie lit candles and switched off the overhead lamp. Dixie waved her hand, making her big diamond sparkle in the candlelight. Trey, now in law school at Vanderbilt, had given it to her in July. She was already planning her wedding. We would all be bridesmaids, of course. (That marriage would last for only a few years, and Dixie would divorce once more before she went to law school herself.) Donnie told us about her mother's new boyfriend. We gossiped on as the hour grew late and bugs slammed suicidally into the porch light. The moon came up big and bright. I kept playing "The Sounds of Silence" over and over; it matched my mood, my new conception of myself. I also liked "I Am a Rock."

Then Lily announced that she was in love, *really in love* this time, with a young poet she'd met that summer on Cape Cod, where she'd been waitressing. We waited while she lit a cigarette. "We lived together for two months," Lily said, "in his room at the inn, where we could look out and see the water." We stared at her. None of us had ever lived with anybody, or known anyone who had. Lily looked around at us. "It was wonderful," she said. "It was heaven. But it was not what you might think," she added enigmatically, "living with a man."

I started crying.

There was a long silence, and the needle on the record started scratching. Donnie got up and cut it off. They were all looking at me.

"And what about you, Charlene?" Lily said softly. "What happened to you this summer, anyway?"

It was a moment I had rehearsed again and again in my mind. I would tell them about my affair with Dr. Pierce and how I had gone to New York to find him, and how he had renounced me because his wife was pregnant. I had just added this part. But I was crying too hard to speak. "It was awful," I said finally, and Dixie came over and hugged me. "What was awful?" she said, but I couldn't even speak, my mind filled suddenly, surprisingly, with Don Fetterman as he'd looked in high school, presiding over the Glee Club.

"Come on," Dixie said, "tell us."

The candles were guttering, the moon made a path across the lake. I took a deep breath.

"Bubba is dead," I said.

"Oh, God! Oh, no!" A sort of pandemonium ensued, which I don't remember much about, although I remember the details of my brother's death vividly. Bubba drowned in a lake in Canada, attempting to save a friend's child who had fallen overboard. The child died, too. Bubba was buried

there, on the wild shore of that northern lake, and his only
funeral was what his friends said as they spoke around the
grave one by one. His best friend had written to me, describ-
ing the whole thing.

"Charlene, Charlene, why didn't you tell us sooner?"
Donnie asked.

I just shook my head. "I couldn't," I said.

Later that fall, I finally wrote a good story—about my
family, back in McKenney—and then another, and then
another. I won a scholarship to graduate school at Columbia
University in New York, where I still live, with my husband,
on the West Side, freelancing for several magazines and
writing fiction.

It was here, only a few weeks ago, that I last saw Lily,
now a prominent feminist scholar. She was in town for the
MLA convention. We went to a bistro near my apartment
for lunch, lingering over wine far into the late-December
afternoon while my husband babysat. Lily was in the middle
of a divorce. "You know," she said at one point, twirling her
tulip wineglass, "I have often thought that the one great
tragedy of my life was never getting to meet your brother.
Somehow I always felt that he and I were just meant for each
other." We sat in the restaurant for a long time, at the window where we could see the passersby hurrying along the
sidewalk in the dismal sleet outside, each one so preoccupied,
so caught up in his own story. We sat there all afternoon.

BLUE WEDDING

Sarah can't keep her mind on the spoons. So she starts over, counting right out loud, "One, two, three, four," pursing her lips in that way she has, fitting each newly polished spoon carefully into its allotted space in the big mahogany silver chest. Thirty-six spoons, all accounted for. Normally this is the kind of job Sarah just loves, but today it's so hot, hotter than the hinges of hell in here, and she is distracted because Gladiola Rolette, who's polishing the spoons and handing them over to her one by one, will *not* shut up, not for a single minute. Gladiola beats all! She does not seem to understand that it's her fault it's so hot in here, that she should have called a repairman the instant the air conditioner went on the blink. Gladiola does not even seem to understand that it's her fault Sarah has to count the silver in the first place. But Gladiola just let it all go during the last six months of Daddy's illness, forks and spoons jumbled up together, the butter knives scattered to the four winds. And furthermore, it is perfectly clear that Gladiola has been giving her trashy family the entire run of this house.

Sarah has seen the signs everywhere—unfiltered cigarette butts in the flower beds, a beer can stuck in a planter on the portico, a lipstick smudge on the drinking glass in the downstairs bathroom—why, even the furniture has been rearranged! Gladiola herself would never think of doing such a thing. But her daughters, both of them hussies, *would*. They've got ideas, Gladiola's girls. Sarah has watched them grow up.

Right now Roxanne, the younger one, could not possibly be a day over seventeen but could pass for thirty, she looks so cheap and jaded with that spiky black hair and all those holes in her ears. Gladiola's older daughter, Missy, is down in Atlanta getting certified to be a massage therapist, or so she says. A massage therapist, ha! Sarah can just imagine. Of course Missy has already had one baby out of wedlock, that fat little girl out there digging in the mint bed right now with a spoon. Probably a silver soup spoon, Sarah would not be one bit surprised.

Little Bonnie comes to work with Gladiola every day, and eats everything in the house. This is a pure fact. Sarah had no idea until she came back to bury Daddy and stayed on to clean out this house. *Somebody* had to! Oh, a lot has been going on here that Sarah didn't know anything about. These Rolettes have practically taken over.

But of course it is all Hubert's fault. Hubert is Sarah's brother, the district attorney, a rumpled, distracted man. All Hubert cares about is his job, and all his northern egghead wife, Mickey, cares about is taking classes at the community college, where she earns degree after degree, or claims to. So Hubert was perfectly happy to hire as many Rolettes as it took and close his eyes to the havoc they wrought, just as long as everybody stayed out of his hair. Hubert! Hubert has no standards.

Sarah practically slams the knives into the silver chest, thinking of Hubert, Hubert who talked *so mean* to her the last time she came home and tried to make some reasonable suggestions about what to do with Daddy. Hubert wears wrinkled suits and horn-rimmed glasses way down on the end of his nose. He looked at her over the rims. "Hell, Sarah," he said, "Dad's fine. Just leave him alone. He *likes* to pile newspapers all over the house, he *likes* to have Gladiola's granddaughter around, it keeps him company. He likes to stay up and watch the talk shows and then sleep until noon, so what's the harm in it?"

"People ought to get up in the mornings," Sarah said. "A regular schedule never hurt anybody." Sarah herself has not slept past seven a.m. in twenty years. She eats one half-cup of bran cereal with banana for breakfast every morning of her life.

Gladiola, on the other hand, fed her father Pop-Tarts and instant grits. This is a fact. Pop-Tarts and grits! Lord knows what kind of shape his bowels were in by the time of his death; Sarah did not discuss this with Hubert.

But she did bring up the hat. "I just don't think we ought to let him go around looking like that," she said.

Hubert laughed. "Hell, he's eighty-five years old. I think he ought to wear whatever damn kind of a hat he wants to."

So Hubert had destroyed her influence with Daddy, Hubert having his way as usual, Hubert who was possibly even more spoiled than Ashley, God rest her soul, however.

Suddenly Sarah feels awful.

She sits down abruptly on a Chippendale chair at the dining room table. She's so hot! Maybe it's a hot flash, maybe she's getting the change of life. "Is there any ice tea?" she asks Gladiola, who tuns to get it.

Thank God! There *ought* to be iced tea in any decent household in the summertime of course, anybody knows that. Mama was nuts on the subject. And among the three children, Sarah is the only one like Mama, that soft pretty woman Sarah can hardly remember right now, sweet Mama who died of a racing heart twelve years ago.

Sarah left work the minute she got the message, and drove all night long to get home in time to see to every detail of

Mama's funeral. Then she volunteered to stay home to take care of Daddy, who was just lost without Mama, it was really the saddest thing. You can't imagine how he carried on.

But instead, here was Ashley back from California, flat broke, to recuperate from the second of her two divorces.

So Sarah stayed on in Richmond, where she is a buyer for the housewares section of Miller and Rhoads, a perfectly elegant downtown department store with branches in all the suburbs. In Richmond, Sarah has her book group, her bridge club, and a whole host of lovely friends. To be perfectly honest, Sarah was *glad* to stay in Richmond, in her new condominium with its eggshell walls and its silk ficus in the foyer. Daddy was disorderly and always had been, not to mention his drinking. Drunk and disorderly, ha!

Come to think of it, they were *all* disorderly—Daddy, Hubert, and Ashley—not to mention all of Hubert's and Ashley's spouses and children, a great straggling parade which Sarah loses track of. *Lost*, Sarah corrects herself. Which she has lost track of, as Ashley herself is lost.

Poor Ashley wasn't even married to the man who caused her last, fatal pregnancy. At the time, she wasn't married at all, and he was married to somebody else. But she was sure he *would* marry her, Ashley had confided to Sarah that summer morning nine years ago. They were sitting in the kitchen after breakfast, drinking coffee. It was already hot. Mama's climbing rose was blooming profusely all over the trellis.

Sarah remembers that morning like it was yesterday. Ashley leaned forward, so excited that spots of color stained her porcelain cheeks. She looked like a person running a fever. She spilled coffee on her flowered robe.

"He loves me so much," she said. "You can't imagine." Two weeks later she was dead of an ectopic pregnancy.

Sarah drinks her iced tea. She finishes with the knives: thirty-six of them, all accounted for. She smiles at Gladiola. "There now," she says.

Gladiola grins back. She's a fat, foolish woman, poor white trash if Sarah ever saw it, of course up here in the mountains this is common. People spill over from one social class into another all the time—it's hard to know who's nice. This is not true in Richmond, where the help is black and a proper distance can be maintained.

Sarah has been absent from her job at Miller and Rhoads for five days now, but she will be back on Monday. She can't afford to stay any longer. As it is, they will begin carrying three new lines of china during her absence, all of them informal: Pietri, heavy painted pottery from Italy, covered with fanciful animals and fish; Provence, oversize French china patterned in wild flowers; and Hacienda-Ware from the Southwest, all earth colors (terra-cotta, sagebrush, sunset, and dawn, ha!), which looks like hell in Sarah's opinion. All of it looks like hell. So does that new girl they've hired to "help" Sarah with the expanded china department, a girl with rat's-nest hair and dead-white makeup and some kind of a degree in "design." Sarah knows she will hate everything this girl likes.

What Sarah loves with all her heart is her mother's delicate bone china right over there in the breakfront, china so thin you can practically see through it. It will just kill her to split up the set with Hubert, who is totally unable to appreciate it. Well, a salad fork is missing, no surprise. Also two butter knives—no, *three* butter knives!

Out the window, Sarah sees Everett Sharp drive past in his little green car. Everett Sharp is the undertaker who buried Daddy two days ago. Sarah had lost touch with him since their high school days, but she was pleasantly surprised by his manner: respectful, attentive, but not unctuous. Not *pushy*. Everett Sharp is a tall, thin balding man, with a red beard and a high potbelly. Sarah has to start over on the soup spoons.

"Let's us stop for lunch now and I'll tell you about the wedding," Gladiola says. Gladiola knows how to get Sarah's attention.

"What wedding?" Sarah is a fool for weddings. She stops counting and wipes her face with a napkin. Actually, she's so hot, she's *glad* to stop for a while.

"Let's us go on in the kitchen and I'll tell you," Gladiola says.

Sarah closes the lid of the silver chest and goes to sit in the old kitchen rocker while Gladiola makes pimiento cheese sandwiches, Sarah's favorite since childhood.

"Well, you knew Roxanne was fixing to get married," Gladiola begins.

Sarah stares at her. "You mean Missy," she says automatically. It's a shame how Gladiola's face has fallen in like spoonbread around her mouth. She used to be a pretty woman.

"No ma'am," Gladiola answers emphatically. "I mean *Roxanne*."

"But Roxanne is only seventeen," Sarah says. "Isn't that so?"

"Yes ma'am," Gladiola says. "But can't nobody do a thing with Roxanne once she takes it in her head to do something. She's been like that ever since she was a little girl, ever since she was Bonnie's age."

As if on cue, Bonnie comes tracking dirt across the clean kitchen floor on her way to the sun porch, where she turns on the TV. Sarah sighs, bites her lip, says nothing. It is possible to say *too much*, she knows this, and really this pimiento cheese is very good.

"Tell me about the wedding," she reminds Gladiola.

"Well, I don't know where Roxanne got this idea, mind you, but she took it into her head that she just had to have a blue wedding."

"A what?"

Gladiola hands Sarah another sandwich, then sits down and grins at her. "A blue wedding! All blue! See, blue is Roxanne's favorite color, always has been, why last year when she was head majorette she forced them to let her make herself a new uniform, blue with gold trim instead of gold with blue."

"Do you mean to tell me that Roxanne had a *blue* wedding dress?" Sarah fans her face with a copy of *Time* magazine.

"*Ordered* it," Gladiola corrects her. "We ordered everything through Judy's Smarte Shoppe. You know Judy is real reliable, so usually everything comes in right when she says it will. We ordered a baby-blue wedding dress and veil, and baby-blue tuxedos for Sean and his brother and the two groomsmen, and three baby-blue dresses with an Empire waist and puff sleeves for the bridesmaids."

"My goodness!" It is all Sarah can think to say.

"But then Roxanne and Tammy—that's her best friend, Tammy Bird—had a big falling-out," Gladiola goes on, "and so Tammy said she wasn't going to be in the wedding after all, and Roxanne said that was fine with *her*, for Tammy not to be in the wedding, and so Roxanne called Judy up and canceled Tammy's dress. But Judy happened to be out sick that day, well, actually, she was over at Orange County Hospital getting her tubes tied and her mother was keeping the store for her. You know everybody thinks she's got Alzheimer's."

"*Who?*"

"Mrs. *Dewberry*," Gladiola says. "Judy's mother. But I don't think she's got it. I think everybody just says that because it's popular."

"What is?" Sarah manages to ask.

"Alzheimer's," Gladiola says. "That's one of those diseases nobody ever heard of until it got popular, and now everybody's got it, like that other one, you know the one I mean, the one where you diet until you die, nobody ever heard of that one until it got popular, either."

"Anorexia," Sarah says weakly.

"Whatever," Gladiola says. She lights a cigarette.

"*The wedding*," Sarah says.

"Well, so Judy's mother went and canceled the *whole order*, is what she did, instead of just the one dress, and forgot to say anything about this to Judy, so when the Thursday before the wedding comes and Roxanne's order doesn't come in, Judy calls them up. It's this company in New Jersey."

"Can I have a Coke?" Little Bonnie plants herself in front of Gladiola, but Sarah stands up and gets it herself out of the refrigerator. She gives it to Bonnie, then pushes her back out on the sun porch, where *All My Children* is on TV. Sometimes Sarah actually watches that show herself, back home in Richmond on her rare days off, of course she'd never admit it to a soul.

"What about the wedding?" Sarah asks when she returns.

"They couldn't have it," Gladiola says. "Judy had to reorder everything."

"But I would have thought that since the church was already reserved, I would imagine, and the minister all lined up, and the *invitations sent*, for heaven's sake . . ." Horror crosses Sarah's face. "I would have thought that they would hold the wedding regardless, and just find something else to wear. Perhaps something more traditional," she adds hopefully.

"Not on your life!" Gladiola laughs. "Roxanne had her heart set on a blue wedding." Gladiola shakes her head. She acts like it was all out of her hands, every bit of it, like she is powerless in the world. But Gladiola was the Mother of the Bride! Sarah cannot say a word, she just stares at Gladiola, who goes right on with the story. "Well, Preacher Sizemore said he could marry them anytime they took a notion to do it, so they set another date, and Judy reordered everything, and we got on the telephone and called up everybody we could think of, and so we put it off. But then, do you know what those rascals done?"

"Who?"

"Roxanne and Sean."

"What? What did they do?" Sarah cannot imagine.

"They went ahead and moved in together just like they had gone and gotten married after all! I was mad as fire. But there wasn't nothing I could do of course, you can't do a thing with Roxanne, and they already had this trailer that Sean's uncle had gave them after he built himself a new brick home out on the Bluefield road. It's got an aboveground swimming pool," Gladiola says, "which I think are so ugly."

Sarah unbuttons the top two buttons of her blouse and rolls up the sleeves. "Then what?"

"Well, so they move into this trailer, which is already decorated real cute, and Sean buys them a new car, which he's real proud of, that he bought cheap in a bankruptcy auction. A black Trans Am, they were both crazy about that car."

"How old is Sean?" Sarah asks.

"Nineteen," says Gladiola. "So anyway, they get all moved in together, and the wedding is set for two months off, and then Roxanne signs up for that nursing program at Mountain Tech. You know she was always so smart."

Sarah nods. *Too smart for her own good*, is what Sarah thinks.

"Well, this is when the trouble really starts." Gladiola lights another cigarette. "Sean's a real jealous person, it turns out. He can't stand for her to go anyplace without him, and he especially can't stand for her to drive off anyplace in the car without him. He gets downright peculiar about that car. So anyway, on the day that Roxanne has to register over at Mountain Tech, there's a big thunderstorm, and the computers go down. So it takes her forever to get registered, and it's nearabout dark when she gets back to the trailer."

"Can I have one of those?" Sarah reaches for Gladiola's pack of Salems.

Gladiola nods absently. "All I can say is that Sean Skeens went temporarily insane because she was over at Mountain Tech so long. Why, as soon as she pulled up in the road, he came busting out of that trailer hollering all this crazy stuff about Roxanne going off in the car to see other men, and such as that, and then you won't believe what he did next!"

"*What?*" The nicotine is making Sarah feel high, dizzy.

"He picks up this two-by-four that was laying right there, that they were fixing to build a deck with onto the trailer, see, they had them a big pile of treated lumber that they got on sale from Wal-Mart, and Sean's brother was going to help them build the deck."

Sarah leans back in the rocker and shuts her eyes. It crosses her mind that Gladiola is trying to drive her crazy. "Go on," she says. She blows smoke in the air.

"Well, Sean Skeens proceeds to lay into that car something terrible. He busted ever window *clean out*, he was so mad, and then started in on the dash."

Sarah sits bolt upright. "But that's terrible! What did Roxanne do?"

Gladiola is putting things back into the refrigerator now. "I'm ashamed to own it," she says, "but Roxanne picks up this *other* two-by-four and hits Sean Skeens right upside the head, just as hard as she can."

"*Good heavens!*" Sarah is suddenly, horribly agitated. She feels like she has to go to the bathroom. Instead she reaches for another cigarette.

"Yes ma'am. Broke his nose and one cheekbone and some little bone right up here." Gladiola points to her eyebrow. "I forget what you call it. Anyway, blood went all over the place, it was the biggest mess. Now they've got Sean Skeens wired up till he can't eat no solid food, he can't have nothing but milk shakes. He's still in the hospital. His mother has gone and charged Roxanne with assault and battery, and Roxanne has charged Sean with destruction of personal property. I tried to talk her out of it, I said, 'You'll have to pay that lawyer out of your own pocket,' but you know how she is."

"So what happened then?"

"Nothing yet. They're all going to court next week." Gladiola wipes off the kitchen counters and spreads her dish-rag on the sink to dry.

"And the wedding is off?" Sarah feels an overwhelming sense of loss.

"You're damn right!" Gladiola says. "They was too young to marry in the first place. Plus they was *too crazy* about each other, if you know what I mean. They would of wore each other out or killed each other, or killed somebody else. It wasn't no way they could of stayed together."

The front doorbell rings and Gladiola goes to answer it, leaving Sarah alone in the kitchen, where she rocks back and forth slightly, hugging herself. Sarah feels like she is hovering over her whole life in this rocking chair, she feels way high up, like a hummingbird. It occurs to her that the change of life might not be so bad. *No* change of life might be worse.

"What is it?" She struggles to her feet.

Everett Sharp has to repeat himself.

"I do hope I haven't come at a bad time," he says,

"although no time is *good*, in such a season of sorrow. I just wanted to thank you for your business and tell you I hope that everything met with your standards. I guess we probably do things different up here in the mountains. . . ." Everett Sharp trails off, looking at her. He has to look *down*, he's such a tall man; this makes Sarah feel small, a feeling she likes.

"*Sally Woodall*," he says suddenly, with a catch in his voice. "Aren't you Sally Woodall? From high school?"

And then Sarah realizes he didn't know who she was at all, not really, he hadn't even connected her with her teenage self of so many years before. Everett Sharp moves closer, staring at her. His long white bony arms poke out of his short white shirtsleeves; his forearms are covered with thick red hair. Sarah feels so hot and dizzy she's afraid she might pass out.

"My wife died last year," Everett Sharp says. "I married Betty Robinson, you might remember her. She was in the band."

Sarah nods.

"Clarinet," says Everett Sharp. Then he says, "Why don't I take you out to dinner tonight? It might do you good to get out some. They've got a seafood buffet on Fridays now, at the Holiday Inn on the interstate."

"All right," Sarah says, but she can't take in much of what happens after that. Everett Sharp soon leaves. It's so hot. Gladiola leaves. It's so hot. Sarah takes a notion to look for her father's vodka, which she finally finds in the filing cabinet in his study. She pours some into her iced tea and goes out on the porch, hoping for a breeze. She sits in the old glider and stares into the shady backyard, planning her outfit for tonight. Certainly not the beige linen suit she's worn practically ever since she got here. Maybe the blue sheath with the bolero jacket, maybe the floral two-piece with the scoop neck and the flared skirt. Yes! And those red pumps she bought on sale at Montaldo's last month and hasn't even worn yet, it's a good thing she just happened to throw them into her traveling bag. This strikes her as fortuitous, an omen. She sips her drink. The glider trembles on the edge of the afternoon.

Then Sarah remembers something that happened years ago, she couldn't have been more than seven or eight. Oddly enough, she was sitting right here on this glider, watching her parents, who sat out on the curly wrought-iron chairs beneath the big tree drinking cocktails, as they did every evening. Sarah was the kind of little girl who sat quietly, and noticed things. Actually she spied on people. Her mama and her daddy were leaning forward, all dressed up.

Mama's dress is white. It glows in the dark. Lightning bugs rise from the grass all around, katydids sing, frogs croak down by the creek. Sally has already had her supper. She wants to go back inside to play paper dolls, but something holds her there on the porch, still watching Mama and Daddy as they start to argue (jerky, scary movements, voices raised), and then as they stand, and then as Daddy kicks over the table, moving toward Mama to kiss her long and hard in the humming dark. Daddy puts his hands on Mama's dress.

The force of this memory sends Sarah back inside for another iced tea and vodka, and then she decides to count the napkins and place mats, and then she has another iced tea and vodka, and then she realizes it's time to get ready for her dinner date, but before she's through dressing she realizes she'd better go through the whole upstairs linen closet just to see what's in there, so she's not ready, not at all, not by a long shot, when Everett Sharp calls for her at seven, as he said.

He rings the front doorbell, then waits. He rings again. He doesn't know!—he couldn't even *imagine!*—that Sarah is right on the other side of the heavy door, not even a foot away from him, where she now sits propped up against it like a rag doll, her satin slip shining in the gloom of the dark hallway, with her fingers pressed over her mouth so she won't laugh out loud to think how she's fooled him, or start crying to think—as she will, again and again and again—how Sean must have felt when his very bones cracked and the red blood poured down the side of his face, or how *she* must have felt, hitting him.

LIVE BOTTOMLESS

In 1958, when my father had his famous affair with Carroll Byrd, I knew it before anybody. I don't know how long he'd been having the affair before I found out about it—or, to be exact, before I realized it. Before it came over me. One day I was riding my bike all over town the way I always did, and the next day I was riding my bike all over town *knowing it*, and this knowledge gave an extra depth, a heightened dimension and color, to everything. Before, I'd been just any old thirteen-year-old girl on a bike. Now, I was a *girl whose father was having an affair*—a tragic girl, a dramatic girl. A girl with a burning secret. Everything was different.

All my conversations, especially my conversations with

my mother, became almost electrical, charged with hidden
import: "pregnant with meaning," in the lingo of the love
magazines and movie magazines she was constantly reading.
Well, okay, *we* were constantly reading. For my mother
loved the lives of the stars above all else. She hated regular
newspapers. She hated facts. She also hated club meetings,
housework, politics, business, and her mother-in-law. She
was not civic. She adored shopping, friends, cooking, gardening, dancing, children and babies and kittens (all little
helpless things, actually), and my father. Especially she
adored my father. Mama's favorite word was "sweet." She'd
cry at the drop of a hat, and kept a clump of pink Kleenex
tucked into her bosom at all times, just in case. She called
people "poor souls."

That spring, Elizabeth Taylor was the poorest soul
around, when Mike Todd was killed in a plane crash one
week before the Academy Awards. Elizabeth, clutching their
tiny baby, Liza, was in shock as her Hollywood and New
York friends rallied to her side. The industry had never seen
such a dynamo as Todd, whose electric energy sparked
everyone. Just a few weeks before Todd's death, he had cel-
ebrated Elizabeth's twenty-sixth birthday by giving her a
dazzling diamond necklace at the Golden Globe Awards
dinner.

Not a "poor soul" was Ava Gardner, who had divorced
Frank Sinatra for the Italian actor Walter Chiari and now
was trying to steal Shelley Winters's husband, Anthony

Franciosa, playing opposite her in *The Naked Maja*, currently being filmed in Rome.

"Can you *imagine?*" My mother, clutching *Photoplay*, was outraged. "Isn't Ava ever satisfied? Just think how Shelley Winters must feel!"

"It's terrible," I agreed. *If you only knew*, I thought. I sat down on the edge of the chaise longue to peer at the pictures of Ava and Shelley and Tony in a Roman nightclub.

"Look at that *dress*." Mama pointed to Ava.

"What a bitch," I said loyally. *If you only knew*, I thought.

"Honestly, Jenny, such language!" But Mama was giggling. "I don't know what I'm going to do with you."

Nothing, was the answer to that, already clear to both of us. The fact is, I was just too much for Mama, coming along to them so late in life (a "surprise"), after my two older sisters had already "sapped her strength" and "lowered her resistance," as she said, to all kinds of things, including migraine headaches, asthma, and a heart murmur. These ailments required her to lie down a lot but did not prevent her from being perfectly beautiful, as always.

My mother was widely known as one of the most beautiful women in Virginia, everybody said so. Previously she had been the most beautiful girl in Charleston, South Carolina, where she had grown up as Billie Rutledge and lived until she married my father, John Fitzhugh Dale, Jr., a naval officer stationed there briefly during the war. "Just long enough to sweep me off my feet," as she put it. He was a divine dancer, and my most cherished image of my parents involved them waltzing grandly around a ballroom floor, she in a long white gown, he in a snappy uniform, her hair and the buttons on the uniform gleaming golden in the light from the sparkling chandeliers.

Thus she became Billie Rutledge Dale, in a ceremony I loved to imagine. It was a wedding of superlatives: the handsomest couple in the world, a wedding cake six feet high, a gown with a train fifteen feet long, ten bridesmaids, a horse and buggy— not to mention a former suitor's suicide attempt the night before, while everybody else was dancing the night away at the rehearsal dinner. I was especially fascinated by this unsuccessful project, which had involved the young man's trying to hang himself from a coat rack in a downtown men's club, after which he was forever referred to as Bobby "Too Tall" Burkes.

Some people said Mama looked like Marilyn Monroe, but I didn't think so; Mama was bigger, blonder, paler, softer, with a sort of inflatable celluloid prettiness. She looked like a great big baby doll. People also said I took after Mama, but this wasn't true, either, at least not yet, and I didn't want it to become true, at least not entirely, as I feared that taking after her too much might eventually damn me into lying down a lot of the time, which looked pretty boring.

On the other hand, I was simply dying to get my period, grow breasts, turn into a sexpot and do as much damage as Mama, who had broken every heart in Charleston and had a charm bracelet made out of fraternity pins to prove it. She used to tick them off for me one by one. "Now that was Smedes Black, a Phi Delt from UVA, such a darling boy, and this one was Parker Winthrop, a Sigma Chi at W and L, he used to play the ukulele. . . ." I was drunk on the sound of so many alphabetical syllables. My mother had "come out" in Charleston; my sisters had attended St. Catherine's School and then "come out" in Richmond, since nobody did such a thing in Lewisville, outside Lynchburg, where we lived. I was expected to follow in my sisters' footsteps.

But then our paths would diverge, as I secretly planned to go up north to college before becoming (to everyone's total astonishment) a *writer*. First I would write steamy novels about my own hot love life, eventually getting world-famous like Grace Metalious. I would make millions of dollars and give it all away to starving children in foreign lands. I would win the Nobel Prize. Then I would become a vegetarian poet in Greenwich Village. I would live for Art.

I had a big future ahead of me. But so far, nothing doing. No breasts, no period, no sex, no art. Though very blond, I was just any skinny, pale, wispy-haired kid on a bike, quick as a rabbit, fast as a bird, riding invisible all over town, bearing my awful secret.

I KNEW WHO SHE WAS, OF COURSE. EVERYONE KNEW. Her father, Old Man Byrd, had been the county judge for forty years. After retirement, he became a hermit—or as

close to a hermit as it was possible to be in Lewisville, which
was chock-full of neighborly curious people naturally bound
and determined to look after one another all the time. ("I
swear to God," my father remarked once in exasperation,
"if the devil himself moved into this town, I guess you'd
take *him* a casserole, too!") Judge Byrd was a wild-looking,
white-haired, ugly old man whose eyebrows grew all the
way across his face in the most alarming fashion; he walked
bent over, leaning on a walking stick topped by a carved
ivory skull, yelling at children. He smelled bad. He did not
socialize. He did not go to church, and was rumored to be
an atheist. When he died, everyone was shocked to learn that
there would be *no funeral*, unheard of in our town. Furthermore, he was to be *cremated*.

I remember the conversation Mama and Daddy had about
it at the time.

"Cremated . . ." Mama mused. "Isn't that sort of . . . com-
munist? Don't they do it in Russia and places like that?"

"Lord, no, honey." Daddy was laughing. "It's perfectly
common, in this country as well as abroad. For one thing,
it's a lot more economical."

"Well, it certainly isn't *southern*," Mama sniffed. "And I
certainly don't intend to have it done to *me*, are you listening, John? I want my body to remain as intact as possible,
and I want to be buried with all my rings on. And a nice
suit, or maybe a dress with a little matching jacket. And I
want lots of yellow roses, as in life."

"Yes, Billie." Daddy hid a smile as he went out the door. He was Old Man Byrd's lawyer, and so was in charge of the arrangements. I couldn't believe my own daddy was actually getting to go inside Old Man Byrd's house, a vine-covered mansion outside town, which everyone called "The Ivy House." But of course my father *was* the best lawyer in town, so it followed that he'd be the judge's lawyer, too. And since he was the soul of discretion, it also followed that he'd never mentioned this to us, not even when my cousin Jinx and I got caught trying to peep in Old Man Byrd's windows on a dare. I still remember what we saw: a gloomy sitting room full of dark, crouching furniture; a fat white cat on a chair; the housekeeper's sudden furious face.

Jinx and I were grounded from our bikes for a whole week, during which I completed a paint-by-numbers version of Leonardo da Vinci's *Last Supper*, done mostly in shades of orange and gold, and presented it to my daddy, who seemed surprised.

"I'm sorry for trespassing," I said. "I'll never do it again."

But I wasn't sorry, not in the least. The incident marked the beginning of my secret career.

I lived to spy, and this was mainly what I did on my bike trips around town. I'd seen some really neat stuff, too. For instance, I had seen Roger Ainsley, the coolest guy in our school, squeezing pimples in his bathroom mirror. I'd seen Mr. Bondurant whip his big son Earl with a belt a lot harder than anybody ever ought to, and later, when Earl dropped out of school and enlisted in the Army, I alone knew why. I had seen my fourth-grade teacher, prissy Miss Emily Horn, necking on the couch with her boyfriend and smoking cigarettes. Best of all, I had seen Mrs. Cecil Hertz come running past a picture window wearing nothing but an apron, followed shortly by Mr. Cecil Hertz himself, wearing nothing at all and carrying a spatula.

It was amazing how careless people were about drawing their drapes and pulling their shades down. It was amazing what you could see, especially if you were an athletic and enterprising girl such as myself. I wrote my observations down in a Davy Crockett spiral notebook I'd bought for this purpose. I wrote down everything: date, time, weather, physical descriptions, my reaction. I would use this stuff later, in my novels.

I saw Carroll Byrd the very first time I rode out there to spy on her, after the old man's death. It was a cold gray day in January, and she was burning trash. The sky was so dark that I didn't notice the smoke at first, not until I was halfway down the long lane that went from the road to the house—*her* house, now. In spite of the cold, she had opened the windows, flung the shutters outward, and left the front door wide open, too. Airing everything out, I guessed. The whole house wore a rattled, astonished expression. She had a regular bonfire going on the patio in the side yard—cardboard boxes, newspapers, old magazines. She emerged from the house with armful after armful of old papers to feed the yellow flames.

I had ditched my bike earlier, up the lane; now I dodged behind giant boxwoods, getting closer and closer. This was interesting. Neither my mother nor any of her friends would *ever* have acted like Carroll Byrd. In the first place, they all had constant help and never lifted a finger carrying anything. In the second place, Mama "would not be found dead" dressed the way Carroll Byrd was dressed that day: she wore work boots, just like a field hand; men's pants, belted at the waist; and a tight, long-sleeved black sweater (*leotard* was a word I would not learn until college). Her dark hair, longer than any woman's in town, was pulled back severely from her high forehead and tied with a string, and fell straight down her back. Indian hair, streaked with gray. I knew instinctively that she didn't care about the gray, that she would never color it. Nor would she ever wear makeup. Her face was lean and hard, her cheekbones chiseled. She had inherited her father's heavy brows, like dark wings above the deep-set black eyes.

While I watched, she paused in the middle of one of her trips to the house, and my heart leaped up to my throat as I thought that I had been discovered. But no. Carroll Byrd had stopped to eye an ornate white trellis, nonfunctional but pretty, which arched over the path between the house and the patio. Hand on hip, she considered it. She walked around it. Then, before I could believe what she was doing, she ripped it out of the ground and was breaking it up like so many matchsticks, throwing the pieces into the fire. Red flames shot toward the lowering sky. She laughed out loud. I noted her generous mouth, the flash of white teeth.

Then Carroll Byrd sat down on an iron bench to watch her fire burn for a while. She lit a cigarette, striking the match on her boot. Now I noticed that she wasn't wearing a brassiere, something I had read about but never seen done among "nice" women. When she leaned over to stub out her cigarette on the patio tiles, I saw her breasts shift beneath the black sweater. Immediately I thought of "Selena's brown nipples" on page 72 in Jinx's and my dog-eared, hidden copy of *Peyton Place*. I was both disgusted and thrilled.

There in the cramped and pungent safety of the giant boxwood bush, I fell in love. We watched her fire, the two of us from our different vantage points, until it burned itself out. She ran a hose on the ashes before she went inside her father's house and shut the door.

I sneaked back to my bike and rode down the long lane and then home, pedaling as fast as I could, freezing to death. But my own house seemed too warm, too bright, too soft—now I hated the baby-blue shag rug in my room, hated all my stuffed animals. I wanted fire and bare trees and cold gray sky. I went straight to bed and wouldn't get up for dinner. After a while, Mama came in and took my temperature (normal) and brought me a bowl of milk toast on a tray. This was what you got in our house when you were sick, and it was delicious.

• • •

MAMA WAS A GREAT COOK. SHE ALSO LOVED TO TALK
on the phone, and during the next weeks, I strained to over-
hear any mention of Carroll Byrd. I got plenty of material.
But since Mama generally stayed home and was the recipient
rather than the purveyor of news, it was sometimes hard for
me to figure out what had actually happened.

"She *what*?"

"You're kidding! Why, those rugs are worth a fortune!
That furniture came from England!"

"Oh, he did *not*!"

"Well, that is the strangest thing I have ever heard in my
whole life. The strangest!"

"You're kidding!"

Et cetera.

I had to decipher the news: Carroll Byrd had given away
the downstairs furnishings and the Oriental rugs to several
distant relations, who showed up in U-Hauls to claim them
and cart them away. Then she fired the housekeeper.
She hired Norman Estep, a local ne'er-do-well and jack-
of-all-trades, to knock down the walls between the
kitchen and the dining room and the parlor, and paint
everything white, including "that beautiful paneling."
("Have you *ever*?") Next, several huge wooden crates arrived
for Carroll Byrd from Maine, and Norman went to the train

station and picked them up in his truck and took them to her house.

For Carroll Byrd was a painter, it developed. Not a housepainter, of course, but the other kind—an *artist*. The minute I heard this, a long shudder ran from the top of my head to my feet. An *artist*. Of course! She had decided to stay on in her father's house because she loved the light down here as spring came on.

"The what?" Mama asked, puckering up her mouth as she talked on the phone to Jinx's mother. "I mean, it's light up in Maine, too, isn't it?"

Well, yes, but Carroll Byrd feels that there is a *special quality* to the light here in Virginia that she just has to capture on canvas. So now Norman Estep is building frames, huge frames, for her canvases. And now he's going all around to junkyards for pieces of iron, and now he's buying welding tools at Southern States Supply. For her *sculptures*—turns out she's a sculptor, too. Newly elevated to a position of importance by his privileged relationship with Carroll Byrd, Norman Estep is grilled mercilessly by all the women in town, and clams up. Now he won't tell anybody anything. Neither what she's painting, nor what she wears, nor what in the world she does out there all day long by herself. Norman Estep buys groceries for her in the Piggly Wiggly, consulting a list penned in a stark angular hand. He won't even tell anybody what she eats! He is completely loyal to Carroll Byrd.

But the women turn against her. They drive out there to welcome her, two by two, carrying cakes or pies or casseroles or congealed salad, to be met cordially at the door by the artist herself, who does not ask them in. She responds politely to their questions but does not initiate any topics herself. Finally, in some consternation, the women turn on their heels and lurch off down the long walk, but not before noticing that she's made a huge mess of the patio—why, it's got an old iron gate and pieces of junk from the junkyard piled right in the middle of it, some of them welded together into this awful-looking construction that Mama swears is a human figure but Jinx's mama says is no such thing—and not before seeing that Carroll Byrd's gotten Norman Estep to plow up all that pretty grass in front of the house for a big vegetable garden, of all things! No lady has a vegetable garden, and no person in their right mind would put such a garden *in front* of a nice house, anyway. ("Lovely home," Mama always says.)

Several weeks after accepting the food, Carroll Byrd sends Norman around to deliver the plates and containers back to their original owners, each with its terse little thank-you note attached, written on fine creamy paper with raised initials.

This paper seems to make Mama madder than anything yet. ("I'll swear! It's certainly not like she *doesn't know any better*.") By then it is clear to all that Carroll Byrd is determined to be as much of a hermit as her father was, even more of one, and in the way of small towns, everybody stops badgering her and even begins to take a perverse pride in her eccentricity. "See that long driveway goes right up that way?" a visitor might be told. "There's a world-famous woman artist lives up there all by herself. Never goes past the gate."

BUT MOST PEOPLE, INCLUDING MAMA, FORGOT ABOUT Carroll Byrd as spring turned into summer and more recent events claimed everyone's attention. Susan Blackwelder had a miscarriage, then fell into a depression; old Mr. Bishop retired and then sold his downtown Commercial Hotel to two young men from Washington who were reputed to be "homos," which interested me, naturally, and led to some fascinating observations. Best of all, Miss Lavinia Doolittle knelt *but never rose* from taking Communion at the altar in the Episcopal church on Palm Sunday. She *died* with her wafer in her mouth. I loved this, and was furious that we had missed it by attending the eleven-o'clock service rather than the nine-o'clock, just because Mama always said nine o'clock was "too early for God or anybody."

Still, *I* didn't forget about Carroll Byrd. I rode my bike about once a week all summer long, with time off for camp and Bible school and the beach. I'd usually find her outside, wearing a halter and cutoff jeans, working in the garden with her braided hair wound on top of her head. She was brown as a berry, strong as a man. The garden thrived, with shiny red tomatoes and big-leafed tropical-looking squash plants and enormous sunflowers that nodded on their stalks like happy idiots. I could have stepped right up and spoken to her, and often I thought I *would*, but somehow I never did. One time she put a plateful of fresh vegetables from the garden on a table outdoors and set up an easel to paint them. I couldn't see the painting, but I could see her face: dire, ruthless, beautiful.

It stayed with me all summer while I went off to 4-H camp and then Camp Nantahala and then to Virginia Beach with my mother and Jinx and Jinx's mother. Virginia Beach was loud and bright and fun, though Jinx and I were dismayed to find that a boy from our very own class back in Lewisville, Buddy Womble, was staying down the beach, and would not let us alone. He liked to sneak up on us while we were lying out in the sun with little wet pads of cotton over our eyes, as suggested by *Teen* magazine. "Gotcha!" Buddy Womble would holler, kicking sand, which stuck to our baby-oiled arms and legs and made us look like sandpaper girls. Then he'd run off down the beach laughing his big fake laugh, "Har-dee-har-har," at the top of his lungs. Jinx and I hated him. We went spying on his cottage one night and were appalled to witness Buddy's fat father, sitting alone on the porch, bury his face in his hands and sob as if his heart would break. This violated every known rule of conduct. Men were not supposed to cry, especially not fathers. "Yuck," Jinx mouthed at me, her round white face like a horrified little moon in the shadows. I felt my own heart drop to my feet in a long, sickening fall. The next day, we were a lot nicer to Buddy on the beach.

Our mothers played bridge and went on a gin-and-tonic diet, which meant that they walked up and down the beach a lot with insulated plastic tumblers in their hands. Jinx and I won cheap jewelry by throwing softballs at stuffed cats in the amusement park, rode rented bikes, and drank some gin of our own with three girls from Durham, North Carolina, who had stolen it from their parents. We bleached our hair with lemon juice. We got real tan, and did not burn our eyelids. The weather was perfect every day except for the last one, which dawned rainy, and so we packed up and drove home early to surprise our daddies.

They would be at work, of course, when we got there. Mama dropped Jinx and her mother off first, then let me out at home and went on to the grocery store. I let myself in with the key and took my bag upstairs to my room, which looked *smaller* now, a baby's room. I put my bag on the bed and turned to the mirror and then stopped still, in shock—I almost failed to recognize myself! My bleached blond hair, grown out longer than it had ever been, curled all around my dark face, which looked different, too . . . thinner, not so babyish.

I raced outside and got my bike out of the garage and rode off to see Carroll Byrd. It was a drizzly, humid August day; I was covered by a fine mist of rain, like my own sweat, by the time I turned down her lane. I rode until I reached the hedge where I always hid my bike, then slipped behind the farthest boxwood, looking toward the house.

But I went no closer.

For there, parked right in front, was Daddy's car, the familiar big gray Oldsmobile with the AAA and Rotary Club stickers. Even from where I was, I could see his old canvas hat stuck under the back windshield.

I waited and waited. At first I thought, *Oh well, Daddy's her lawyer. This is a lawyer visit.* Then I stopped thinking anything, as gradually it came over me. I didn't move a muscle. I stayed behind that boxwood for one hour and forty minutes by my watch, and then dodged back to the hedge and got my bike and rode home. When I went to bed that night, after Mama's special supper and Daddy's big hello, my arms and legs ached and ached, as if I had run a race, or climbed a mountain.

I NEVER RODE MY BIKE TO CARROLL BYRD'S HOUSE again. But the horrible thing was that I didn't really blame Daddy. I could see why he would love her. For in a sense, Daddy was *like* her: a loner, an observer, an outsider . . . despite the fact that he'd been born and brought up in Lewisville, despite the fact that he was doing exactly what he was supposed to be doing and had been at it for decades.

Daddy had run the mill, Dale Industries, since he was only twenty-eight years old, when his own father killed himself.

One day I asked Daddy to tell me about this. We were down at the mill, in the very office where my grandfather had done it. It was after hours, and Daddy was trying to finish up some paperwork, at the same desk where his father had kept the gun in the bottom drawer. "Why?" I kept asking. "Why did Granddaddy shoot himself?"

But all Daddy would say was, "Oh, Jenny, honey, there are pressures, circumstances, that you can't possibly understand at your age"—the kind of response that infuriated me. I went right out in front of the mill and broke the aerial off Daddy's car, then lied about it. I said it had been done by some kids in a blue van with Ohio tags. Daddy always underrated me. As a future novelist and student of the human soul, I knew a lot more than he thought I did. I was capable of understanding anything he had to tell me.

I alone understood that Daddy was a hero, a tragic figure. He stood six-foot-three and looked like Gregory Peck, with a rangy body, a prominent nose, dark thick hair, and sad gray eyes that seemed to see *everything*. Perhaps to make up for his father's lapses, Daddy was the most responsible man in the world. He worked harder than anybody I have ever seen, involving himself not only in the daily business of the mill but also in the lives of the families who had been working there for generations: tirelessly attending funerals, weddings, graduations, wakes. My mother rarely went with him to these events, as she had "better things" to do, and also found "those people" depressing. Daddy served on every board in town and belonged to every organization, or so it appeared to me.

He also took care of my mean old grandmother and my shy maiden aunt Chloë, who lived with her, visiting them nearly every day. Aunt Chloë had had polio, and leaned to the left as she walked. My grandmother Ernestine Dale enjoyed absolutely *nothing* as far as I could see, except television; Daddy had bought them the first set in town. Grandmother claimed to watch only the quiz shows, calling them "educational," but in fact she watched that television all the time. She had trained Aunt Chloë to hop up and turn it off the moment a visitor arrived on the porch; by the time Aunt Chloë had let the visitor into the parlor, my grandmother would be reading the *Upper Room* or the Bible.

Oh, she *acted* simpery-sweet, but she didn't fool me for a minute—she was a fake, an old bitch. I didn't like her and she didn't like me much, either, complaining that I was a "tomboy" and a "roughneck," criticizing my nails, which I bit to the quick, and trying to convince me that I should like Charles Van Doren better than Elvis Presley. My grandmother was a fool! She wore big black dresses and smelled like Mentholatum. I used to put baby powder in her tapioca and rearrange everything on her night table whenever I went to her house, so she would think she was going crazy.

I felt sorry for Daddy. He had to take care of Grandmother's and Aunt Chloë's affairs as well as our own; he also had to shepherd his other sister, my silly aunt Judy (that's Judy Dale Tuttle Miller Hall), in and out of one crazy marriage after another, while back at home he had two daughters to raise and then *me* (the surprise). Daddy had his work cut out for him. He had a beautiful wife who required a lot of coddling and catering to, something I'd always assumed he enjoyed, but after my observations of Carroll Byrd, I realized that Mama was *too* soft, *too* sweet, *too* safe for Daddy, like one of those pink satin pillows on her huge unmade bed. A man could sink down in there and never get out.

Now I saw Daddy as stifled, smothered by all that pink. I saw him as a restless cowboy in Grandmother's parlor, as a hawk among knickknacks.

No wonder he loved Carroll Byrd.

I still loved her, too; and in a way, I felt, this love brought me closer to my father, though he didn't know it, of course. But I was trying to *stop*, out of loyalty to my mother and also because I knew that Carroll Byrd would never love me back. She'd never even know me. The affair would not last long—these things never did, I told myself.

Anyway, I was used to loving people who didn't love me back. After all, I'd been in love with Tom Burlington, my sister's husband, for years and years. Three years, to be exact, but it seemed like an eternity.

• • •

MY SISTER CAROLINE *DID NOT DESERVE* TOM BURLING-
ton. I couldn't imagine how she had tricked him into marrying her in the first place. My grandmother always called
Caroline a flibbertigibbet; and for once, I agreed with her.
Caroline was simply too bouncy. She wore everybody out.
Of course she was a cheerleader at St. Catherine's, of course
she was "Most Popular" in the yearbook; of course she was
president of her class twice in a row at Hollins before trans-
ferring to Carolina in her junior year, where of course she
pledged Tri Delt. She made solid B's and majored in elementary education. Caroline had a bouncy ponytail, boundless
enthusiasm, and the whitest teeth I've ever seen. By Christmas of her senior year, she was engaged to Tom; right after
graduation, they got married.

Caroline's wedding was the biggest event in our family
that I could remember. My oldest sister, Beth, had married
quietly (in the Little Chapel of St. Michael's Episcopal
Church) before moving to California, where her young husband had gotten a very good job in the computer industry,
which nobody had ever heard of. She had one child already,
and was expecting another. I didn't know Beth at all, though
I'd always felt that I'd *like* her, because of the sweet way she
held her baby in the photographs she sent home. And when
she and her husband came east for Caroline's wedding, Beth
was the only person thoughtful enough to bring *me* a

present: a silver ring with a turquoise flower. (I cried and cried when I lost it in the lake at Camp Nantahala the following summer.)

I was the youngest bridesmaid in Caroline's wedding. I got to wear a white organdy dress with a pink satin sash, a picture hat, and pearl earrings. I got to carry a bouquet of pink rosebuds and baby's breath. I even got to wear Cuban heels—my first high heels ever—over my grandmother's objections. She said I was too young. My mother said, "Oh, Ernestine, I'm sure you're right," and let me wear them anyway. I looked perfectly beautiful at Caroline's wedding, much prettier than Caroline herself, who was a bit too wholesome for white. Caroline looked like a nurse.

But her groom, Thomas Burlington, looked like Troy Donahue. He was the handsomest boy I'd ever met, and the nicest, possessing all of Daddy's sensitivity without the aloofness.

I had been predisposed toward him anyway, after Mama's discussions about him on the telephone: "Well, he doesn't have a penny to his name, but he's real *smart*, he's gotten all these scholarships. . . . Oh yes, we like him. You can't help but like him. . . . He's got a master's degree in English literature, have you *ever*? . . . Well, I don't know. Teach school, I reckon." Mama's tone betrayed what she thought about teaching school, and I was sure Caroline held the same opinion. A schoolteacher would never be able to support Caroline, not even the cutest schoolteacher in the world, which

Tom was. He didn't know what he was getting into. (Though they did receive so many wedding presents that they could have sold them off and lived for a year or two on the proceeds, it looked like to me.)

The wedding reception was held at our house, under a huge white tent set up in the backyard. In the house, the wedding presents were displayed in the family room and the downstairs guest suite, a sea of silver, china, and crystal. I had earlier pocketed a nifty jade paperweight sent by one of Tom's relatives that nobody had ever heard of, to keep as a souvenir.

I started loving Tom Burlington at the wedding reception, and never stopped. The party was all but over. Tom and Caroline had cut the cake, made the toasts, and everybody was dancing to terrible music (Percy Faith). Caroline had gone upstairs to put on her "going-away outfit." My feet were killing me. I shifted from foot to foot to keep my heels from sinking into the grass as I waited in the front yard, clutching my net package of rice, wishing I hadn't gotten so grown up all of a sudden, so I could run down the road playing tag with my little cousins.

"Why don't you just take them off?" There was Tom at my elbow. He pointed to my shoes.

"Oh, I'm fine," I said. "Just fine. I wear heels all the time," I said.

"I was just thinking of taking my own shoes off," Tom said. "In fact, I believe I will." He stepped out of his loafers and leaned down to peel off his socks. He had changed to a seersucker suit with a white shirt and a striped tie.

"Me too, then." My feet sank into the cool thick grass.

"And now, Miss Jennifer, I wonder if you would do me the honor of accompanying me to get another bite of that cake," Tom said formally. "There's plenty of time. You know how long it takes your sister to get dressed."

He held his arm out to me the way people do in movies, and I took it. We walked off, leaving our shoes where they were, and went over to the huge delicious complicated cake on its own table, attended by a waiter. "Which layer, Miss?" the waiter asked, and I said, "Chocolate, please." There was a white layer, a yellow layer, and a chocolate layer. Trust Caroline to have a fancier cake than anybody in Lewisville had ever had before.

Tom chose chocolate, too. "Now how about a drink?" he asked.

"I'd love some champagne," I said.

Tom didn't bat an eye. He disappeared and came right back with a glass of champagne for me and one for himself. He clinked my glass in an elegant toast: "To the lovely Miss Jennifer." This is the exact moment I fell in love. Then he quoted a real poem, which began: "A sweet disorder in the dress . . ." It was very long and very beautiful.

I held my breath the whole time. At the end of the poem, I raised my glass and drained it. The champagne went straight up my nose. I started crying, and couldn't stop.

Tom was not at all disconcerted by my tears. He did not say "Don't cry" or "There now." Instead, he wiped at them gravely, scientifically, with a linen napkin. Then he took my arm again and escorted me gallantly across the grass to the front yard, where the whole crowd had gathered, with Mama up on the steps in her billowing satin gown, her hand to her forehead like an explorer, anxiously scanning the crowd.

"*Here* he is!" she called inside. "Okay, dear!" And then Caroline emerged in a beige suit with a corsage, carrying her bouquet. Before I knew it, Tom had moved to her side, and flashbulbs were popping, and then she threw the bouquet straight to me. Everybody cheered. I clutched it tight, forgetting to throw my own rice, while Tom and Caroline ran the gauntlet out to their waiting limo and were rushed away to the Mountain Lake Hotel, where they would *do it* all night long. (Do *what*? I had no idea.) I saved that bouquet, though. I have it still.

When the wedding pictures came, everybody was amused to see that Tom had gone off on his honeymoon *barefooted*. Nobody but me knew why. Nobody but me ever knew that he had toasted me with champagne, and said a poem to me.

From that day forward, I loved Tom with a rapt, fierce, patient love. Sometimes I even talked myself into believing, for an hour or so at least, that Tom had married Caroline only to get closer to *me*, to wait for me to grow up. Other times, even I had to admit that their marriage seemed to be going okay.

Tom got a job teaching English at a boys' boarding school outside Charlottesville, which afforded them a nice free bungalow on campus, which Caroline immediately fixed up like a doll-house version of Mama's house. Tom got a promotion, then another promotion and a raise. Caroline taught second grade and joined the Junior League and gave little dinner parties using all her wedding presents. When Mama and I drove up for a Saturday visit, Caroline served us shrimp salad on bone china plates with a scalloped gold edge. She told us that she and Tom were very happy, which I had no reason to doubt.

Yet unrequited love is the easiest sort of love to hang on to, and I'd cherished mine for three years now, until it had become not only a passion but a habit. Whenever I heard Debbie Reynolds's hit recording of "Tammy," for instance, I'd change the words to "Tommy" in my mind:

> *The old hootie-owl*
> *Hootie-hoos to the dove,*
> *Tommy, Tommy,*
> *Tommy's in love . . .*

with *me*! His bare feet in the wedding pictures provided all the proof I needed. Of course I also liked the wedding pictures because I was in them, looking terrific.

However, I hated looking at Mama and Daddy's wedding pictures because I was *not* in them, because I hadn't even existed then, a fact which threw me into as much terror as the thought of my own death. I had tried to explain this to Jinx, but she didn't get it. Nobody got it.

I saw myself as an island with time stretching out before me and behind me, all around me like a deep lake, mysterious and never-ending, like Lake Nantahala, where I lost my ring, where a person might lose anything. This precarious view made everything that happened to me seem very, very important. I had to see as much as I could see, learn as much as I could learn, feel as much as I could feel. I had to live like crazy all the time, an attitude that would get me into lots of trouble later. So it didn't matter, not really, whether or not Tom loved me back. Sometimes—I knew this from observing Mama and her baby brother, Mason—you're bound to love most the one who loves you least, and least deserves it.

MASON WAS JUST NO GOOD. EVERYBODY KNEW IT, SINCE he had come to live with Mama and Daddy when his parents—my grandparents—died unexpectedly in the same year, many years ago. Seventeen years older than I, Mason was grown and gone by the time I was born. He had graduated from our local high school by the skin of his teeth, distinguished by nothing—no sports, no clubs. Nice girls would not date him. College was out of the question. Mason wore T-shirts and the same old leather jacket all through high school; his swept-back hair was long and greasy. Even

Daddy could not get a button-down shirt or a sports jacket on him.

Mason had been a *juvenile delinquent*. This thrilled me. Of course, I would have adored him if he'd been nice to me at all, but his interest in me was confined to ruffling my hair at infrequent intervals throughout my childhood and mumbling "Hey now" out of the side of his mouth. That was *it*. And now, after some awful fight, he and Daddy had had a "parting of the ways," as Mama put it. Daddy was a man who stood on principle, though the rift broke Mama's heart. I wasn't sure what the final straw had been. I knew that Daddy had bailed Mason out of debt numerous times and had set him up in two businesses, which had, however, failed. Somewhere along the way, Mason had married "disastrously," Mama said, a much older woman of no consequence, with three children. Her name was Gloria, but I had never met her, or even laid eyes on her. I hardly ever laid eyes on Mason, either. He lived someplace near Norfolk and worked in the shipyards, I think. He no longer showed up for holidays, and had not attended Caroline's wedding.

So by the time of this story, a sighting of Mason was as rare as a comet, taking place only during the daytime when Daddy was not at home. On those few occasions, Mason scared me a little—he'd grown fat and scruffy, and needed a shave. He didn't look like a juvenile delinquent anymore but like some guy you'd see on the side of a road hitchhiking. He looked older than he was, down on his luck.

Daddy was still officially waiting for Mason to "come around." In the meantime, Mama gave him money. That's what these visits were all about: money. I knew it, though Mama never said so. She received Mason privately—in her bedroom or the Florida room or the living room—anywhere I was *not*, which she made sure of by closing whatever door existed between me and them. When Mason left, looking shifty, Mama always seemed to have her purse nearby—on her bed, or the coffee table, or the sofa. Wherever they'd just been. I could put two and two together. She didn't have to tell me not to tell Daddy, either; I already knew that. Just as I knew that Mason never came to see her unless he needed money, and this must have hurt her deeply.

Mama always had a good cry the minute he left. "Oh, Jenny, honey, come here and hug your mama," she'd call, and I would go do it, patting her plump shoulder ineffectively while she sobbed into her pink Kleenex. "That poor soul," she'd wail, "that poor, poor soul!"

I didn't even like Mason by then, and couldn't understand why Mama would waste her tears on him when she had such a brilliant and adorable daughter right there on the premises. Now, so many years later and a parent myself, I understand that there is no anguish like the anguish of not being able to make a loved one become the person you think he ought to be. It can't be done, of course. But they had not given up on him yet, not Mama and not even Daddy. Why, Mason was barely thirty years old! Surely he'd come to his senses. Surely he'd shape up.

In the fall of 1958, Mama and Daddy were still expecting this to happen.

JINX AND I WERE IN MY ROOM LISTENING TO RECORDS when the call came. It was a Saturday afternoon, bright and blowing outside, leaves flying everyplace. We lay stretched out flat on the shag carpet trying to figure out what in the world "*Nel blu, dipinto di blu*" meant, and sighing over "Fever" by Peggy Lee. We knew what that meant. I had just put "Love Me Tender" on when the phone rang. Jinx jumped up. She was hoping to hear from Stevie Burns, who had said he'd call her this weekend; I knew Jinx had made her mother promise to give him our number before she'd agree to come over to my house at all. Since summer, Jinx had, one, started her period and, two, gotten popular, just like that. She wouldn't go spying with me anymore.

I had a phone in my room, and Jinx grabbed it on the first ring. "Hello," she said. Her new poodle cut gave her a heart-shaped face, eager now.

I sat up, too, vicariously excited, thinking I might pick up some useful pointers for handling future dates. So I was watching closely as Jinx's smiling mouth went into that frozen O, as she shut her brown eyes for a long moment before carefully replacing the receiver on its cradle.

Downstairs, Mama started to scream.

"Oh, Jenny." Jinx finally spoke. "Your uncle is dead."

"What?" I had to think for a moment to figure out who she was talking about.

"Mason," she said. "Isn't his name Mason? Mason's been shot."

"Shot," I repeated.

"Murdered," Jinx said.

The word hung in the air in my bedroom, quivering along with Elvis's voice. I turned the record player off just as Mama rushed through the bedroom door, swooping me up, smothering me with her sobs and tears.

The story, what we could learn of it, went like a country song. Mason's wife had left him for another man, and Mason had gone out looking for her. He'd found them at last in some bar in Norfolk, where things had turned ugly fast. Mason had pulled a knife and cut the man's face. Then the man shot him.

"Shot him dead?" I asked Mama.

"No, honey. Shot him *four times* before he died." Mama collapsed on my canopied bed, wailing. "He was the most adorable little boy," she cried. "I was just a newlywed myself when he came to live with us, you know. Just a girl. Your daddy was always working, always gone. So it was just Mason and me. We grew up together. He was the sweetest

boy, you can't imagine. Maybe he was *too* sweet, maybe that
was the problem, he just never could get along. And then all
that drinking, oh Lord, it started so soon. If only—if only
we—" Mama went on and on.

Jinx sneaked out, looking panicked. She waved from the
door. I sat on the side of my bed hugging Mama for what
seemed like hours, until Jinx's mother arrived. I was never
so glad to see anybody in my life. Then suddenly my wild
aunt Judy was there, too, serious for once; and our minister,
Mr. Clyde Vereen; and then Dr. Nevins, who gave Mama
some pills which shut her up all right but made her *too calm*,
I felt.

Mama sat downstairs on a tufted velvet love seat, where
she had never sat before, at least not in my memory, vacant
and glassy-eyed, asking for Daddy. Meanwhile, Aunt Judy
was on the phone constantly, and Jinx's mama answered the
door.

"Where is John?" Mama kept asking. "I just can't understand where John is."

Nobody else could understand this, either. Aunt Judy
couldn't reach him out at Granddaddy's old hunting cabin,
where Daddy had gone for the night. He did this occasionally, though he'd read and reflect instead of hunt. It was his
retreat.

Finally Aunt Judy dispatched his good friend George
Long to get him, but an hour and a half later George called
back with the perplexing message that Daddy was not at the

hunting cabin, and it didn't look like he'd even gotten there yet. Our house was filling up with people and food; I was amazed at how fast the news spread. Jinx came back over to "be with me." It was not until I saw her in her church dress that I realized the seriousness of what had happened.

The phone kept ringing and people kept coming in and going out. Arrangements were made. They were sending Mason's body over from Norfolk in a hearse. It would arrive at our local funeral home by evening. Mr. Joines, the under-taker, came in. He talked to Mama, who did not seem to understand what he was saying. She smiled and smiled, in a way that scared me. My grandmother arrived, all dressed up, and started bossing everybody around.

There was so much going on that I barely registered the arrival of Mr. Kinney, Daddy's foreman and "right-hand man" from the mill, still in his work clothes, holding his hat in his hands. Mr. Kinney went straight to my aunt Judy and took her aside for a whispered conference, then left without speaking to Mama or me. He ducked his head as he went out the door. And the afternoon wore on, the longest day I had ever lived through, the longest day in the world.

It was almost night when Daddy finally came home. Jinx and I were sitting in the windowseat in the living room, balancing plates of ham sandwiches and potato salad on our knees, when a red car pulled up and stopped at the end of our walk. I thought I had seen the car before, but I couldn't remember where. I peered out through the gathering dark.

Daddy got out on the passenger side of the car and then I could see him plain in the light at the end of our walk. He looked years older than he had the day before.

Daddy stared at our house, then opened the door and leaned down into the car to say something. He straightened up and looked at the house again. The other door of the car opened and Carroll Byrd got out, wearing pants, her hair streaming down her back. She walked around the front of the car to Daddy, who put out his arms and held her for a long time, so long I couldn't believe it.

Didn't he *know* that this house was full of people who could look out the windows and see him, and see what he was doing? Didn't he *care*? Didn't he even care at all about Mama, or me, or anybody except himself?

Finally, Carroll Byrd stepped away from Daddy, who touched her cheek once and then turned and came slowly up the walk, as if to his own execution. Carroll Byrd got back in her car and drove away, and I never saw her again.

The funeral was held two days later at St. Michael's Episcopal Church, though Mason had not been there or to any other church for many years, as far as we knew. The church was packed anyway, with Mama and Daddy's friends and lots of people from the mill. Mason's wife did not show up, but two of her daughters did, trashy girls in their late teens with curly red hair who cried like they meant it and told Mama that Mason had been a great stepfather to them. I know this was more important to Mama than anything else that was said at Mason's funeral. She clung to their arms, and gave them money later.

My oldest sister Beth could not come for the funeral, as she was nearing the end of a difficult pregnancy, but Caroline came, of course, with Tom—my beloved Tom, who immediately made himself indispensable to everybody, with his good sense and calm, reasonable manner.

After the funeral, Tom and Grandmother stood by the door and shook hands and talked to everybody who came to our house, while Mama and Caroline sat together on the love seat and cried. They looked like beautiful strangers to me—the big disheveled blonde, the pretty girl with mascara streaking her face. My old terror came back as I realized I didn't have a clue as to what their family had been like, how they had acted with each other, who they were before I was born. I got the same feeling in my stomach that I'd had at the beach when Jinx and I spied on Mr. Womble. Daddy talked on the telephone back in his study with the door closed, though Aunt Judy tried several times to get him to come out and "act responsible." (Imagine *Aunt Judy* saying this to *Daddy*!)

At length Grandmother left her post in the front hall and walked to Daddy's study, magisterial in her black suit. I followed, slipping into the stairwell. I understood that Grandmother had been dressing for a funeral for years, and now was in her element. Grandmother went into the study and shut the door behind her. I am not sure what she said to

Daddy, but it all ended with her marching out and him shouting, "Goddamnit, Mama!" and slamming the door.

"But John!" Grandmother had apparently thought of something else to say. She turned and tried the knob. He had locked the door. She was furious, I knew, but when she saw me, her face fell into its customary haughty expression, and she sailed into the living room without another word, to shake hands and smile some more.

I headed to the kitchen for a Coke, and there I discovered Aunt Judy in the process of getting drunk. She'd done absolutely as much as she *could*, Goddamnit! she said. Now it was out of her hands entirely. Nobody could blame her.

It seemed to be out of *everyone's* hands.

I got back to the living room just in time to hear Caroline announce her own pregnancy. Tom stood beside her, straight as a soldier, grinning from ear to ear, the bastard. I felt like I'd been kicked in the stomach.

"Oh, John," Mama began calling. "Oh, John!" She blew her nose on her pink Kleenex. "Oh, John, come here, darling, we've got some *good* news after all, even on this awful day! Oh, John . . ." she kept calling, but Daddy never came.

I spent the night at Jinx's. Locked in the bathroom, we smoked a whole pack of her mother's Kents, which tasted awful. Then I slept for twelve hours solid. I awoke to find both Jinx and her mother sitting on the end of Jinx's extra twin bed staring fixedly at me.

"Oh, thank goodness," Jinx's mother said in a fuzzy,

distracted way, which was not like her at all. "Oh, Jenny, honey."

I could tell that she knew everything, all about Daddy and Carroll Byrd, which probably meant that everybody else knew everything, too. What a big relief! I didn't realize how hard it had been to keep such a secret until I felt the weight of it leave me like a physical thing, like a rock being lifted off the top of my head. For the first time in months, I could cry—and I did. I cried and cried and cried, for Mama and Daddy and Carroll Byrd and poor terrible scary dead Mason, who had been the sweetest child, and for myself and especially for the loss of Tom Burlington, who would never be free to love me now.

THIS IS WHERE EVERYTHING GETS ALL HAZY IN MY MIND. By the time I went home from Jinx's, Daddy was gone. I did not have to be told where he was. I knew he was with her. Mama was brightly, determinedly cheerful, wearing that same crazy smile which had scared me so much before. She was in the kitchen cooking up a storm, banging the pots around, while Dot, our maid, watched her anxiously.

"Oh, hello, dear," Mama said to me. "I'm making some potato soup, I think potato soup is just so *comforting*, and Lord knows, we can all use a little comfort, isn't that right, Dot?"

"Yes ma'am," Dot said.

Mama wore a green knit suit with lots of gold jewelry, including her famous charm bracelet. I looked to see if Daddy's Deke pin was still on it. It was.

"Jenny," she said brightly to me, stirring. "Did you hear that your daddy has had to go out of town on an extended business trip? He said to give you his love and tell you he'll be back before long. I made this potato soup for you, honey," she added. "I know it's your favorite."

It was the first time in my life that I had ever been unable to eat. Mama didn't even try. She just sat across from me drumming her beautiful red nails on the table, rat-a-tat-tat, and sipping from a tall Kentucky Derby glass.

I thought she had water in the glass, but it was vodka, and she filled it again as soon as the level dipped below half, and did not put it down for the next two weeks. She never quit talking, either, to me or Dot or Jinx's mother or one or another of her friends. They had arranged it among themselves so that someone was always with her, and every day when I came home from school, there they'd be, Mama and her visitor (Buffy, Bitsy, Helen, Jane Ann, etc.), talking a mile a minute, with Dot hovering in the background. Mama kept cooking those nice little suppers for me, which we never ate. Dinnertime was my time to entertain her, though, while Dot and Mama's friends went home to their own families, before Aunt Judy showed up to spend the night.

Mostly we read movie magazines and talked about the lives of the stars. So much had happened lately that we had a lot to catch up on. Judy Garland was divorcing Sid Luft, and that "ideal couple," Cary Grant and Betsy Drake, had parted, amicably though. Jean Seberg was engaged to some Frenchman she'd met in the romantic resort town of Saint-Tropez, on the French Riviera, while she was filming *Bonjour Tristesse*. Tyrone Power married Debbie Minardos in a little chapel in her hometown of Tunica, Mississippi.

We were still reveling in Grace Kelly's fairy-tale wedding to Prince Rainier, and in the Robert Wagner—Natalie Wood marriage. We could tell that Janet Leigh and Tony Curtis were truly in love; Mama explained to me that their union had brought Tony (born Bernard Schwartz) "up into a better class of people." And Kim Novak was dating Sammy Davis, Jr., which outraged Mama. I didn't care. I thought Kim Novak was beautiful, and planned to paint my entire room lavender, just like hers, whenever Mama would let me.

I still could not understand how the gorgeous Marilyn Monroe could have married such a dried-up pruny old guy as Arthur Miller, though Mama said he was a brilliant egghead intellectual. "They have their charms," she told me, sipping from her glass, ignoring the fried chicken she had just cooked.

This was as close as Mama ever came to mentioning Daddy.

After supper we watched television together, an unaccustomed treat since Daddy didn't like for the television set to be on in the evenings except for *Huntley—Brinkley* or an occasional dramatic production. But now Mama and I watched everything, and she kept up a running commentary. Her favorites were the variety shows, where she could see the most stars. I thought *Ed Sullivan* and *Your Hit Parade* were okay, but I personally liked the Dinah Shore show the best, especially the end, where she sang, "See the *U*.S.A. in your *Chev*rolet," and blew a big, smacking kiss to the studio audience. Mama invariably turned to me at this point and whispered, "Of course, you know Dinah has Negro blood."

"How do you know that?" I'd asked the first couple of times Mama said this, but all she ever answered was, "Oh, honey, *everybody* knows it!" Whether everybody did or not, Mama believed it implicitly, as she believed in flying saucers and reincarnation and segregation and linen napkins and Chanel No. 5 and not going swimming for one hour after eating and not having milk with fish.

Mama and I watched television together until about nine o'clock, when Aunt Judy would show up to give Mama her pills and I'd be free to do my homework or go to bed and read for as long as I liked. I was reading *By Love Possessed* (pretty hot stuff), which had just arrived in a package from the Book-of-the-Month Club. I kept it under my bed.

We went on this way for about three weeks, until that awful night when we were watching *What's My Line?* together. Now, I really liked *What's My Line?* I felt that its question-and-answer format offered some good pointers for a combination spy and novelist such as myself. First "the challenger" would come into the studio and sign in on the blackboard. The challenger could be a man or a woman, either one. Then words would flash up on the screen, telling the audience what the challenger did for a living. The job was always far out—one man polished jelly beans, another put sticks in Popsicles, another was a bull de-horner. I loved these jobs, which made me feel that the world was a much more open place than I had been led to believe thus far. It was clear that I was destined to go to St. Catherine's and make my debut, but after college, who knows? I imagined going on the show myself someday as the challenger, the youngest best-selling author in the world. Anyway, the panelists asked questions to figure out the challenger's line, such as:

"Are you self-employed?"

"Do you deal in services?"

"Do people come to you? Men and women both?"

"Are they happier when they leave?"

"Do you need a college education to do what you do?"

I imagined Carroll Byrd as the challenger, squirming while she tried to answer this question, cringing when Dorothy Kilgallen pointed a finger at her and cried: "You are an *adulteress*!"

On the night I am thinking about, the challenger was a professional fire-eater and the panel was closing in. "Oh, he'll get it now," I said to Mama, because it was Bennett Cerf's turn and he was the smartest. "Don't you think? Hmmm? Don't you think?"

When Mama didn't answer, I turned and saw that she had slumped over to one side in the easy chair, her head too far down on her shoulder, exactly like a bird with a broken neck. Her overturned drink made a spreading stain on her silk print dress. I watched while the Kentucky Derby glass rolled slowly off her lap and onto the carpet and under the coffee table. Then I got up and went to the telephone to call Aunt Judy, who didn't answer. I let it ring and ring. Finally I realized: Aunt Judy was already on her way. I stood by the front door, not moving, until she got there.

LOTS OF THINGS HAPPENED IMMEDIATELY AFTER THAT. Daddy appeared and took Mama out of the local hospital and drove her to a "lovely place" in Asheville, North Carolina, for a "nice little rest." I wouldn't even speak to him. I stayed in my room smoking cigarettes until they left. Then I had a big fight with my grandmother, refusing to stay with her and Aunt Chloë, claiming I'd rather be dead and would kill myself with a knife if they tried to make me. Nobody knew what to do. I had become a "problem child." I hoped to stay with Jinx, of course, but Jinx's mother announced unexpectedly that she thought this would not be a good idea just now, that Jinx and I were "not good influences" on each other. And furthermore Aunt Judy had "*had* it" with all of us, she said, and was off to Bermuda for a much-needed vacation. So I stayed at our house and Dot stayed in the guest room until Daddy came back and got me and took me down to visit Mama's cousins in Repass, South Carolina, where I had never been. I wouldn't go until Mama begged me on the phone, and then I had to. I had to do anything she wanted me to do. My mother's cousin was named Glenda. They were sending me to her because she was a school principal whose home had "structure," which I "needed," and because she had a daughter about my age, who was a "model girl" and would be my friend.

I doubted this, and didn't speak to Daddy the entire way down to South Carolina in the car, though he tried and tried to talk to me and never lost his patience, not even when he saw me spit in his Coke at a Howard Johnson's. He looked at me sadly, solemnly, like a tragic hero. Daddy had dark circles beneath his eyes now, and his hands shook. He was supposedly living for love, but it seemed to me more like he was dying of it. I hated him. I hated him for being so weak, for loving her more than he loved us. I also hated Mama—for letting this happen, for getting sick, for going in the hospital. For abandoning me. I hated Aunt Judy for going to Bermuda, and my sisters for being so involved with their own jobs and babies and lives. I hated Jinx because she got to stay with her own happy family while I had to go live with complete strangers in South Carolina.

I already hated everybody I knew, so I was prepared to hate cousin Glenda on sight. And what a sight she was! Though I was told I had met her before, when I was little,

I couldn't remember . . . and surely I would have remembered anybody as awful as this. Cousin Glenda looked like a fire-plug, or maybe a built-in barbecue grill. She was five-by-five, and wore an orange suit with a flowered blouse and brown lace-up shoes when I first saw her. They were the ugliest shoes in the world. Her hair was a bright yellow lacquered helmet squished way down on her head. It was impossible for me to believe that she was related to Mama, or that they had grown up together. I had heard Mama say that she and Glenda "did not always see eye to eye" on things. Now I understood this was a huge understatement. Cousin Glenda was as hard as Mama was soft, as practical as she was flighty, as ugly as she was pretty, as mean as she was sweet.

Cousin Glenda stood in the driveway with her arms crossed and her feet planted wide apart as we drove up. Behind her, their house was completely square, as square as she was, as if it were made out of building blocks. It was a plain two-story brick house with no shutters and no shrubbery, sitting smack in the middle of a square green yard, with a walk going up to the front door and a maple tree planted on each side.

"I don't want to stay here." It was the first thing I had said all day.

Daddy turned off the car. "Honey, it's only for a little while. You know that. It's just until your mama gets out of the hospital."

"I can't stay here," I said.

"Honey, please."

It occurred to me that *Daddy* might cry.

"Let's get your things out," he said. "This won't be for long, I promise."

"*Sure*." I sounded every bit as sarcastic as Buddy Womble.

Cousin Glenda rolled toward us like a tank. "I'll take that," she said to Daddy, grabbing my suitcase. "Come on now, Jennifer," she said to me, and I surprised myself by getting out of the car. She grabbed my elbow. Her grip was iron. "Okay, John, I'll take care of her. Send a check every week, and call her every Sunday night. That's it, then."

Cousin Glenda was talking *at* my father instead of *to* him, as if he were some lower order of being, and suddenly I felt my allegiance shifting in an alarming about-face, back toward Daddy. I felt that I could be as mean to him as I wanted to, as mean as he deserved, but I couldn't stand for anybody else to be mean to him.

"Daddy, Daddy, Daddy," I said, and he stepped over to me quickly and gave me a tight, fierce hug. "It'll be all right, Jenny. It will. It won't be long, you'll see." Close up, Daddy smelled like cigarettes and Aqua Velva, his old smell, and then I loved him more than anybody in the world and wanted to die for hating him so much and spying on him and spitting in his Coke at Howard Johnson's and for the many other awful things I'd done.

"Come along now, Jennifer." Cousin Glenda had a voice that made you do everything she said.

"You're hurting my arm." I tried to shake her off, but she held on like a bulldog.

"I know all about *you*, Miss," she announced with a great deal of satisfaction, pulling me toward the house. "We're going to put the quietus on you."

The quietus! What was *THAT*? I was terrified. But I soon learned that this was simply one of cousin Glenda's favorite sayings. She was always going to "put the quietus" on somebody, or telling somebody to "get a grip." She'd say, "Your mother called today, Jennifer, and said how much she hated doing all the things she has to do up there, such as exercise, and I said to her, 'Billie, get a grip!' I just hope she was taking it in."

Cousin Glenda quoted herself endlessly, infatuated with her own good advice. She'd say, "That new substitute teacher came in my office all upset because we had to cut fifteen minutes off of second period for the fire drill, and I said, 'Mr. Johnson, get a grip!'" Cousin Glenda reminded me of a blowfish, all puffed up and blustery, and I soon understood that I didn't really need to be afraid of her. She was all hot air and good intentions. Growing up as one of Mama's poor relations in Charleston, she had idolized Mama for her sweetness and generosity. Now that Mama was in trouble and had no brothers and sisters of her own, cousin Glenda was more than willing to step in and help her out. She would shape me up. She would *make* me get a grip. And for a fact, it was easier to get a grip in that household than in our own, where so many things were too slippery to hold on to and so many words were never spoken and the rules were always changing.

The rules in cousin Glenda's house were inflexible, and everybody toed the line. "Everybody" included her husband, Raymond, long-faced and lantern-jawed but clearly nice, who didn't have a chance to get a word in edgewise with cousin Glenda around, repeating word for word every conversation she'd ever had. I can't remember hearing Raymond speak once during the whole time I was there, though this can't be true. He grinned a lot, however, as if he got a big kick out of cousin Glenda—out of us all, in fact. Raymond would never leave *his* wife. They had been married since they were both eighteen, and he had worked at the same job in the post office for twenty-three years. He wasn't going *anywhere*.

Rayette, my model cousin, turned out to be a junior version of her mother. One year older than I, freckled, sturdy, and curly-haired, she had a wide plain face and big cornflower-blue eyes and not one ounce of irony or guile. I knew immediately that Rayette would never understand my spying, which I would never tell her about. I hid my Davy Crockett notebook under my mattress. Rayette was fascinated by me, and especially by all my cool stuff: the red plastic case containing my 45-rpm records, my Tangee lipstick and fashionable clothes, especially the crinolines and my two appliquéd circle skirts; my castle-shaped jewelry

box with its own lock and key, containing my add-a-pearl
necklace and Captain Midnight decoder ring and jade paperweight and fourteen separate items (such as a ballpoint pen
and a jujube wrapper) that had been touched by Tom Burlington. But Rayette did not have a jealous bone in her body.
She seemed as glad to have me there as her parents were, and
curiously enough, I did not mind being there, either, or
obeying all the rules or following the rigid schedule.

I loved this schedule, which included getting up at the
crack of dawn because we had to catch the school bus, saying
the blessing and sitting down to eat a huge breakfast of eggs
and bacon and grits, and then making our own beds and
washing the dishes (no Dot) before we set out through the
foggy chill of the lowland South Carolina morning to stand
by the road and stamp our feet and blow out our breath in
puffy clouds and wait for the big yellow school bus to come
blasting out of the mist like an apparition and carry us away.
Back home, Daddy or Dot had always driven me to school.

Rayette's school was a hick school, as Jinx had predicted
it would be, but as the new girl, I was more popular than I
had ever been, and reveled in this development. All the girls
wanted to sit next to me at lunch. All the boys bumped into
me in the hall, acting dumb. A's were easy to come by. After
school, I'd stay late with Rayette for her 4-H and Tri-Hi-Y
meetings—clubs I would have scorned back home. They
were just beginning a sewing project in 4-H, and so I, too,
got to make a terrible-looking bright yellow blouse with a

scoop neck, and sleeves that did not fit the armholes, and darts in the wrong place. I was intensely proud of myself.

Rayette was president of Tri-Hi-Y, a Christian service club that pledged itself to goodness at every meeting and did good deeds all over the county. While I was there, they were raising money to buy an artificial leg for a little boy named Leonard Pipkin. Rayette called each meeting to order by banging on a table with a gavel. This gavel impressed me so much that I gave up espionage and literature on the spot, and vowed to be just like her. I wanted to bang on a table with my gavel, to run clubs, to wear a huge cross around my neck every day, a cross so big it would pitch me forward and weigh me down, and most of all, to be *absolutely sure* about everything in the world.

The main criterion in cousin Glenda's house was, "What would Jesus think of this?" Jesus did not think much of rock and roll, for instance. Specifically, He did not like fast records that caused young people to move their bodies in sinful ways. He hated "Whole Lot-ta Shakin' Goin' On," "Wake Up, Little Susie," and "Blue Suede Shoes," so these had to stay in my special case, but I was allowed to play "Que Será, Será," "April Love," and (strangely) "The Great Pretender." Jesus was very picky.

He apparently prized neatness, cleanliness, and order above all things; I imagined that the plastic runners on the living room carpet and the cellophane covers on all the lampshades were His idea. I liked them myself, as they gave the living room such a weird, ghostly aspect, and the runners popped and crinkled nicely when you walked on them. Lots of things had covers in cousin Glenda's house—the toaster, the Mixmaster, and the blender wore matching piqué jackets with rickrack around the edges; the Kleenex box and the Jergens lotion bottle had crocheted skirts; the toilets featured big fuzzy pads.

And everything had its place. I learned this fast. Rayette burst into tears the third day I was there because I had borrowed her hairbrush (without asking) and put it back in the wrong place, and so it wasn't *exactly where it was supposed to be* when she needed it. Pearl Harbor! This threw Rayette for such a loop that I never did it again, striving for a Jesusy order as great as hers. I got into it. I put my shoes in a row in my closet, as if some dainty princess were going to step into them at any minute. I rolled my socks into balls. I learned where all the dishes went, and everything in the refrigerator. I loved to fill the bird feeder and put away the groceries, both tasks that had to be done just so.

Another virtue right up there with order was *being prepared*. "Jesus will look after you, honey," cousin Glenda often said, "but He expects you to do what you can." Therefore the family was prepared for any possible crisis, with a first-aid kit, emergency flares, a snakebite kit, a shotgun, and—wonder of wonders—a Bomb Shelter!

Rayette didn't appear to care too much about the Bomb Shelter one way or the other—I guess she was used to it—but

I thought it was the coolest thing I had ever seen, the coolest place I'd ever been. You went down into the Bomb Shelter through a trap door in the garage. This was an orange metal door with three black X's on it. It was impervious to radiation. You had to go down a dozen steep steps into the cave-like Bomb Shelter itself, which was equipped with all the necessities for nuclear war, including:

A Geiger counter with its $98.50 price tag still attached

A two-way portable radio

A pick and shovel

A chemical toilet (Rayette explained that you would put a blanket over yourself, for privacy, when you used it.)

Mattresses and blankets

A Sterno stove

A fire extinguisher

Paper products

Canned water

Canned food and drinks

It was always cold down there, and it was lit by a faint blue light that buzzed with a thrillingly extraterrestrial sound. I loved to sit in the Bomb Shelter. I also loved to survey the backyard from the kitchen window while I washed dishes, thinking, *The Bomb Shelter is right out there! Nobody knows it, nobody can possibly tell, nobody knows it but us!* I spent as much time in the Bomb Shelter as I could get away with, without attracting too much attention to myself, whenever we weren't at school or doing chores or praying or going to church.

We went to church a lot. We went to church every time they cracked the door; but even at home, we'd pray at the drop of a hat. We prayed over everything: that I would make an A on my math test, that the lady up the street would see the light (*what* light?), that Mama would get well soon and Daddy would see the error of his ways and Jesus would forgive him, that the family's old station wagon would make it through the winter without a new clutch, that the upcoming Tri-Hi-Y bake sale would be a big success and Leonard Pipkin would get a new leg. Cousin Glenda would throw one hand up, bow her head, and set into praying whenever she felt like it, and then we'd all have to bow our heads and pray, too. Used to the sedate and abstract *Book of Common Prayer*, I was as startled by the personal nature of these prayers as by their frequency.

The church itself was even more unnerving. It was very plain, a cinder-block building that looked as if it might have once been a grocery store. There was nothing about it now to suggest that it was a church except for a hand-painted sign over the front door that read "Bible Church of God, All Enter In." I knew that "enter in" was redundant, like "Ford car," yet I found it mysteriously compelling, an invitation to a foreign country. And I was fascinated by what went on inside: clapping, singing, crying, hugging, and shouting amen—I had never seen anything like it at St. Michael's, that's for sure. "Bible" was the key to everything. "If it's not Bible, we don't believe in it, and we don't do it," cousin Glenda explained.

"But the Bible was written a long time ago," I pointed out. "Before airplanes or electricity or anything. How do you know Jesus wants you to have electricity?" I asked. "How do you know He wants you to have a phone? How do you know He doesn't like the Everly Brothers? How do you know He doesn't like eye makeup? There wasn't any makeup back in the Bible days, so—"

"Jennifer, Jennifer," cousin Glenda said, hugging me, "get a grip."

I tried to. I had given up spying entirely, except for one quick peep into Rayette's bedroom window to ascertain that, yes, she really did have breasts as big as softballs, obscured by the homemade shirtwaist dresses and shapeless blocky sweaters she always wore. I did not have the heart to spy on cousin Glenda and Raymond, however. The prospect of either one of them actually taking off their clothes was too awful to contemplate, much less their *doing it*. (What was *it*? I still didn't know.) But I was sure they had done it only once, whatever it was, in order to conceive Rayette and populate the earth.

Rayette (big as a woman, dumb as a post) soon became my personal servant and bodyguard. She carried my books to school, ironed my clothes, and once even hemmed a skirt for me. Cousin Glenda shook her head at this, smiling. "That's exactly how I was with your mama," she said. "Just exactly. I was three years younger than Billie, and if Billie said 'Jump!' I said 'How far?' I used to follow her around everyplace, but if I got on her nerves she never let on, at least she never let on to me."

"What was Mama like, as a little girl?" I asked. I couldn't imagine this.

"An angel," my tough cousin Glenda answered immediately. "Oh, Jennifer, she was an angel."

I was no angel, but I was *trying*—trying not to spy, trying to get a grip, trying to be good. Now that I realized how good it was possible to be, I realized how bad I'd always been; and I got the idea that it was all my fault somehow, everything that had happened, and that if I could just be *good enough,* Mama and Daddy might get back together. So I was almost killing myself being as good as I could possibly be, which did not come naturally to me; but before long, sure enough, it worked.

One Sunday, Daddy reported that he had good news, that Mama was improving, and that we might all take a vacation together when she got out of the hospital. He did not mention Carroll Byrd. I was elated. I knew I had done this by being so good. I doubled my efforts, making three dozen brownies to sell at the Tri-Hi-Y bake sale to buy Leonard Pipkin that new leg.

There was a boy in the Tri-Hi-Y club who liked me, and I sort of knew it, though we had not exchanged two words. His name was Harlan Boyd. Everybody knew who he was because he was a big deal, the star football player. A *jock*. His neck was as thick as his head, which made his head and his neck together look like one single unit, like a fencepost topped off by his fuzzy brown flat-top. He had square jock shoulders and wore his red satin letter jacket all the time, with blue jeans. (Nobody cool wore blue jeans yet, this was before they got popular. Then, in Repass, blue jeans meant you were poor.) Harlan Boyd was in Rayette's grade, though he was in my math class. He was big for his age, and came from a "troubled home." He lived someplace out in the swamp with his uncle, under conditions too awful to imagine, yet he could catch a football like a dream and run like hell. These skills would be his ticket out of there, but he didn't know it yet, had not thought that far ahead. In fact, he probably hadn't thought much about anything yet, at age fifteen, that day at the bake sale.

The sale was held downtown in front of the courthouse, in the center of Repass, one Saturday in early December. Cousin Glenda, the Tri-Hi-Y sponsor, brought two card tables from home in the station wagon. Rayette rode over with her, and they were just getting everything set up when I arrived. Though I was trying my dead-level best to be good, I did not really like to be identified with cousin Glenda in public situations and so had turned down her offer of a ride and walked to the square by myself, bearing my platter of brownies. I hung back behind the giant live-oak tree, while cousin Glenda, wearing the world's largest car coat, bossed everybody around.

"Susan, put that right there!" she barked. "Rayette, pull the tablecloth down! Peter, go get some change from the Rexall!" Cousin Glenda was a world-class expert on bake sales, as on everything. Rayette, too innocent to know she ought to be embarrassed, did everything her mother told her, smiling placidly. (Oh, *she* was the angel, not me; I could never be that good!) I stayed hidden where I was until everything had been set up to cousin Glenda's satisfaction.

"All right now, boys and girls," she announced in a voice like a trumpet, raising her arm, "let us join hands and pray together, and ask our Heavenly Father to bless this bake sale and all this good food and all the proceeds therefrom, and may Leonard Pipkin get his new leg a.s.a.p., amen."

Looking sheepish, all the kids dropped one another's hands like hot potatoes while cousin Glenda stomped off to her station wagon for a cigarette (Jesus did not mind for adults to smoke), and I sallied forth with my brownies.

I'm still not sure how it happened. All I know is that one minute I was holding the brownies out in front of me like a sacrificial offering, and the next minute they were flying through the air like miniature UFOs and I was pitching forward, forward, forward in horrible slow motion forever, until I slammed into the wide solid chest of Harlan Boyd, propelling him backward, overturning one of the card tables and sending pound cakes and homemade bread and fudge everywhere. It was awful. It was the most awful and embarrassing thing I had done in my life up to that point, and it ended at last with me and Harlan Boyd splayed out on the ground against the card table, my cheek smashed into the letters on his football jacket, RR for Repass Rattlers. The letters felt scratchy and wonderful against my cheek. I could hear my own heart beating in my ears, so loud I thought briefly I might be having a heart attack.

"Jennifer, Jennifer, Jennifer!" squealed Rayette. "Are you okay?"

Then cousin Glenda was there, too, pulling us up, brushing us off, getting everything to rights. I wanted to die, of course. I stood to the side with Rayette cooing over me, and would not even look at Harlan Boyd, who kept trying to say something to me. I had gotten pink icing on my blouse and mud on my crinoline, which hung way down below my skirt so everyone could see. Cousin Glenda drove me home to change. I told her I'd walk right back, though I had no intention of going back, *ever*, or of ever speaking to any of those kids again, especially not to Harlan Boyd, whose athletic letters had made a red mark like a rope burn on my cheek.

After I showered I kept touching it, looking at my face in the mirror. I put on some clean slacks and a sweater, but I couldn't find it in me to start back over to the bake sale. Instead I wandered around the still, sunny house. It was the first time I had been there alone, and it put me in mind of home, where I had often been the only child and had had the run of the house, and had done whatever I wanted. I started feeling spacy, detached from myself, between things.

The doorbell rang.

I opened it to find Harlan, letter jacket and all, there on the stoop. Though red-faced, he spoke up bravely: "I just wanted to see how you was," he said.

"I'm okay," I told him. "Come on in." I grabbed his sleeve and pulled him inside the house quickly, and shut the door. Now that I had him inside, however, I had no idea what to do with him. "My name is Jenny," I said stupidly.

"I know that," Harlan said. "You're not from around here, are you?"

"No," I said. "I'm just staying with my cousins until my parents get out of the hospital. They were in a train wreck," I added.

"Aw, shoot," Harlan said. "That's awful. Are they going to be okay?"

"Nobody knows," I said dramatically, mysteriously. "Come here, I want to show you something."

I grabbed his hand, which felt as big as a ham, and led

him down the hall and through the kitchen and into the empty garage, over to the orange XXX door. We paused before it. I was breathing hard.

"Do you know what this is?" I asked him.

"You sure are pretty," Harlan said loudly. This announcement appeared to surprise him as much as it surprised me. He immediately turned fiery red and ducked his head and started stamping his feet in their big uncool work boots.

Hick, I thought. *Swamp boy.* "Come on," I said, and pulled the door up and pushed him ahead of me, down the stairs. "This is the Bomb Shelter," I said.

"No kidding," Harlan said. "Well, I'll be darned."

I was thrilled to see the entwined rattlesnakes on the back of his jacket disappearing into the gloom. I shut the door behind myself and followed, showing him everything: the Geiger counter, the supplies, etc., though I did not go into any details about the chemical toilet.

"Let's sit here." I patted the pile of mattresses. "Let me get you something to drink." I opened a can of orange juice for him and one for myself and clinked mine against his in a toast. "Cheers!" I said. I knew my sophistication was knocking him out. He just kept grinning at me, forgetting to drink his juice, while I downed mine in one sophisticated gulp and broke open a package of Fig Newtons.

"Care for a cookie?" I said, knowing that cousin Glenda would kill me. "A little refreshment?" There in the humming blue light of the Bomb Shelter, I turned into the perfect hostess, exactly as prescribed in *Teen* magazine. ("When he comes to your home, have refreshments ready.")

Harlan Boyd set his juice can down carefully on the Sterno stove. "C'mere," he said.

I didn't think about being good or not being good. I didn't think about anything. I dropped the Fig Newtons on the floor and scooted over there to get myself kissed by a boy for the first time ever, and I have to say it was just fine, and the whole world dropped out from under me for I don't know how long while Harlan Boyd and I mashed our lips together, mouths closed, and then open as he stuck his tongue into mine. (*Teen* magazine had not mentioned tongues.) I was lying partway back on the mattress by now, with him on top of me, when suddenly I felt this hard thing like a stick between us. What was it? I struggled upward like a swimmer surfacing through thousands of feet of water. *Uh-oh.* What would Jesus think of *that?*

But it was all over, anyway, because cousin Glenda's station wagon pulled into the garage, and then we could hear the car doors slamming and cousin Glenda and Rayette calling my name, getting closer and closer. Of course, cousin Glenda knew where I was. Cousin Glenda always knew everything.

Since there was no other way to get out of the Bomb Shelter, Harlan and I just sat there side by side, buddies at the end of the world, until the orange door opened and cousin Glenda came clomping downstairs like the wrath of God.

By the time Daddy appeared to retrieve me, Christmas had come and gone and I had repented of my behavior in the Bomb Shelter and was being totally good again, or as good as possible, newly aware of my potential for backsliding. Harlan Boyd never spoke to me again. He dropped out of Tri-Hi-Y and wouldn't even look at me in math class, where he got a D-minus for the semester.

It was over. I knew he still loved me, though, with a hopeless love, the kind of love my uncle Mason had felt for his wife, a love so strong it had caused him to go out and cut somebody. I didn't think Harlan would do that, though I sort of wished he would. But he was too nice. Also, he had basketball practice every day after school, so he was very busy. Anyway, I would be far, far away soon, in Key West, Florida, where Mama and Daddy were going to "patch up their marriage": a geographical cure prescribed by Mama's doctors.

But I hated to leave Repass. This astonished Mama and Daddy, who looked puzzled as they stood waiting while I sobbed, hugging first Rayette and then cousin Glenda. Raymond stood like a tree by the door.

"Now come on, Jennifer." Cousin Glenda finally

disentangled herself from my frantic arms. "What did I tell you?"

I had to smile.

Rayette smiled.

"*Get a grip,*" we all said together, and I started laughing in spite of my tears.

EVEN THOUGH DADDY HAD BOUGHT US A NEW CAR FOR the occasion, a silvery-gray fishtailed Cadillac, the long drive down to Florida was grim. Mama and Daddy sat up front, and I had the wide backseat all to myself. There was a seat divider, which I could pull down to make a table if I wanted to draw or write. I had a shopping bag containing a white New Testament with my name embossed on the front in gold, a good-bye gift from my cousins; a copy of *'Twixt Twelve and Twenty* by Pat Boone, a gift from my grandmother; Rayette's Rattler yearbook from the year before; the yellow blouse I had made in 4-H; and *The Search for Bridey Murphy,* which I had been dying to get my hands on. Mama had just finished reading it. At the bottom of the shopping bag was my old jewelry box, all locked up, and a big new auxiliary jewelry box containing the stale package of Fig Newtons and the empty orange juice can touched by Harlan Boyd. I had resurrected my notebook and brought it along, too, to record my thoughts and observations, though I had still given up both espionage and literature at least for the time being, until I could get my parents through this crisis.

I had made a new chart in the back of my notebook. It said "Good Deeds" at the top and then had the days of February numbered down the left-hand margin with a line drawn out from each date. I had done this laboriously, with a ruler, before leaving my cousins'. We would be gone for one whole month, and I planned to do a good deed every day—twenty-eight good deeds, which ought to be enough to bring even Mama and Daddy back together.

I had my work cut out for me. It would be a challenge. Mama and Daddy sat as far apart as possible from each other on the big front seat, as remote as planets. They were both smoking a lot (Mama, Newports; Daddy, Winstons), making the air in the new Cadillac dense and blue and wavy, making my eyes water all the way down through South Carolina and Georgia, until it grew warm enough in Florida for us to crack the windows.

Cousin Glenda's reaction upon seeing Mama had been the same as mine: "Oh, Billie, you poor thing!" for Mama had simply lost her luster. She had become a thinner, paler version of herself, quieter and more hesitant. Cousin Glenda's final instructions for us ("Now you all just forget about everything and have a good time, you hear me?") seemed more and more impossible to follow, the farther we traveled.

It became clear that I was absolutely necessary to this

trip, as the only remaining link between Mama and Daddy. They were trying to patch up their marriage for me, and the only way to do it seemed to be *through me*. So I was consulted on everything: where to spend the night, for instance, hotel or motel? I picked the Palm Courts, a pink stucco motel where Mama and I shared a tiny square room and bath, while Daddy had the same to himself. Mama got ready for bed as if she were in a trance—brushing her teeth, creaming her face with Noxzema, taking a lot of pills. As my good deed, I folded up the clothes she had just thrown over a chair, and was rewarded for this when she put them all back on the next morning, the same exact outfit—something she would never have done in the past.

My parents asked me where we should eat lunch, whether to play the radio or not, whether to stop at the Bok Singing Tower or not (no), whether to stop at Weeki Watchee Springs or not (yes). I loved Weeki Watchee Springs, where beautiful girls swam around in underwater caverns with oxygen tanks on their backs, among the brilliant angelfish. I determined to go back when I was grown and get a swimming job.

My parents did not come with me into the underwater viewing room at Weeki Watchee Springs. They did not appear to be at all interested in the girl divers, or the fish, or anything. They sat on the low stone wall outside the entrance waiting patiently for me to emerge, not talking, smoking. They looked like prisoners blinking in the sun. I made them wait an extra hour, until shark-feeding time, and they didn't even complain about that.

This is when I realized that I could make them do anything I wanted on this trip. *Anything*. I was in charge.

Mama pulled out her compact and looked at herself the minute we got back in the car after Weeki Watchee Springs. "Oh, no!" she started sobbing. "I got *sunburned*! I didn't think I could get sunburned so early in the year, but this Florida sun is just so *hot*. . . ." Mama went on and on. I didn't see what she was all upset about, myself, but at least it was more than she had said so far on the whole trip. "Honey, ask your daddy if he can get me some Solarcaine and some more Noxzema," she said to me.

"Daddy, can you do that?" I said to Daddy, who pulled off at the very next drugstore, a huge Rexall with a big Coppertone sign over it.

"I'll go in," I volunteered, and Mama thrust a ten-dollar bill over the seat at me.

"No, I'll go, Jenny," Daddy said.

"No, *I'll do it*, Daddy!" I had already decided to count this as my good deed for the day. "Solarcaine and Noxzema, right?" Daddy jumped out of the car and made a grab for the money, but I danced away, waving it. "I'll be back in a minute," I yelled.

"Damn it," Daddy said.

"Jenny, get me some more cigarettes, too," Mama called after me.

I took off.

"Goddamnit," Daddy said behind me.

I got the Solarcaine and the Noxzema (a smell I will forever associate with Mama), plus some peanut M&M's for myself, and went back to the car, where Mama sat bowed with her head in her hands and Daddy stood leaning against his door, smoking furiously. They had been arguing, I could tell. The words hung in the Florida air. They had started arguing probably the very minute I disappeared into the Rexall. I couldn't leave them alone for even a minute! What a responsibility! I went around to Mama's side of the car and put the paper bag from the Rexall and the wad of change in her lap. "Oh, honey, just keep the change," she said, so I put it in my pocket along with the M&M's. Good deeds are always rewarded, as cousin Glenda had told me.

"Did you forget my cigarettes?" Mama asked.

I cleared my throat. "No," I said, fidgeting from one foot to the other. "You don't need any more cigarettes, either one of you," I announced. "You are both smoking too much, and you'll make yourselves sick."

Mama gasped and started to cry.

Daddy walked around the fancy front grillework of the Cadillac. "Now listen here, Miss," he said, "you don't talk to your mother that way, in case you've forgotten. You apologize to her, and get in the damn car, and let's get the hell out of here." He looked at his watch as if we had some big schedule to keep, but I knew we didn't have any schedule at all.

I stood my ground. "Don't say 'hell,' " I said. "You curse too much, too."

"Now just a minute," Daddy said. "What's going on here?" For the first time, he really looked at me.

Mama stuck her head out the window and squinted at me, too—suddenly seeming, in spite of her puffy eyes, almost herself again. "Just what *is* going on here?" she asked. "And take off that damn cross, for God's sake, Jenny. Where in the world did you get that ugly old thing, anyway?"

"Don't say 'for God's sake,' " I said. "What would Jesus think of that?"

"Get in the goddamn car!" Daddy was gritting his teeth.

I got in and slammed the door and prayed that Jesus would not punish Mama and Daddy for taking His name in vain, and that I could stay good enough for long enough to get them back together, and that Rayette would not miss her cross too much.

CENTRAL FLORIDA WAS PRETTY BORING, BUT I LOVED Miami, with lots of traffic and lots of people in the streets shouting and gesturing, speaking Spanish. "Lock all the doors," Mama instructed. "Jenny, don't stare." I couldn't help it as we cruised slowly through the city in our huge, shiny, smoke-filled car like a shark at Weeki Watchee Springs, like a submarine from another civilization.

My father never took his eyes off the road ahead. He

seemed infinitely, infinitely sad to me, full of his grim
resolve. He was doing the only thing he *could* do—I see this
now—given the time and the place they lived in, and the
circumstances, and all the women who depended upon him,
and all the people at the mill, which Mr. Kinney was gamely
running even now, in Daddy's absence. For my father, being
the man he was, no other choice was possible.

And Mama—what was *she* thinking over there with her
pretty blond cap of curls and her milk-glass baby-doll face
wreathed in smoke, so far from everything familiar? Did she
really want to patch up her marriage? Did she even understand that she had any choice in the matter? I couldn't tell.
She remained vacant-eyed and silent. When they spoke to
each other, it was with an exaggerated politeness that I soon
adopted, too, as if we were *all* sick.

The drive was interminable. Finally I asked Daddy why
we were going *there* for our prescribed vacation, anyway,
when there were so many other places to go that were so
much closer. "Well, Jenny," Daddy said, "you know I was
in the Navy"—I nodded—"in fact, I met your mother when
I was in the Navy, stationed in Charleston"—I nodded again,
while Mama merely widened her big blue eyes as if this were
news to her—"and before Charleston, I was stationed in Key
West, and I'll tell you, I've always wanted to go back. It's
not like anywhere else, you'll see. It's very exotic. I thought
it would be good for us to take a trip together to someplace
completely different, the three of us, after what we've been

through this past year. I thought we could use a little adventure."

Daddy stubbed out his cigarette as he said "adventure," glancing over at Mama. She looked out the window. I was mad at him for saying "what we've been through this past year," as if none of it were his own fault, as if we'd all been hit by a truck. I had to rub my cross and count backward from one hundred in order to stay good, to keep from saying something mean.

It was easier once we could see the water. This happened after Miami. Suddenly we were on a bridge with blue water under us and on either side, and then we were on Route 1. "Originally the only way you could get to Key West was by boat or by rail, Jenny. A man named Henry Flagler started the railroad in 1905, and it took him seven years to get all the way down to Key West. You can still see the tracks right over there, see that old trestle? A storm blew the railroad away sometime in the thirties," Daddy was saying, when Mama started to shriek.

"Key Largo! Look, John, that sign says 'Key Largo'! You didn't tell me we were going to Key Largo, John. Oh, Jenny, isn't this exciting?"

I sat up. *Key Largo* was one of Mama's and my all-time favorite movies.

"Oh, *stop*, John! I want to take a picture."

Mama had a brand-new Brownie camera, which Daddy had bought her especially for this trip, but until now she hadn't shown any interest in it. We had to pull over on the sandy side of the road while she rummaged through her overnight case to find it, and then Daddy had to read the instructions to figure out how to load it. I shaded my eyes from the sun and breathed in the fishy air and looked at a long-legged bird that hopped nearer and nearer. It expected us to give it something, so I got a nab out of Mama's pocketbook. Mama freshened her lipstick and fluffed up her curls.

"Okay, now." She walked over and leaned against the sign that said 'Key Largo' and smiled, a big red smile that came out of nowhere.

Daddy snapped the picture.

"Now you get in it *with me*, honey," she said to me, and I did, and Daddy took that picture, too. I still have it. There's a palm tree behind us, and the sun is in our eyes. Then we all got back in the car and drove through Key Largo, which wasn't much, as it turned out. It only took about two minutes.

"I'm not sure they actually filmed it here," said Daddy, who knew they hadn't.

"Oh, of course they did!" Mama said. "It's named *Key Largo*, isn't it? *Silly*." For a moment, she sounded like herself again.

Humphrey Bogart had died of cancer not even two years earlier, in 1957, ending a marriage that Mama and I were just crazy about. We knew the facts by heart. Everybody had thought Lauren Bacall was too young for him when they met in 1943 (she was only nineteen, he was forty-four), but they had been blissfully happy together, against all odds, and she had nursed him devotedly when he got cancer; on his deathbed, Bogey's last words were for her: "Good-bye, kid." Lauren Bacall never got over him, of course. How could she? I thought about it. Clark Gable never got over Carole Lombard, either, after she died in that tragic plane crash, though he *tried* to. He kept marrying other people, but nobody else ever really *took*. And what about Spencer Tracy, who loved Katharine Hepburn for years yet never left his wife?

Then I had this awful thought: Why should it be any different for Daddy and Carroll Byrd? What if Daddy was just *pretending* to patch up the marriage, knowing he would never be able to live without Carroll Byrd? Or what if he was really *trying* to give her up, and couldn't? What if he just *couldn't*? I watched him carefully as he drove us down the Keys. But unlike Mama, who was all on the surface, all open, too open, I could never guess what Daddy was thinking. His face betrayed nothing.

We ate lunch at a place called the Green Turtle Inn, which had a cannery (named Sid and Roxie's) right across the road, where they canned turtle meat. Yuck! It was on the menu, too—turtle steak, turtle soup. Daddy ordered the turtle soup. Mama ordered a Manhattan and a cup of clam chowder, staring defiantly at Daddy. I ordered a hamburger. It was a confusing, jumbled-up restaurant, with tables and chairs that didn't match, and all kinds of people, some of them very loud. Nobody was dressed up. It was not like any restaurant I had been to before. As we were leaving, a fight broke out at the bar. "Don't look at anybody," Mama said, clutching my shoulder and pushing me ahead of her, and we got out of there, and we did not look at anybody, or mention Mason.

None of us mentioned Mason's death, or Mama's stay in the hospital, or Carroll Byrd. All the way down the Keys, what we did not say seemed as real as what we did say, like the shadowy railroad alongside the highway with its ghost bridges spanning the sea. I kept wishing cousin Glenda had come along, to haul everything out in the open and pray over it.

I started getting really excited on the Seven Mile Bridge, a span so long over a stretch of water so wide that it seemed we were entering another world. It had not occurred to me that water could be so many different colors of blue. I saw dark shadows (sharks? rays?) moving under it, and cloud shadows moving over it.

We touched land briefly at Bahia Honda, then crossed the water again to Big Pine. Daddy solemnly read the road signs out loud to us, as if he were a travel guide or we were illiterate: Little Torch Key, Niles Channel, Summerland Key, Cudjoe, Sugarloaf. By now I had abandoned even *Bridey*

Murphy and was sitting up against the front seat, so I could see everything as soon as they did.

We crossed Stock Island and drove into Key West around suppertime. After the long stretches of water and the scruffy unpopulated keys we'd come through, Key West was disorienting, a bright buzz of color and noise.

"Did *you* have a uniform like that?" I asked Daddy as a young sailor dodged in front of our big car.

"Pretty much," Daddy said. "In fact, that young man might have been me, thirty years ago." This thought seemed to make him sad. He cleared his throat and went on. "You'll see a lot of Navy personnel here right now because of the situation in Cuba, which is only ninety miles away. A dictator named Batista has just been ousted, and the rebels have taken over."

"Castro, right?" I already knew about this from the *Weekly Readers* we had to read in civics class at Repass Junior High.

Daddy looked impressed. "Why, that's right, Jenny. Fidel Castro is the rebel leader, a genuine hero." Daddy was always for the people, for the underdog. His own father had kept the union out of the mill, but after Granddaddy killed himself, Daddy welcomed it. This was only one of Grandmother's many longtime grievances against Daddy.

We stopped for the red light at Truman and White, which gave me a chance to get a good look at all the boys in uniform along the sidewalk. Several of them were as cute as Harlan

Boyd, in that same sweet country way, which made me feel funny deep down in my stomach. But nobody was as cute as Tom Burlington. Nobody would ever be as cute as Tom Burlington.

"Well, I like Ike," Mama said irrelevantly. This had something to do with Castro, I believe.

It was the kind of remark that used to make Daddy smile, or pinch her cheek. Not now. Instead, he curled his lip in an ugly way. Luckily Mama did not notice; she was staring out the open window. "I just wish you'd look at all these flowers!" she said. "I have never seen such vines."

I hadn't, either. Nor had I ever seen anyplace that looked like Key West, with old frame houses covered and sometimes hidden by lush vegetation, with dogs and cats and chickens running around in the streets, and piano music and laughter pouring out of open doorways. I had never seen adults riding bicycles before, yet it seemed to be a common form of transportation here. People sat on their porches and balconies or stood chatting on the sidewalks beneath big-leafed trees. The light was green and golden. Everybody seemed to have all the time in the world.

I observed these people carefully.

Nobody looked like us.

"We're almost there," Daddy said.

Mama reapplied her lipstick. We turned left onto Duval Street, and now I could see a glistening patch of ocean ahead. Daddy pulled into a motel called the Blue Marlin, with a huge fish on its sign. Mama and I waited in the car, under the entrance portico, while he headed for the office, tucking his shirt down in back as he went. The motel was made of blue-painted concrete, two stories in a U shape around a good-size pool featuring a diving board and a water slide and lots of lounge chairs and palm trees. "Wow, this is really nice, isn't it?" I said to Mama, who was lighting a cigarette and didn't answer. Still, I was hopeful. The Blue Marlin *was* nice. But was it nice enough to get Mama and Daddy back together? Mama smoked that whole cigarette and lit another, blowing smoke rings out her window. I watched a neon-green lizard zip up a blue concrete wall.

"Why is this *taking so long*?" Mama said finally. She looked like she was about to cry.

I was halfway out of the car, on my way to find out, when Daddy came through the plate-glass doors jingling two keys, with a funny look on his face. "Jenny, get back in the car," he said abruptly, and I did. Then Daddy got in and closed his door and turned to look at us instead of starting the car.

"You're not going to believe this, Billie," he said slowly.

"What? What is it? Are the girls okay?" Mama's pretty face was an instant mask of alarm. She had had too much bad news.

"Oh no, nothing like that." Daddy smiled his new, distant smile. "It appears that almost this entire motel has been taken over by the cast and crew of a movie that they are shooting on location right now in Key West, over at the

Navy yard. There are only four rooms they're not occupy-
ing, and it turns out we've got two of them." Daddy jingled
his keys again. "They asked me a lot of questions. I had to
swear that we weren't journalists or photographers in order
to stay here."

"Who did you say we are?" I asked. It was exactly what
I had been trying to figure out.

Daddy looked at me. "An American family," he said
firmly. I felt something very deep inside myself relax. "But
Jenny," he added in a no-nonsense voice, "I promised that
man that you *would not bother* the stars, do you hear me?
Or the crew, or anybody else. I promised because I knew
that you and your mother would want to stay here. There
are no other children at this motel, so you'll just have to
amuse yourself. You can meet some other kids down there,
I imagine"—Daddy pointed to the beach at the end of the
street—"but you can't bring them here, and you *cannot*
bother anybody at this motel. Is that clear?" He had his key
in the ignition, yet did not turn it. I knew he was speaking
as much to Mama as to me.

"Yes," I said.

"Which stars?" Mama asked.

"Well, there's Dina Merrill," Daddy said, "and Tony
Curtis . . ."

"*Tony Curtis!*" Mama and I squealed together. Tony Curtis had just been voted the most popular young actor in

Hollywood, after the recent success of *The Defiant Ones*. Mama and I were crazy about Tony Curtis.

Daddy had to grin in spite of himself. "And you just missed Janet Leigh," he said. "She left yesterday. She was here for two weeks, apparently, on vacation. She's not in this movie, though."

"She's gone back to California to be with the children," Mama said automatically. "Kelly and Jamie."

Daddy looked at her for a while. Then he cleared his throat and said, "That's not all."

"*Who?*" Mama and I breathed together. Over the top of the seat, I clutched her hand.

"Cary Grant." Daddy was trying to sound offhand.

"*Cary Grant!*" We couldn't believe it. The most gorgeous, the most elegant, the biggest star in Hollywood!

"He's got the bungalow and several of those end units." Daddy pointed. "His secretary is here, and a number of other people, his whole staff. The man at the desk says he's a real gentleman."

"Of course he is," Mama said.

I was not so sure of that. I sucked in my breath, thinking of his recent affair with Sophia Loren.

Mama and I peered in Cary Grant's direction but couldn't see any particular activity over there beyond the pool and the pink bougainvillea, which grew in profusion, shielding the bungalow.

"They're still on location today," Daddy said. "They don't get back until about eight o'clock. They're filming down at the Navy yard, where they've painted a submarine pink for this movie. The movie is called *Operation Petticoat*. So if everything is understood, Jenny"—I bobbed my head vigorously—"then let's get unpacked, girls!" Daddy finally started the car and drove around back.

Our rooms were on the second floor. I insisted on helping Daddy carry the bags, even though he said I didn't have to. It was my good deed for the day. My room, 208, had a connecting door into Mama and Daddy's room, 209, which was actually a suite with two beds and a rattan settee and coffee table and two armchairs and a tiny kitchenette. I was utterly charmed by the kitchenette, with its two-burner stovetop and miniature refrigerator. It had four of everything—four spoons, four forks, four knives, four plates, four glasses.

"You can go swimming before supper if you want to," Mama told me, so I went in my room and put on my bathing suit and headed for the pool, while Daddy fixed gin and tonics for himself and Mama and pulled two chairs out onto the balcony.

"Honestly, John," Mama was saying behind me as I took off down the concrete stairs, "is that really true, about the movie company? Or did you make all that up?"

"Scout's honor, Billie," Daddy said.

At least they were talking to each other.

I took a running dive into the water.

• • •

IF WE RARELY SAW CARY GRANT, IT WAS NOT FROM LACK of trying. He had his own chef, and took his meals mostly in his bungalow, where he held private parties as well. He rode to and from the set in a chauffeured limousine, which had been written into his contract, according to Mr. Rudy, the motel manager, our informer. Sometimes I sneaked out to the parking lot in the early morning to wash the windshield and polish the hubcaps of the limousine, though I was discouraged in this particular good deed by Rocco Bacco, Mr. Grant's chauffeur.

Cary Grant often gave other cast members, and the pretty young script girls and makeup girls, a ride in the limousine. Mama considered this very democratic of him; she pronounced him a "perfect gentleman." I was a little disappointed in his looks, personally. He was so old, for one thing. I thought he looked pretty much like any other old guy, for instance Dr. Nevins, our family physician back in Lewisville, or Ronnie Tuttle, Aunt Judy's first husband. Cary Grant was not even as good-looking as Daddy.

I *did* like his accent, however. I liked the way he said "hot dog" on the night they had the cast cookout by the pool. He said "hot dog" as if the *o*'s were long instead of short. Mama said this was English. On the night of the cookout, Mama and I sat on our balcony, suspended over the crowd, so we could see everything: the gorgeous girls in their two-piece bathing suits, the muscly young men, two guys with beards (was one of them the director?), the tall bitchy woman with red hair and glasses who seemed to be in charge of herding everybody around. We were there to see her break into a terrible tap dance (everybody clapped politely) and to see Tony Curtis do his Cary Grant imitation at Mr. Grant's request, and then to see Tony Curtis get thrown in the pool by most of the crew, who soon joined him, swimming around in their clothes. Mama and I pulled our chairs up to the rail and hung over it to watch. By then it was dark and the lighted aqua pool glowed like a jewel in the fragrant night, full of impossibly attractive people trailing wet clothes through the water.

Mama nudged me. "Hollywood high jinks," she said.

Behind us, in their room, Daddy lay on one of the beds reading some big book, a biography. Sometimes he seemed amused by our reaction to the movie stars; other times he seemed disgusted; and that night, when we wouldn't leave our vantage point to go out for dinner, he had gone without us. We didn't care. We were perfectly happy to have potato chips and Fritos for dinner. We weren't about to leave the balcony, that was for sure, especially after they all jumped into the pool. I thought they might peel off their clothes at any moment, but nobody did. The party broke up soon after the swimming part. People disappeared into their rooms or sat quietly in the lounge chairs around the pool, where there were so many plants and it was so dark that Mama and

I couldn't see who they were anymore; all we could see was the occasional flare of a match, and all we could hear was a low laugh now and then.

In fact, we never did see as many high jinks as we expected. The biggest surprise about the movie business was how hard everybody worked. The bus was waiting under the portico every morning at seven-thirty; by seven forty-five, everybody, even Cary Grant, was gone.

Though I was always there to witness their departure, it was much too early for Mama, who had to make do with peeping from behind the venetian blinds. Then she'd fall back asleep for two more hours while Daddy took a long walk around the island or went fishing with Captain Tony. This left me free to roam the streets, or swim in the pool, or talk to Mr. Rudy, or do anything else I wanted, and often I'd fit in my good deed right then, so I'd have it over with.

Sometimes I walked around the corner to the big scary church and prayed with the Catholics. I loved the gory statues and the candles. I loved the feel of the scratchy cold stone floor on my knees when I knelt to pray. I loved the old people dressed in black, bent over and mumbling their prayers. Where did all these old people come from, anyway? I never saw them on the beach or in the streets, that's for sure. They looked dark and sad. I knew they would die soon. The Jesus in the Catholic statues was a lot less peppy than the one back at St. Michael's—and certainly than the Jesus in my cousins' church in Repass, who looked like a Ken doll.

This Jesus' brow was encircled by thorns, and He was always bleeding.

It was hard to imagine what He would think of anything. He was too busy suffering.

But I loved the way *I* felt, clean and new and bursting with goodness, when I popped back out of that church into the sunny Key West morning, like a girl in a cuckoo clock. I always took some money to donate, and if I could scrounge up enough, I'd buy a candle from the sad lady and light it in honor of my uncle Mason and Carroll Byrd and Harlan Boyd. Whenever I did this, I'd check in throughout the day to see my candle flickering in its red glass holder in the bank of candles burning in the alcove. I liked to see how long my candle would last in comparison with the others, and make sure I got my money's worth. The money came from Daddy, who left change from his pockets scattered on top of the bureau. I'd gather this up and take it with me on my morning good-deed run.

Other times I'd give the money away to the bums who slept on the beach at the end of the street, or to the children who lived on top of the Cuban grocery where I went to buy cigarettes for Mama and café con leche for myself. I came to love café con leche, and usually that was what I'd have for breakfast, café con leche and a Hershey bar.

It thrilled me to walk down the alley behind the Havana Madrid nightclub, where strippers worked and "unimaginable things" went on in the back room, according to Mama.

One of the signs on the front of the club said "Live Bottomless, Friday Only"—a show I'd have given anything to see. By mid-morning, the strippers were often out on a wooden porch behind the nightclub, sunning themselves and smoking cigarettes and giggling like high school girls. Two of them, sisters maybe, even looked like high school girls, not much older than I.

One day they were sitting together on a ratty chaise longue, looking at a fashion magazine, when I came walking along. "Hi!" I said loudly, on impulse. Immediately I could feel myself turning red all over.

"Hi!" they said right back. They jumped up and came to the rail. Their fresh morning faces, without makeup, were open and friendly. "Me Luisa," the thin one said. "Me Rosa," said the other, blinking into the sun. Over the rail, they stared at me curiously. I felt like an exhibit—an American Girl, member of an American Family, suddenly exotic in this locale.

"Me Jenny," I said, thumping my chest in a gesture so awkward it made us all break into giggles.

"You smoke a cigarette?" Luisa offered her crumpled pack of Camels.

I loved the way she said "seegarette," and resolved on the spot to say it that way for the rest of my life.

"Don't mind if I do," I said, and took one.

"Rosa! Luisa! What are you doing? This little girl doesn't smoke!" An older woman wearing a purple silk kimono stepped up behind them. She had a hard leathery face and dyed red hair.

"Oh yes I do," I assured her, putting the cigarette in the pocket of my camp shirt. "I've just been trying to quit."

The woman grinned at me. "You have, huh?" she said. "Well, as long as you're here, why don't you make yourself useful, and get me a newspaper." She flipped me a fifty-cent piece.

When I came back with the paper, she said, "Aw, honey, keep the change," and I did. Then I got to go up on the porch and sit in a chair and smoke my cigarette and get my stubby fingernails painted by Rosa, who was doing everybody's, while the woman turned to the crossword puzzle and worked it in a flash, just like Daddy. Her name was Red.

Rosa and Luisa had other, stripper names (Candy Love, Nookie) for their acts. The billboard on the sidewalk in front of the Havana Madrid featured a photograph of Luisa/Nookie, wearing only a G-string. She was much too thin, with no breasts to speak of. (Rayette could have made a fortune at the Havana Madrid.) Luisa and Rosa both looked tired, too. I was always worried about their health. Sometimes I brought them oranges, and one morning I left a bottle of vitamins for them on the porch rail. The bottle had disappeared by afternoon, but Rosa and Luisa never mentioned the vitamins to me. Of course, they didn't know I was the person who had brought them. But this didn't matter; it was still a good deed.

Another place I loved to go was the graveyard, where I could always clean off a grave or two. There were about a million graves over there, a million people buried above the ground in white concrete boxes that you could walk on or sit on, and some of them had not been cleaned off for the longest time, you could tell. You could tell that nobody cared about those people anymore at all. Maybe everyone who ever knew them was dead. I'd push the brown leaves off the graves into little piles, then scrape green mold off them with the snow scraper from Daddy's new car. Then I'd walk around the graveyard admiring the statues—swans, angels, lambs, cutoff tree trunks, and even some stone dogs on dogs' graves. *Those dogs are all dead now*, I'd think, and a thrill would shoot through me. I liked to subtract the dates and figure out how long the people had lived and try to imagine what they had died of. I liked to read the names and inscriptions, my favorite being:

HERE LIES OUR HEART

What if I died right now? What if I was hit by a car on my way back to the motel? What would they write on *my* grave? I hoped it would be "Our Jenny, a good girl." The very thought of this made me cry and cry. Mason's stone had only his full name on it, Henry Mason Rutledge, and the dates of his birth and death, and the carving of a bird in flight. They had buried him in our family plot at St. Michael's,

next to Granddaddy who had killed himself, and a whole
bunch of other old dead people in our family, people so old
that even their names were all but gone from their stones. I
wanted to be buried in the nifty aboveground graveyard in
Key West, and informed Mama of this one morning when
I got back to the motel and found her out sunning by the
pool.

She took off her dark glasses and sat up in the lounge
chair to stare at me. "You what, honey?" she said.

"Bury me in Key West," I said. "In case I die, I mean. I
want to be buried in the cemetery here, in one of those cool
white concrete boxes, with an angel. A big angel."

"Oh, honestly, Jenny, where do you get these crazy ideas?
And for heaven's sake, take off that awful blouse," Mama
said. "I swear, it looks like somebody *made* it."

WE FELL INTO A ROUTINE. I'D GO FISHING WITH DADDY,
and I'd shop or sun or watch the movie stars with Mama.
This way, I got to have plenty of everybody's undivided
attention, though I kept wishing my parents would do more
things together. Sometimes they did, though Daddy always
looked like a man fulfilling a duty, even after Mama started
wearing flowers in her hair.

I loved those rare nights they went out without me. I'd
swim in the pool or run errands for Mr. Rudy or smoke
Mama's cigarettes or hide in the shrubbery by the pool in

order to keep up with several romances I had taken an interest in. Then, of course, I would have to do a lot of good deeds to make up for all that. Then I'd read *East of Eden*, which somebody had carelessly left by the pool (I had finished *Bridey Murphy*), and then I'd have to read my New Testament to make up for *that*. I was really busy, and was often completely exhausted by my efforts.

I couldn't tell whether or not the good deeds were working. My parents were endlessly cordial to each other now, but so far they had never slept in the same bed. I knew this for a fact. I checked their room every morning.

So I doubled my efforts—buying more candles, cleaning more graves, using up all Mama's Kleenex on Cary Grant's hubcaps, donating a jar of her Noxzema to the Havana Madrid girls. But we seemed to have reached a stalemate. Entranced by the stars, Mama was becoming herself again. But would this ever be enough for Daddy? Could it be? I knew that Frank Sinatra still loved Ava Gardner right now, even though she was now in Spain living with a bullfighter. The bullfighter meant nothing to Frank. He was peanuts; he was toast. Frank would *always* love Ava.

I prayed it would not be so for Daddy and Carroll Byrd.

It was hard to stay mad at Daddy, however. His lawyer-like quality of paying close attention was flattering; he was winning me over again. I especially liked our fishing trips. Once we got up at four a.m. to drive up the Keys and go out with a one-eyed man named Captain Lewjack who gave me a mug of black coffee and a jelly glass of brandy and strapped me into a fighting chair and kept chanting, "C'mon, baby, c'mon, baby, hootchie-koo," when I hooked a dolphin.

"Not a *dolphin*!" I cried out at first, though Daddy and Captain Lewjack assured me it wasn't *that* kind of dolphin but the other kind, a game fish. Still, the dolphin was so beautiful that it took my breath away when it leaped out of the water for the first time, its lovely colors like a rainbow in the sun. It turned iron gray the instant Captain Lewjack hit it on the head with a hammer after I pulled it in, with Daddy's help.

This was the same day Daddy caught a marlin after a three-hour struggle, and I still have the photograph that was taken of him and the marlin on the dock when we went back in: Daddy bare-chested and grinning from ear to ear, cigarette dangling from the corner of his mouth, wearing a Panama hat. It is impossible to tell that he had a broken heart, or that anything at all was the matter with him.

I have another photograph, of myself beside a giant jew-fish which I hooked when we went out on Captain Tony's party boat. This picture ran in the Key West newspaper, even though I didn't actually catch the fish; it was brought up with block and tackle by several of Captain Tony's crew members. It was the ugliest fish I had ever seen. In the picture, I'm nearly invisible behind somebody's enormous sunglasses; the caption reads "Va. Miss Gets Big Jew."

Daddy and I were fools for fish. We also took the

glass-bottom boat trip out to the reef, where we peered down into another world, another universe, with its softly waving sea fans and giant brain coral and gorgeous deadly fire coral and silly octopuses and squids with big round doll-baby eyes. Daddy took me to the old aquarium at Mallory Square, and later I went again and again by myself. I liked to touch the barracudas and turtles. I especially liked the sharks, and never tired of leaning way over their open pen to watch them glide by (constantly, endlessly, they *could not* be still), knowing that they would kill me if they could. They would *love* to kill me, and I loved to think about this. For a nickel, you could feed them, which counted as one good deed.

What I did with Mama never varied. Shortly before nine o'clock every evening, just after dinner, we'd go into the lobby of the Blue Marlin and settle ourselves on a large rattan sofa, which she called "the davenport."

" 'Lo, Miz Billie," Hal, the skinny night clerk, would say, and Mama always said, "How are you, Hal?" as if she really cared. Now restored to something approaching her old self again, Mama had everybody at the motel eating out of her hand. Hal adored her. Everyone did.

Mama carried a newspaper. I carried a magazine or a book. (Once I brought my New Testament, but Mama said, "Honestly, Jenny! Take that thing back to your room," rolling her eyes, so I did.) We'd sit down ostentatiously on the davenport and begin to read. Right behind us stood a row of potted plants. Right behind them stood a table with an

ashtray and a telephone on it, the only telephone at the Blue
Marlin available for guests to use. An old armchair was next
to the table.

And every night, at exactly nine o'clock, here came Tony
Curtis through the plate-glass doors. He nodded to Hal,
then walked to the table, where he sat down and lifted the
receiver and asked for a long-distance operator. Mama rattled her paper, reading. Sometimes there'd be a brief wait,
during which Tony lit a cigarette, until Janet Leigh answered
the phone in Hollywood, all the way across the continent.

"Hello, darling," Tony said.

Mama sighed. I sighed. We kept on reading.

Tony talked about what had happened on the set that
day; he referred to Cary Grant as a fine fellow. Then he'd
ask about the kids, and about the rest of the family, and about
their friends. They seemed to have a lot of friends. Sometimes they'd talk about really boring things, such as money.
Janet Leigh always had a lot to say, and Tony chuckled
intimately into the phone and smoked another cigarette
while he listened to her. Then he always told her how much
he missed her. At this point, Mama and I would take deep
breaths and straighten up: here came the moment we were
waiting for.

First Tony said, "I love you," and then listened, while
(we guessed) Janet Leigh said, "I love you," back.

Then he said, "God bless you, darling," and hung up.

By then Mama was breathing so hard she could barely

hold her paper, and I felt just as I had felt in the Bomb Shelter when Harlan Boyd stuck his tongue in my mouth. Mama and I were so rattled that we didn't even notice when Tony Curtis strode back through the lobby and out the door. "Thanks, Hal," he'd say, giving Hal a mock salute. Tony Curtis was *so cute*. I even thought old bucktoothed Hal was cute, by then. I thought everybody was cute.

Romance was in the very air here—in the lush bright flowers, the seductive vines, the lazy twirling overhead fans, the snatches of song on the soft, soft breeze. Surely Mama and Daddy would *catch it* somehow. Surely they would fall in love again.

I had everything riding on this.

Then came the big night—when Tony Curtis had just said, "God bless you, darling," and Mama and I were still in a fever state—the night that Tony Curtis paused before going out the door and then turned on his heel in a military way (his role was that of Navy Lieutenant Nick Holden) and walked to the davenport, right up to Mama and me. He was wearing white shorts and a red knit shirt, I will never forget. He cleared his throat. "Ladies?" he said.

Mama and I went on reading as though our lives depended on it.

"Ladies?" Tony Curtis said again.

I looked up into those famous blue eyes and suddenly had to pee.

Mama folded her newspaper and stuck out her hand. "I'm

Billie Dale, from Virginia," she said, "and this is my daughter
Jenny."

Tony Curtis shook Mama's hand, bowing slightly from
the waist, and then took mine. "So pleased to meet you," he
said. He was smiling. "From Virginia," he repeated. "A beautiful state."

"Yes, it is," Mama said.

"Are you in Key West on business or pleasure?" Tony
Curtis asked.

"Oh, it's just a vacation," Mama said.

"Actually, my parents are trying to patch up their marriage," I blurted out. All of a sudden I was determined to
spill the beans, to tell Tony Curtis the *whole thing*. He had
such a good marriage himself that maybe he could fix up
Mama and Daddy's, give them some good Hollywood
advice—a hot tip from the stars.

"Jenny, don't you dare!" Mama shrieked.

Tony Curtis looked very surprised. "Well," he said, inch-
ing back, "I was going to say, if you've got the time, and if
you're interested, we'll be shooting crowd scenes for the next
two days, and we need extras. Your daughter"—he rolled
those big blue eyes at *me*—"might get a kick out of being in
the movie."

I threw my book on the floor and started jumping up
and down. "In the movie? I'd *love* to be in the movie!"

Behind the desk, Hal started laughing.

"It's a deal, then," Tony Curtis said to Mama. "You and

your husband can be in it, too, ma'am, if you want to see what it's all about. Just show up at the Navy dock tomorrow morning at nine. We need a big civilian crowd to wave hello at the submarine when it comes into the port."

"All right," Mama said. You could barely hear her.

Tony Curtis left for good then, waving to me from the door before he spun militarily on his heel and vanished into the shrubbery. I gathered up his cigarette butts from the ashtray, for my collection.

"Maybe you'll be discovered." Hal winked at me.

"Oh, don't be silly," Mama said. "Don't give her any ideas."

But I already had ideas. Why not? Jean Seberg, the daughter of an Iowa druggist, had been picked from eighteen thousand hopefuls to be Joan of Arc.

"Anyway, who knows?" Mama flung back over her shoulder to Hal. "Maybe *I'll* be discovered!"

I RAN ALL THE WAY TO OUR ROOMS, MAMA FOLLOWING. Daddy sat in one of the wicker armchairs, reading in a yellow pool of light from the Chinese lamp with the tassels. The rest of the room was dark. A drink sat sweating on the glass table beside him. Overhead, in the darkness, the fan went around and around, making a whispery noise like wind in the fields at home.

"Daddy, Daddy, Daddy! Guess what? You'll never believe

it! We get to be in the movie!" I stood panting just inside the door.

Daddy looked up at me very slowly then, as if he were coming back from somewhere far away, as if I were speaking a foreign language. In the light from the Chinese lamp, his face looked haunted, lined, and old; his eyes were bleak and dark in their deep sockets. My heart went down to my feet. I had caught Daddy out, surprised him. This was the way he *really* felt, and all the fishing trips and good deeds in the world could never change it.

"What is it, Jenny?" he said.

I had to say it, to blunder on. "All of us—you and Mama and me—get to be in the movie tomorrow if we go down to the docks. They need extras. Tony Curtis said."

Daddy looked at me. I realized that the last thing in the world he'd ever want to do was be in a movie. He put a piece of paper in the book to mark his place, and put the book on the table.

"Come on, Daddy, *please* can we do it?"

A gray smile came and went at the sides of his mouth. "Well, honey, *of course* you and your mother can go down there—"

In the middle of that sentence, I felt his attention shift away from me, and I realized he was speaking now to Mama, who must have come in behind me as he spoke. "—but I believe I'll pass on it."

"John—" Mama was still breathless from her climb up the stairs. "John, come on, this is the chance of a lifetime."

"Mr. Kinney has sent me some figures I have to look over in the morning." Daddy's face was gray, his long cheeks shadowy and hollow.

Of course. How *could* he do it? I thought. How could he? A man who voted for Adlai Stevenson and loved Carroll Byrd? A man whose own father had killed himself? Of course he couldn't do it.

Behind me, Mama started to cry. I heard her ragged breathing and those snuffly sounds she always made. *Get a grip!* I wanted to scream at her. Didn't she understand him at all? Didn't she understand *anything*?

Daddy did not get up from the chair. "Jenny, go on to bed," he told me. "It's late. Go on, so you can be in the movie in the morning."

I spun around, pushing Mama aside. "I hate you!" I screamed from the balcony. "I hate you both!" I tore off into the dark and ran all the way to the cemetery, where I threw myself down on somebody's grave, and cried and cried and cried. The concrete was still warm from the sun; I could feel its heat down the length of my body. It felt strange, good. Finally I rolled over on my back and looked at the starry bowl of the sky. I took a deep breath. There was a full moon coming up, so I could see the white graves in their orderly rows, the palms, the urns, and all the angels. I would never

be an angel. I knew that now. Mama was an angel, and Rayette was an angel, but I would never be one, not in a million
years, no matter how many good deeds I did. I was suddenly
sick of good deeds, and vowed never to do another one. They
hadn't worked, anyway. Nothing had worked, and nothing
was ever going to work. Mama and Daddy would never
patch up their marriage. They would never get back together.

I would be an orphan, like Jane Eyre. I would wander
alone in the world, doing bad deeds. I would become a stripper. A prostitute. A love slave. Who cared? Not Jesus, obviously, who hadn't done a damn thing for me in spite of all
my efforts. I probably didn't even believe in Him, as a matter
of fact. He was too damn picky. Too hard to please.

I lay on my back on top of a dead person, thinking this
stuff.

Bats swooped around overhead. A cat stole up to rub
against my drooping arm, and I petted it till it purred. The
longer I stayed there, the brighter the moonlight grew, and
the more I could see. I could see everything.

It was after midnight when I got back to the Blue Marlin,
where I found Mama and Daddy and Mr. Rudy and a young
Cuban policeman all sitting around in room 209 waiting for
me. They jumped up when I came in.

"Oh, thank goodness! Oh, thank God!" Mama rushed
over to smother me in tears and Chanel No. 5.

Daddy said, "I guess we won't be needing your services

after all," and shook hands with the young Cuban police-man, who left looking disgusted. Mr. Rudy clicked his tongue disapprovingly at me before he slipped out the door, too.

"I'm sorry," I started, though I wasn't, but Daddy put his finger to my lips. "Hush, Jenny. It's all right. Just go to bed now, okay? It's late. We'll talk about this in the morning."

But in the morning there was no time to talk. Mama woke me by shaking my shoulders and saying, "Jenny! Jenny! Come on, get up! We're going to be in the movie! Wake up, honey, you'll want to wash your hair—" I opened my eyes to find her sitting on the edge of my bed looking as beautiful as any movie star, hair fixed just so, fire-engine-red lips smiling. She wore a fresh dose of perfume and a full-skirted red-flowered dress.

"You look beautiful, Mama," I said.

"Come on, Jenny, hurry." Daddy stood behind her. He was dressed for the movie, too, in a clean white shirt and khaki pants. I didn't ask any questions. I jumped up and took a shower and put on my middy-blouse outfit and some of Mama's dusting powder. I parted my hair and combed it carefully, and made spit curls over my ears. Then I put on a whole lot of Mama's makeup, turning the corners of my eyes into silver points like shark fins, like angel wings. Mama and

Daddy looked at each other but did not say a thing about
my makeup.

They grabbed my hands and we set off down the street
along with the crowd. People poured out of motels and shops
and restaurants—tourists, tramps, artists, merchants and
shopgirls and women wiping their hands on their aprons.
Even the iguana man fell in, with his big lizard circling his
shoulders. It was a holiday. "*Buenos días*, Jenny," called
Luisa, mincing along in yellow short shorts and high heels.
Sleepy-eyed Rosa waved. Mama's eyebrows made little
arches of surprise. She jerked my hand. "Jenny, who *are*
those girls?" But I didn't have to answer, because somebody
started singing: "You had a wife and forty-nine kids, but
you *left*, you *left*, you *left*, right, *left*," and everybody took
it up. We became a parade.

We trooped to the Navy yard and onto the docks, bursting into a spontaneous cheer at the sight of the pink submarine that steamed back and forth in the harbor, decks covered
with actors. I had never seen it under way before. Against
that bright blue water, the pink submarine was miraculous.
Mama squeezed my hand. Pelicans and gulls wheeled overhead. Camera crews were everywhere: on a launch in the
water, on an official-looking truck at the dock, on top of a
warehouse. A man with a beard and a bullhorn was lifted
high above us on a crane.

"Okay!" His amplified voice rang out. "Ladies and gentlemen! Boys and girls! We appreciate your participation

here today! Now, all you have to do is cheer—" At this point, we drowned him out. He had to wave his arms back and forth to restore order. "Good! Very good! All you have to do is cheer—just like that—when the sub comes up to the dock. That's it! Got it?"

We cheered again. My throat was getting sore already, and it didn't even *count* yet.

"Okay! Now save it. Don't do it until I give you the sign. Then you start, and be sure to wave hello. These guys have been out in the Philippines winning a war for you, so you're glad to see them, right? Okay?"

I strained to see Tony Curtis on the deck of the submarine, but it was still too far away. The actors looked like ants. The director held his bullhorn up against the sky, then brought it down. Great puffs of white smoke shot out of the smokestacks as the pink sub headed toward shore, toward us, toward home. I started crying and couldn't stop. The crowd went wild. I could hear Mama's high voice, Daddy's piercing whistle. My makeup was running but I didn't care. I wiped silvery tears off my chin and kept on crying. It was the happiest moment of my life. We waved and cheered until the pink submarine was at the dock, and Tony Curtis looked straight at me, I swear he did, and winked.

So I did it. I pulled it off. We stayed in Key West for an other week, and every day Daddy softened up a bit more, relaxing into his old self again. I could see it happening. My parents paid more and more attention to each other, less to me. When the maid came to their room in the mornings, she had only one bed to make up. I was free to roam all over town by myself, free to get my ears pierced by the oldest of the Cuban children who lived over the grocery—an act which served to unite Mama and Daddy even more, *against* me: "Honestly, Jenny, nice girls in Virginia don't have pierced ears! Only *maids* have pierced ears, don't you know *anything*?" Mama wailed, clutching Daddy's hand for support. They would be together for twenty more years.

Though this ought to be the end of the story, it's not. One more thing happened. One more thing is *always* happening, isn't it? This is the reason I have found life to be harder than fiction, where you can make it all work out to suit you and put The End wherever you please. But back to the story.

A few days before we left for home, Caroline and Tom flew down to Key West for a weekend visit, bringing their brand-new baby (Thomas Kraft Burlington, Jr.—then called Tom-Tom) with them. I couldn't wait to see Tom Burlington again, especially now that I had gotten such a nice tan and a new haircut and had my ears pierced and did not have to be good anymore. I had *grown up*, I felt. I had been tongue-kissed, and lived among stars.

I was ready for him.

But when they arrived, Tom wouldn't pay a bit of

attention to me, no more than Mason ever had. All he would do was wait on Caroline hand and foot, and make goo-goo eyes at his stupid little pointy-headed baby. It made me sick! Tom-Tom had colic, and spit up his milk, and cried all the time. I was dying to show Tom around Key West (I had not specifically invited Caroline), which I couldn't do until Tom-Tom fell asleep, which took forever. But finally he lay curled on his stomach in a little red ball, oohed and aahed over by Mama, and Tom stood up.

"Come on, honey," he said to Caroline. "Let's let Jenny give us this grand tour we've been hearing so much about."

I held my breath, but Caroline shook her head. "No, honey, you go on. I'll just catch a few winks myself, I think. I'm really tired."

Tom looked doubtful, but she squeezed his hand. "Go *on*, silly," she said, and he did.

I showed him the cemetery first, but he seemed preoccupied, and didn't even laugh at the funny tombstone that read "I Told You I Was Sick." Instead he looked sweaty and pale, worried. "I ought to go back," he said.

"No, don't!" I was howling. "Come on. You've got to come down to the docks for the sunset. I want to show you the sharks and the iguana man."

Tom looked uncomfortable now. "Maybe tomorrow," he said, "when Caroline can come, too."

We stood there awkwardly among the tombs and

angels, which I loved, while—for the second time in Tom's presence—I started crying uncontrollably. I don't know what I had thought—that he would say a poem to me in the graveyard, perhaps, something about love and death, or undying love . . . about his undying love for me. Now I knew I was a fool—an idiot.

I turned and took off running through the cemetery without another word.

"Hey!" Tom yelled behind me. "Jenny! Stop!"

But I wouldn't have stopped for anything. I ran like the wind, straight through the cemetery and out the gate and into the carnival bustle of late afternoon, all the way down Duval Street to the Havana Madrid, where I nearly crashed into Luisa's billboard. Here I stopped short, panting hard. The door to the bar stood wide open, dark and inviting.

I walked in.

It took a while for my eyes to adjust, but then I could see fine. It was plenty light where the sailors sat with their beers, looking up at a girl who walked the long shiny bar wearing nothing but pasties and a G-string, stopping from time to time to dangle her breasts in their faces. She was a big-legged Cuban girl, nobody I had ever seen before. While I watched, she reached out and grabbed a sailor's hat and rubbed it between her legs while he turned bright red and started grabbing for it. "Gimme that!" he said. "Give it back!" No older-looking than Harlan Boyd, he was mortified. Everybody was laughing at him when the girl smacked the hat back on his head and swayed off down the long bar and exited. I peered at the girls and men sitting at the tables all around the sawdust floor, looking for Rosa and Luisa, but I didn't see them. The unimaginable corners of the cavernous room were dark and vast.

"Are you lost, Miss?" a tall black man at my elbow asked.

"I just came in for a drink," I said, and went over to the bar and climbed up on a wooden stool before he could stop me. Two men sitting to my left elbowed each other, grinning at me. They were old and fat. I grinned back. "Well, hello there, honey," one of them said. A skinny redhead sashayed down the bar in a top-hat-and-tails outfit, then came back without the tails.

I knew exactly what Jesus would think of this place, but since he didn't exist anyway, I ordered a Coke from the flat-chested blond bartender, who was wearing a sort of corset.

"Make that a rum and Coke for the little lady," the man said, and the bartender raised an eyebrow at him but brought it. I took a big drink. The man scooted his stool closer to mine. He touched my knee lightly, with one finger.

"Thank you, this is a delicious cocktail," I said.

"It is, huh!" And suddenly Red is there, too, the other bartender, hands on substantial hips, fiery Medusa hair standing out all around her head, bosom heaving furiously.

"Jenny, you get your ass out of here *right now*!" she yells, and I run out the door, straight into Tom Burlington. He grabs my shoulders and shakes me until my teeth rattle, then hugs me, then shakes me again.

"You little bitch!" he says.

What a relief! I have been recognized at last. I *am* a little bitch, and I will never be an angel, and it's okay. I start laughing, and Tom starts laughing, too.

This is the moment when the street photographer snapped our picture, and Tom paid him for it, and gave it to me, and I have it still. I blew it up. I tend to move around a lot, but I always take this picture with me, and keep it right here on my desk.

In the picture, Tom Burlington and I cling together in the jostling crowd, our arms wound tightly around each other. We look like lovers, which we never were. Behind us is the Havana Madrid sign with the winking lady's face on it. There is something she knows that I don't know yet. But I will learn. And I will get my period, and some breasts. I will also *do it* plenty, thereby falling into numerous messy situations too awful to mention here. I will never be really good again. I am not good. I am as ornery and difficult and inconsolable as Carroll Byrd.

I don't know whatever happened to her, or to Tom Burlington, who left my sister for another woman, an English teacher at his school, when Tom-Tom was still small. Caroline is happily remarried now, to a lawyer in Charleston,

South Carolina, where she has raised four children and is the head of the Historical Society. Our lives are very different, Caroline's and mine, and I regret that I don't see much of her now, except for her children's graduations and weddings. My oldest sister Beth is still married and still living out west; I don't see much of her, either. Tony Curtis and Janet Leigh are long divorced. He's an artist now. Cary Grant is dead. Grandmother and Aunt Chloë and Aunt Judy are dead. Mama is dead, too, of ovarian cancer in 1979. After she died, Daddy turned the mill into a co-op and gave it to his employees; Mr. Kinney's son is running it today. Then Daddy surprised everybody by moving to Boca Raton, Florida, where he "up and married" (as Mama would have said) the real estate woman who sold him his condo. This woman has a black spiky hairdo, and everybody calls her "The Shark." Daddy takes Elderhostel courses and seems very happy; his current personality bears no relation, that I can see, to his former self, to the person who is in this story. Cousin Glenda ran a rest home for many years after Raymond's death; now she is *in* the rest home, and Rayette and her husband are running it. Rayette sends me a long chatty Christmas letter every year, even though I never did get a grip. I don't know what happened to Harlan Boyd. Jinx is still my friend, and we keep in touch by phone, and meet at a spa in Sedona once a year.

For some reason, I can't quit writing this story, or looking at this picture, in which the sun is so bright, and Tom

Burlington and I are smiling like crazy. I guess it reminds me of Mama and Daddy in love, of the day when Mama and Daddy and I walked down to the docks to be in the movie, and cheered when the pink submarine came in, and waved hello.

The

SOUTHERN CROSS

Mama always said, "Talk real sweet and you can have whatever you want." This is true, though it does not hurt to have a nice bust either. Since I was blessed early on in both the voice and bosom departments, I got the hell out of eastern Kentucky at the first opportunity and never looked back. That's how Mama raised us, not to get stuck like she did. Mama grew up hard and married young and worked her fingers to the bone and wanted us to have a better life. "Be nice," she always said. "Please people. Marry rich."

After several tries, I am finally on the verge of this. But it has been a lot of work, believe me. I'm a very high-maintenance woman. It is *not easy* to look the way I do.

Some surgery has been involved. But I'll tell you, what with the miracles of modern medicine available to our fingertips, I do not know why more women don't go for it. *Just go for it!* This is my motto.

Out of Mama's three daughters, I am the only one that has gotten ahead in the world. The only one that really listened to her, the only one that has gone places and done things. And everywhere I go, I always remember to send Mama a postcard. She saves them in a big old green pocketbook which she keeps right by her bed for this very purpose. She's got postcards from Las Vegas and Disney World and Los Angeles and the Indianapolis 500 in there. From the Super Bowl and New York City and Puerto Vallarta. Just this morning, I mailed her one from Miami. I've been everywhere.

As opposed to Mama herself, who still cooks in the elementary school cafeteria in Paradise, Kentucky, where she has cooked for thirty years, mostly soup beans. Soup beans! I wouldn't eat another soup bean if my life depended on it, if it was the last thing to eat on the earth. Give me caviar. Which I admit I did not take to at first as it is so salty, but now have acquired a taste for, like scotch. There are some things you just have to like if you want to rise up in the world.

I myself am upwardly mobile and proud of it, and Mama is proud of me, too. No matter what kind of lies Darnell tries to tell her about me. Darnell is my oldest sister, who goes to church in a mall where she plays tambourines and dances all around. This is just as bad as being one of those old Holiness people up in the hollers handling snakes, in my opinion. Darnell tells everybody I am going to hell. One time she chased me down in a car to lay hands on me and pray out loud. I happened to have a new boyfriend with me at the time and I got so embarrassed I almost died.

My other sister, Luanne, is just as bad as Darnell but in a different way. Luanne runs a ceramics business at home, which has allowed her to let herself go to a truly awful degree, despite the fact that she used to be the prettiest one of us all, with smooth creamy skin, a natural widow's peak, and Elizabeth Taylor eyes. Now she weighs over two hundred pounds and those eyes are just slits in her face. Furthermore, she is living with a younger man who does not appear to work and does not look American at all. Luanne claims he has Cherokee blood. His name is Roscoe Ridley and he seems nice enough, otherwise I never would let my little Leon stay with them, of course it is just temporary until I can get Larry nailed down. I feel that Larry is finally making a real commitment by bringing me along this weekend, and I have cleared the decks for action. Larry has already left his marriage psychologically, so the rest is just a matter of time.

But speaking of decks, this yacht is not exactly like the Love Boat or the one on *Fantasy Island*, which is more what I had in mind. Of course, I am not old enough to remember those shows, but I have seen the reruns. I never liked that weird little dwarf guy, I believe he has died now of some unusual disease. I hope so. Anyway thank goodness there is nobody like that on *this* boat. We have three Negroes who are nice as you please. They smile and say yes ma'am and will sing calypso songs upon request, although they have not done this yet. I am looking forward to it, having been an entertainer myself. These island Negroes do not seem to have a chip on their shoulder like so many in the U.S., especially in Atlanta, where I live. My own relationship with black people has always been very good. I know how to talk to them, I know where to draw the line, and they respect me for it.

"Well, baby, whaddaya think? Paradise, huh?" This is my fiancé and employer Larry Marcum who certainly deserves a little trip to paradise if anybody does. I have never known anybody to work so hard. Larry started off as a paving contractor and still thinks you can never have too much concrete.

This is also true of gold, in my opinion, as well as shoes.

Now Larry is doing real well in commercial real estate and property management, in fact we are here on this yacht for the weekend thanks to his business associate Bruce Ware, one of the biggest developers in Atlanta, though you'd never know it by looking at him. When he met us at the dock in Barbados wearing those hundred-year-old blue jeans, I was so surprised. I believe that in general, people should look as good as they *can*. Larry and I had an interesting discussion about this in which he said that from his own observation, *really* rich people like Bruce Ware will often dress down, and even drive junk cars. Bruce Ware drives an old jeep, Larry says! I cannot imagine.

And I can't wait to see what Bruce Ware's wife will have on, though I *can* imagine this, as I know plenty of women just like her—"bowheads" is what I call them, all those Susans and Ashleys and Elizabeths, though I would never say this aloud, not even to Larry. I have made a study of these women's lives which I aspire to, not that I will ever be able to wear all those dumb little bows without embarrassment.

"Honey, this is fabulous!" I tell Larry, and it is. Turquoise-blue water so clear you can see right down to the bottom where weird fish are swimming around, big old birds, strange jagged picturesque mountains popping up behind the beaches on several of the islands we're passing.

"What's the name of these islands again?" I ask, and Larry tells me, "The Grenadines." "There is a drink called that," I say, and Larry says, "Is there?" and kisses me. He is such a hard worker that he has missed out on everything cultural.

Kissing Larry is not really great but okay.

"Honey, you need some sunscreen," I tell him when he's through. He has got that kind of redheaded complexion that will burn like mad in spite of his stupid hat. "You need to

put it everywhere, all over you, on your feet and all. Here,
put your foot up on the chair," I tell him, and he does,
and I rub sunscreen all over his fat white feet one after the
other and his ankles and his calves right up to those baggy
plaid shorts. This is something I will not do after we're
married.

"Hey, Larry, how'd you rate that kind of service?" It's
Bruce Ware, now in cutoffs, and followed not by his wife
but by some young heavy country-club guy. I can feel their
eyes on my cleavage.

"I'm Chanel Keen, Larry's fiancée." I straighten up and
shake their hands. One of the things Larry does not know
about me is that my name used to be Mayruth, back in the
Dark Ages. Mayruth! Can you imagine?

Bruce introduces the guy, who turns out to be his associate Mack Durant, and then they both stand there grinning
at me. I can tell they are surprised that Larry would have
such a classy fiancée as myself.

"I thought your wife was coming," I say to Bruce Ware,
looking at Larry.

"She certainly intended to, Chanel," Bruce says, "but
something came up at the very last minute. I know she would
have enjoyed being here with you and Larry." One thing I
have noticed about very successful people is that they say
your name all the time and look right at you. Bruce Ware
does this.

He and Mack sit down in the deck chairs. I imagine their

little bowhead wives back in Atlanta shopping or getting their legs waxed or fucking the kids' soccer coach.

Actually I am relieved that the wives stayed home. It is less competition for me, and I have never liked women much anyway. I never know what to say to them, though I am very good at drawing a man out conversationally, any man. And actually a fiancée such as myself can be a big asset to Larry on a business trip, which is what this is anyway, face it, involving a huge mall and a sports complex. It's a big deal. So I make myself useful, and by the time I get Bruce and Mack all settled down with rum and tonic and sunscreen, they're showing Larry more respect already.

Bruce Ware points out interesting sights to us, such as a real volcano, as we cruise toward Saint-Philippe, the little island where we'll be anchoring. It takes three rum and tonics to get there. We go into a half-moon bay which looks exactly like a postcard, with palm trees like Gilligan's Island. The Negroes anchor the yacht and then take off for the island in the dinghy, singing a calypso song. It is *really foreign* here! Birds of the sort you find in pet stores, yachts and sailboats of every kind flying flags of every nationality, many I have never seen before. "This is just *not American* at all, is it?" I remark, and Bruce Ware says, "No, Chanel, that's the point." Then he identifies all the flags for Larry and me. Larry acts real interested in everything, but I can tell he's out of his league. I bet he wishes he'd stayed in Atlanta to make this deal. Not me! I have always envisioned myself on a yacht, and am capable of learning from every experience.

For example, I am interested to hear Bruce Ware use a term I have not heard before, "Eurotrash," to describe some of the girls on the other yachts. Nobody mentions that about half the women on the beach are topless, though the men keep looking that way with the binoculars. I myself can see enough from here—and most of those women would do a lot better to keep their tops on, in my opinion. I could show them a thing or two. But going topless is not something which any self-respective fiancée such as myself would ever do.

The Negroes come back with shrimp and limes and crackers, etc. I'm so relieved to learn that there's a store someplace on this island, as I foresee running out of sun-screen before this is all over. While the Negroes are serving hors d'oeuvres, I go down to put on my suit, which is a little white bikini with gold trim that shows off my tan to advantage. I can't even remember what we did before tanning salons! (But then I *do* remember, all of a sudden, laying out in the sun on a towel with Darnell and Luanne, we had painted our boyfriends' initials in fingernail polish on our stomachs so we could get a tan around them. CB, I had painted on my stomach for Clive Baldwin who was the cutest thing, the quarterback at the high school our senior year, he gave me a pearl ring that Christmas, but then after the wreck I ran off to Nashville with Mike Jenkins. I didn't care what I did. I didn't care about anything for a long, long time.)

"You feel okay, honey?" Larry says when I get to the top of the stairs, where at first I can't see a thing, the sun is so bright, it's like coming out of a movie.

"Sure I do." I give Larry a wifely peck on the cheek.

"*Damn*," Mack Durant says. "You sure *look* okay." Mack himself looks like Burt Reynolds but fatter. I choose to ignore that remark.

"Can I get some of the Negroes to run me in to the beach?" I ask. "I need to make a few purchases."

"Why not swim in?" Bruce suggests. "That's what everybody else is doing." He motions to the other boats, and this is true. "Or you can paddle in on the kickboard."

"I can't swim," I say, which is not technically true, but I have no intention of messing up my makeup or getting my hair wet, plus also I have a basic theory that you should never do anything in front of people unless you are really good at it, this goes not just for swimming but for *everything*.

Bruce claps his hands and a Negro gets the dinghy and I ride to the beach in style, then tell him to wait for me. I could get used to this! Also I figure that my departure will give the men a chance to talk business.

There's not actually much on the island that I can see, just a bunch of pathetic-looking Negroes begging, which I ignore, and selling their tacky native crafts along the beach. These natives look very unhealthy to me, with their nappy hair all matted up and their dark skin kind of dusty-looking, like they've got powder on. The ones back in

Atlanta are much healthier, in my opinion, though they all carry guns.

I buy some sunscreen in the little shack of a store which features very inferior products, paying with some big green bills that I don't have a clue as to their value, I'm sure these natives are cheating me blind. Several Italian guys try to pick me up on the beach, wearing those nasty little stretch briefs. I don't even bother to speak to them. I just wade out into the warm clear water to the dinghy and ride back and then Larry helps me up the ladder to the yacht, where I land flat on my butt on the deck, to my total dismay. "It certainly is hard to keep up your image in the tropics!" I make a little joke as Larry picks me up.

"Easier to let it go," Bruce Ware says. "Go native. Let it all hang out."

In my absence, the men have been swimming. Bruce Ware's gray chest hair looks like a wet bath mat. He stands with his feet wide apart as our boat rocks in the wake of a monster sailboat. Bruce Ware looks perfectly comfortable, as if he grew up on a yacht. Maybe he did. Larry and I didn't, that's for sure! We are basically two of a kind, I just wish I'd run into him earlier in life, though better late than never as they say. This constant rocking is making me nauseous, something I didn't notice before when we were moving. I am not about to mention it, but Bruce Ware must have noticed because he gives me some Dramamine.

Larry and I go down below to dress up a little bit for

dinner, but I won't let Larry fool around at all as I am sure they could *hear* us. Larry puts on khaki pants and a nice shirt and I put on my new white linen slacks and a blue silk blouse with a scoop neck. The Negroes row us over to the island. I am disappointed to see that Bruce and Mack have not even bothered to change for dinner, simply throwing shirts on over their bathing trunks, and I am further disappointed by the restaurant, which we have to walk up a long steep path through the actual real jungle to get to. It's at least a half a mile. I'm so glad I wore flats.

"This better be worth it!" I joke, but then I am embarrassed when it's not. The restaurant is nothing but a big old house with Christmas lights strung all around the porch and three mangy yellow dogs in the yard. Why I might just as well have stayed in eastern Kentucky! We climb up these steep steps onto the porch and sit at a table covered with oilcloth and it *is* a pretty view, I must admit, overlooking the harbor. There's a nice breeze too. So I am just relaxing a little bit when a chicken runs over my foot, which causes me to jump a mile. "Good Lord!" I say to Larry, who says, "Shhh." He won't look at me.

Bruce Ware slaps his hand on the table. "This is the real thing!" He goes on to say that there are two other places to eat, on the other side of the island, but this is the most authentic. He says it is run by two native women, sisters, who are famous island cooks, and most of the waitresses are their daughters. "So what do you think, Chanel?"

"Oh, I like it just fine," I say. "It's very interesting," and Larry looks relieved, but frankly I am amazed that Bruce Ware would want to come to a place like this, much less bring a lady such as myself along.

"Put it right here, honey," Bruce says to a native girl who brings a whole bottle of Mount Gay rum to our table and sets it down in front of him, along with several bottles of bitter lemon and ice and drinking glasses which I inspect carefully to choose the cleanest one. None of them look very clean, of course they can't possibly have a dishwasher back in that kitchen which we can see into, actually, every time the girls walk back and forth through the bead curtain. Two big fat women are back there cooking and laughing and talking a mile a minute in that language which Bruce Ware swears is English though you can't believe it.

"It's the rhythm and the accent that make it sound so different," Bruce claims. "Listen for a minute." Two native men are having a loud backslapping kind of conversation at the bar right behind us. I can't understand a word of it. As soon as they walk away, laughing, Bruce says, "Well? Did you get any of that?"

Larry and I shake our heads no, but Mack is not even paying attention to this, he's drinking rum at a terrifying rate and staring at one of the waitresses.

Bruce smiles at us like he's some guy on the Discovery Channel. "For example," he lectures, "one of those men just said, 'Me go she by,' which is really a much more efficient way of saying, 'I'm going by to see her.' This is how they talk among themselves. But they are perfectly capable of using the King's English when they talk to us."

I make a note of this phrase, "the King's English." I am always trying to improve my vocabulary. "Then that gives them some privacy from the tourists, doesn't it?" I remark. "From people like us."

"Exactly, Chanel." Bruce looks very pleased and I realize how much I could learn from a man like him.

"Well, this is all just so interesting, and thanks for pointing it out to us," I say, meaning every word and kicking Larry under the table. He mumbles something. Larry seems determined to match Mack drink for drink, which is not a good idea. Larry is not a good drunk.

But unfortunately I have to go to the bathroom (I can't imagine what *this* experience will be like!), so I excuse myself and make my way through the other tables, which are filling up fast. I can feel all those dark native eyes burning into my skin. When I ask for the ladies' room, the bartender simply points out into the jungle. I ask again and he points again. I am too desperate to argue. I stumble out there and am actually thankful to find a portable toilet such as you would see at a construction site. Luckily I have some Kleenex in my purse.

It is all a fairly horrifying experience made even worse by a man who's squatting on his haunches right outside the door when I exit. "Oh!" I scream, and leap back, and he says

something. Naturally I can't understand a word of it. But
for some reason I am rooted to the spot. He stands up slow
and limber as a leopard and then we are face to face and he's
looking at me like he knows me. He is much lighter-skinned
and more refined-looking than the rest of them. "Pretty
missy," he says. He touches my hair.

I'm proud to say I do not make an international incident
out of this, I maintain my dignity while getting out of there
as fast as possible, and don't even mention it to the men when
I get back, as they are finally talking business, but of course
I will tell Larry later.

So I just pour myself a big drink to calm down, and Larry
reaches over to squeeze my hand, and there we all sit while
the sun sets in the most spectacular fiery sunset I have ever
seen in real life and the breeze comes up and the chickens
run all over the place, which I have ceased to mind, oddly
enough, maybe the rum is getting to me, it must be some
really high proof. So I switch to beer, though the only kind
they've got is something called Hairoun which does not even
taste like beer in my opinion. The men are deep in conversation, though Mack gets up occasionally and tries to sweet-
talk the pretty waitress, who laughs and brushes him off like
he is a big fat fly. I admire her technique as well as her skin
which is beautiful, rich milk chocolate. I laugh to think what
Mack's little bowhead wife back in Atlanta would think if
she could see him now! The strings of Christmas lights
swing in the breeze and lights glow on all the boats in the

harbor. Larry scoots closer and nuzzles my ear and puts his arm around me and squeezes me right under the bust, which is something I wish he would not do in public. "Having fun?" he whispers in my ear, and I say, "Yes," which is true.

I am expanding my horizons as they say.

This restaurant does not even have a menu. The women just serve us whatever they choose, rice and beans and seafood mostly, it's hard to say. I actually prefer to eat my food separately rather than all mixed up on a plate which I'm sure is not clean anyway. The men discuss getting an eighty-five-percent loan at nine percent and padding the specs, while I drink another Hairoun.

The man who touched my hair starts playing guitar, some kind of island stuff, he's really good. Also he keeps looking at me and I find myself glancing over at him from time to time to see if he is still looking, this is just like seventh grade. Still it gives me something to do since the men are basically ignoring me, which begins to piss me off after a while since Mack is *not* ignoring the pretty waitress. The Negro with the guitar catches me looking at him, and grins. I am completely horrified to see that his two front teeth are gold. People start dancing. "I don't know," Larry keeps saying to Bruce Ware. "I just don't know."

I have to go to the bathroom again and when I come back there's a big argument going on involving Mack, who has apparently been slapped by the pretty waitress. Now she's crying and her mother is yelling at Mack, who is pretty damn mad, and who can blame him? Of course he didn't mean anything by whatever he did, he certainly wasn't going to sleep with that girl and get some disease. "Goddamn bitch," he says, and Bruce tells Larry and me to get him out of there, which we do, while Bruce gets into some kind of fight himself over the bill. These Negroes have overcharged us. Bruce's behavior at this point is interesting to me. He has gone from his nice Marlin Perkins voice to a real J. R. Ewing obey-me voice. *Thank God there is somebody here to take charge*, I'm thinking as I stand at the edge of the jungle with a drunk on each arm and watch the whole thing happening inside the house like it's on television. The ocean breeze lifts my hair off my shoulders and blows it around and I don't even care that it's getting messed up. I am so mad at Larry for getting drunk.

"You okay, honey?" Bruce Ware says to me when he gets everything taken care of to his satisfaction, and I say, "Yes." Then Bruce takes Mack by the arm and I take Larry and we walk back down to the beach two by two, which seems to take forever in the loud rustling dark. I wouldn't be a bit surprised if a gorilla jumped out and grabbed me, after everything that's happened so far! Bruce goes first, with the flashlight.

I love a capable man.

When we finally make it down to the beach, I am so glad to see our Negroes waiting, but even with their help it's kind of a problem getting Mack into the dinghy, in fact it's like a slapstick comedy, and I finally start laughing. At this point Mack turns on me. "What are you laughing at, bitch?" he says, and I say, "Larry?" but all Larry says is, "Sshhh."

"Never mind, Chanel," Bruce tells me. "Mack's just drunk, he won't even remember this tomorrow. Look at the stars."

By now the Negroes are rowing us out across the water. "What?" I ask him.

"Look at the stars," Bruce says. "You see a lot of constellations down here that you never get to see at home, for instance that's the Southern Cross over there to your left."

"Oh yes," I say, though actually I have never seen *any* constellations in my life, or if I did I didn't know it, and certainly did not know the names of them.

"There's Orion right overhead," Bruce says. "See those three bright stars in a row? That's his belt."

Of course I am acting as interested as possible, but by then we've reached the yacht and a Negro is helping us all up (he has quite a job with Mack and Larry), and then two of them put Mack to bed. " 'Scuse me," Larry mutters, and goes to the back of the boat to hang his head over and vomit. Some fiancé! I stand in the bow with Bruce Ware, observing the southern sky, while the Negroes say good night and go off with a guy who has come by for them in an outboard. Its motor gets louder and louder the farther they get from us, and I am privately sure that they are going around to the other side of the island to raise hell until dawn.

Bruce steps up close behind me. "Listen here, whatever your real name is," he says, "Larry's not going to marry you, you know that, don't you?"

Of course this is none of Bruce Ware's business, so it makes me furious. "He most certainly *is*!" I say. "Just as soon as . . ."

"He'll never leave Jean," Bruce says into my ear. "*Never.*"

Then he sticks his tongue in my ear, which sends world-class shivers down my whole body.

"Baby—" It's Larry, stumbling up beside us.

"Larry, I'm just, we're just—" Now I'm trying to get away from Bruce Ware but he doesn't give an inch, pinning me against the rail. He's breathing all over my neck. "Larry," I start again.

"Hey, baby, it's okay. Go for it. I know you like to have a good time." Larry is actually saying this, and there was a time when I would have actually had that good time, but all of a sudden I just can't do it.

Before either my ex-fiancé or his associate can stop me, I make a break for it and jump right down into the dinghy and pull the rope up over the thing and push off and grab the oars and row like mad toward the shore. I use the rowing machine all the time at the health club, but this is the first time I have had a chance at the real thing. It's easy.

"Come back here," yells Bruce Ware. "Where the hell do you think you're going?"

"Native," I call back to them across the widening water. "I'm going native."

"Shit," one of them says, but by now I can barely hear them. What I hear is the slapping sound of my oars and the occasional bit of music or conversation from the other boats, and once somebody says, "Hey, honey," but I keep going straight for the beach, which lies like a silver ribbon around the bay. I look back long enough to make sure that nobody's coming after me. At least those natives can speak the King's English when they want to, and I can certainly help out in the kitchen if need be. I grew up cooking beans and rice. Anyway, I'm sure I can pay one of them to take me back to Barbados in the morning. Won't that surprise my companions? Since I am never without some "mad money" and Larry's gold card, this is possible, although I did leave some brand-new perfectly gorgeous shoes and several of my favorite outfits on the yacht.

A part of me can't believe I'm acting this crazy, while another part of me is saying, "Go, girl." A little breeze comes up and ruffles my hair. I practice deep breathing from aerobics, and look all around. The water is smooth as glass. The whole damn sky is full of stars. It is just beautiful. All the stars are reflected in the water. Right overhead I see Orion and then I see his belt, as clear as can be. I'm headed for the island, sliding through the stars.

The

HAPPY MEMORIES
CLUB

I may be old, but I'm not dead.

Perhaps you are surprised to hear this. You may be surprised to learn that people such as myself are still capable of original ideas, intelligent insights, and intense feelings. Passionate love affairs, for example, are not uncommon here. Pacemakers cannot regulate the strange unbridled yearnings of the heart. You do not wish to know this, I imagine. This knowledge is probably upsetting to you, as it is upsetting to my sons, who do not want to hear, for instance, about my relationship with Dr. Solomon Marx, the historian. "Please, Mom," my son Alex said, rolling his eyes. "Come on, Mama," my son Will said. "Can't you maintain a little dignity here?" *Dignity*, said Will, who runs a chain of miniature golf courses! "I have had enough dignity to last me for the rest of my life, thank you," I told Will.

I've always done exactly what I was supposed to do—now I intend to do what I want.

"Besides, Dr. Solomon Marx is the joy of my life," I told them all. This remained true even when my second surgery was less than successful, obliging me to take to this chair. It remained true until Solomon's most recent stroke five weeks ago, which has paralyzed him below the waist and caused his thoughts to become disordered, so that he cannot always remember things, and he cannot always remember the words for things. A survivor himself, Solomon is an expert on the Holocaust. He has numbers tattooed on his arm. He used to travel the world, speaking about the Holocaust. Now he can't remember the name of it.

"Well, I think it's a blessing," said one of the nurses—that young Miss Rogers. "The Holocaust was just awful."

"It is not a blessing, you ignorant bitch," I told her. "It is the end. Our memories are all we've got." I put myself in reverse and sped off before she could reply. I could feel her staring at me as I motored down the hall. I am sure she wrote something in her ever-present notebook. "Inappropriate" and "unmanageable" are some of the words they use, unpleasant and inaccurate adjectives all.

The words that Solomon can't recall are always nouns.

"My dear," he said to me one day recently, when they had wheeled him out into the Residence Center lobby, "what did you say your name was?" He knew it, of course, in his heart's deep core, as well as he knew his own.

"Alice Scully," I said.

"Ah. Alice Scully," he said. "And what is it that we used to do together, Alice Scully, which brought me such intense—oh, so big—" His eyes were like bright little beads in his pinched face. "It was of the greatest, ah—"

"Sex," I told him. "You loved it."

He grinned at me. "Oh, yes," he said. "Sex. It was sex, indeed."

"Mrs. Scully!" his nurse snapped.

Now I have devised a game to help Solomon remember nouns. It works like this. Whenever they bring him out, I go over to him and clasp my hands together, as if I were hiding something in them. "If you can guess what I've got here," I say, "I'll give you a kiss."

He squints in concentration, fishing for nouns. If he gets one, I give him a kiss.

Some days are better than others.

This is true for us all, of course. We can't be expected to remember everything we know.

IN MY LIFE I WAS A TEACHER, AND A GOOD ONE. I taught English in the days when it was English, not "language arts." I taught for thirty years at the Sandy Point School in Sandy Point, Virginia, where I lived with my husband, Harold Scully, and brought up four sons, three of them Harold's. Harold owned and ran the Trent Riverside Pharmacy until the day he dropped dead in his drugstore counting out antibiotic capsules for a high school girl. His mouth and his eyes were wide open, as if whatever he found on the other side surprised him mightily. I was sorry to see this, as Harold was not a man who liked surprises.

I must say I gave him none. I was a good wife to Harold, although I was initially dismayed to learn that this role entailed taking care of his parents from the day of our marriage until their deaths. They both lived long lives, and his mother went blind at the end. But we lived in their house, the largest house in Sandy Point, right on the old tidal river, and their wealth enabled us to send our own sons off to the finest schools, and even, in Robert's case, to medical school.

Harold's parents never got over his failure to get into medical school himself. In fact, he barely made it through pharmacy school. As far as I know, however, he was a good pharmacist, never poisoning anybody or mixing up prescriptions. He loved to look at the orderly rows of bottles on his shelves. He loved labeling. Often he dispensed medical advice to his customers: which cough medicine worked best, what to put on a boil. People trusted him. Harold got a great deal of pleasure from his job and from his standing in the community.

I taught school at first, because I was trained to do it and because I wanted to. It was the only way in those days that a woman could get out of the house without being considered odd. I was never one to plan a menu or clip a recipe out of a magazine. I left all that to Harold's mother and to the family housekeeper, Lucille.

I loved teaching. I loved to diagram sentences on the blackboard, precisely separating the subject from the predicate with a vertical line, the linking verb from the predicate adjective with a slanted line, and so forth. The children used to try to stump me by making up long sentences they thought I couldn't diagram, sentences so complex that my final diagram on the board looked like a blueprint for a cathedral, with flying buttresses everywhere, all the lines connecting.

I loved geography, as well—tracing roads, tracing rivers. I loved to trace the route of the Pony Express, of the Underground Railroad, of de Soto's search for gold. I told them the story of that bumbling fool Zebulon Pike who set out in 1805 to find the source of the Mississippi River and ended up instead at the glorious peak they named for him, Pikes Peak, which my sister Rose and I visited in 1926 on our cross-country odyssey with our brother William and his wife. In the photograph taken at Pikes Peak, I am seated astride a donkey, wearing a polka-dot dress and a floppy hat, while the western sky goes on and on endlessly behind me.

I taught my students these things: the first sustained flight in a power-driven airplane was made by Wilbur and Orville Wright at Kitty Hawk, North Carolina, on

December 17, 1903; Wisconsin is the "Badger State"; the
Dutch bought Manhattan Island from the Indians for
twenty-four dollars in 1626; you can't sink in the Great Salt
Lake. Now these facts ricochet in my head like pinballs, and
I do not intend, thank you very much, to enter the Health
Center for "better care."

I never tired of telling my students the story of the Mississippi River—how a scarlet oak leaf falling into Lake Itasca,
in Minnesota, travels first north and then east through a wild,
lonely landscape of lakes and rapids as if it were heading for
Lake Superior, then over the Falls of St. Anthony, then down
through Minneapolis and St. Paul, past bluffs and prairies
and islands, to be joined by the Missouri River just above St.
Louis, and then by the Ohio, where the water grows very
wide—you can scarcely see across it. My scarlet leaf meanders
with eccentric loops and horseshoe curves down, down, down
the great continent through the world's biggest delta, to New
Orleans and beyond, past the great fertile mud plain shaped
like a giant goose's foot, and into the Gulf of Mexico.

"And what happens to the leaf *then*, Mrs. Scully?" some
student would never fail to ask.

"Ah," I would say, "then our little leaf becomes a part of
the universe"—leaving them to ponder *that!*

I was known as a hard teacher but a fair one, and many
of my students came back in later years to tell me how much
they had learned.

• • •

HERE AT MARSHWOOD, A "TOTAL" RETIREMENT COM-
munity, they want us to become children again, forgoing
intelligence. This is why I was so pleased when the announcement went up on the bulletin board about a month ago:

WRITING GROUP TO MEET
WEDNESDAY, 3 P.M.

Ah, I thought, that promising infinitive "to meet." For, like
many former English teachers, I had thought that someday
I might like "to write."

At the appointed day and hour, I motored over to the
library (a euphemism, since the room contains mostly well-
worn paperbacks by Jacqueline Susann and Louis L'Amour).
I was dismayed to find Martha Louise Clapton already in
charge. The idea had been hers, I learned; I should have
known. She's the type who tries to run everything. Martha
Louise Clapton has never liked me, having had her eye on
Solomon, to no avail, for years before my arrival. She inclined
her frizzy blue head ever so slightly to acknowledge my
entrance.

"As I was just saying, Alice, several of us have discovered
in mealtime conversation that in fact we've been writing for
years, in our journals and letters and whatnot, and so I said

to myself, 'Martha Louise, why not form a writing group?' and *voilà*!"

"*Voilà*," I said, edging into the circle.

So it began.

Besides Martha Louise and myself, the writing group included Joy Richter, a minister's widow with a preference for poetry; Miss Elena Grier, who taught Shakespeare for years and years at a girls' preparatory school in Nashville, Tennessee; Frances Weinberg, whose husband lay in a coma over at the Health Center (a euphemism—you never leave the Health Center); Shirley Lassiter, who had buried three husbands and still thought of herself as a belle; and Sam Hofstetter, retired lawyer, deaf as a post. We agreed to meet again in the library one week later. Each of us should bring some writing to share with the others.

"What's that?" Sam Hofstetter said. We wrote the time and place down on a piece of paper and gave it to him. He folded the paper carefully and put it in his pocket. "Could you make copies of the writing, please?" he asked. He inclined his silver head and tapped his ear significantly. We all agreed. Of course we agreed, we outnumber the men four to one, poor old things. In a place like this, they get more attention than you would believe.

Then Joy Richter said that she probably couldn't afford to make copies. She said she was on a limited budget.

I pointed out that there was a free Xerox machine in the manager's office and I felt sure that we could use it, especially since we needed it for the writing group.

"Oh, I don't know." Frances Weinberg started wringing her hands. "They might not let us."

"I'll take care of it," Martha Louise said majestically. "Thank you, Alice, for the suggestion. Thank you, everyone, for joining the group."

I HAD WONDERED IF I MIGHT SUFFER INITIALLY FROM "writer's block," but nothing of that sort occurred. In fact, I was flooded by memories—overwhelmed, engulfed, as I sat in my chair by the picture window, writing on my lap board. I was not even aware of the world outside, my head was so full of the people and places of the past, rising up in my mind as they were then, in all the fullness of life, and myself as I was then, that headstrong girl longing to leave her home in east Virginia and walk in the world at large.

I wrote and wrote. I wrote for three days. I wrote until I felt satisfied, and then I stopped. I felt better than I had in years, filled with new life and freedom (a paradox, since I am more and more confined to this chair).

During that week Solomon guessed "candy," "ring," and "Anacin." He was getting better. I was not. I ignored certain symptoms in order to attend the Wednesday meeting of the writing group.

Martha Louise led off. Her blue eyes looked huge, like lakes, behind her glasses. "They just don't make families like they used to," she began, and continued with an account of growing up on a farm in Ohio, how her parents struggled to make ends meet, how the children strung popcorn and cut out paper ornaments to trim the tree when there was no money for Christmas, how they pulled taffy and laid it out on a marble slab, and how each older child had a little one to take care of. "We were poor but we were happy," Martha Louise concluded. "It was an ideal childhood."

"Oh, Martha Louise," Frances Weinberg said tremulously, "that was just beautiful."

Everyone agreed.

Too many adjectives, I thought, but I held my tongue.

Next, Joy Richter read a poem about seeing God in everything: "the stuff of day" was a phrase I rather liked. Joy Richter apparently saw God in a shiny red apple, in a dewy rose, in her husband's kind blue eyes, in the photographs of her grandchildren. It was a pretty good poem, but it would have been better if she hadn't tried so hard to rhyme it. Miss Elena then presented a sonnet comparing life to a merry-go-round. The final couplet went:

Lost children, though you're old, remember well
    the joy and music of life's carousel.

This was not bad, and I said so. Frances Weinberg read a

reminiscence about her husband's return from the Second World War, which featured the young Frances "hovering upon the future" in a porch swing as she "listened for the tread of his beloved boot." The military theme was continued by Sam Hofstetter, who read (loudly) an account of army life entitled "Somewhere in France." Shirley Lassiter was the only one whose story was not about herself. Instead it was fiction evidently modeled upon a romance novel, for it involved a voluptuous debutante who had to choose between two men. Both of them were rich, and both of them loved her, but one had a fatal disease, and for some reason this young woman didn't know which one.

"Why not?" boomed the literal Sam.

"It's a mystery, silly," Shirley Lassiter said. "That's the plot." Shirley Lassiter had a way of resting her jeweled hands upon her enormous bosom as if it were a shelf. "I don't want to give the plot away," she said. Clearly, she did not have a brain in her head.

Then it was my turn.

I began to read the story of my childhood. I had grown up in the tiny coastal town of Waterville, Maryland. I was the fourth in a family of five children, with three older brothers and a baby sister. My father, who was in the oyster business, killed himself when I was six and Rose was only three. He went out into the Chesapeake Bay in an old rowboat, chopped a hole in the bottom of it with an ax, and then shot himself in the head with a revolver. He meant to finish the job. He did not sink as planned, however, for a fisherman witnessed the act and hauled his body to shore.

This left Mama with five children to bring up and no means of support. She was forced to turn our home into a boardinghouse, keeping mostly teachers from Goucher College and salesmen passing through, although two old widows, Mrs. Flora Lewis and Mrs. Virginia Prince, stayed with us for years. Miss Flora, as we called her, had to have a cup of warm milk every night at bedtime; I will never forget it. It could be neither too hot nor too cold. I was the one who took it up to her, stepping so carefully up the dark back stair.

Nor will I forget young Miss Day from Richmond, a teacher, who played the piano beautifully. She used to play "Clair de Lune" and "Für Elise" on the old upright in the parlor. I would already have been sent to bed, and so I'd lie trembling in the dark, seized by feelings I couldn't name, as the notes floated up to me and Rose in our attic room, in our white iron bed wrought with roses and figures of nymphs. Miss Day was jilted some years later, we heard, her virtue lost and her reputation ruined.

Every Sunday, Mama presided over the big tureen at breakfast, when we would have boiled fish and crisp little johnnycakes. To this day I have never tasted anything as good as those johnnycakes. Mama's face was flushed, and her hair escaped its bun to curl in damp tendrils as she dished up the breakfast plates. I thought she was beautiful. I'm sure she could have married again had she chosen to do so, but her heart was full of bitterness at the way her life had turned out, and she never forgave our father, or looked at another man.

Daddy had been a charmer, by all accounts. He carried a silver-handled cane and allowed me to play with his gold pocketwatch when I was especially good. He took me to the harness races with him, where we cheered for the horse he owned, a big roan named Joe Cord. On these excursions I wore a white dress and stockings and patent-leather shoes. And how Daddy could sing! He had a lovely baritone voice. I remember him on bended knee singing, "Daisy, Daisy, give me your answer, do," to Mama, who pretended to be embarrassed but was not. I remember his bouncing Rose up and down on his lap and singing, "This is the way the lady rides."

After his death the boys went off to sea as soon as they could, and I was obliged to work in the kitchen and take care of Rose. Kitchen work is never finished in a boarding-house. This is why I have never liked to cook since, though I know how to do it, I can assure you.

We had a summer kitchen outside, so it wouldn't heat up the whole house when we were cooking or canning. It had a kerosene stove. I remember one time when we were putting up blackberry jam, and one of those jars simply exploded. We had blackberry jam all over the place. It burned the Negro girl, Ocie, who was helping out, and I was surprised to see that her blood was as red as mine.

As time went on, Mama grew sadder and withdrew from

us, sometimes barely speaking for days on end. My great joy
was Rose, a lively child with golden curls and skin so fair
you could see the blue veins beneath it. I slept with Rose
every night and played with her every day. Since Mama was
indisposed, we could do whatever we wanted, and we had
the run of the town, just like boys. We'd go clamming in the
bay with an inner tube floating out behind us, tied to my
waist by a rope. We'd feel the clams with our feet and rake
them up, then flip them into a net attached to the inner tube.
Once we went on a sailing trip with a cousin of ours, Bud
Ned Black, up the Chickahominy River for a load of brick.
But the wind failed and we got stuck there. We just *sat* on
that river, for what seemed like days and days. Rose fussed
and fumed while Cap'n Bud Ned drank whiskey and chewed
tobacco and did not appear to mind the situation so long as
his supplies held out. But Rose was impatient—always,
always so impatient.

"Alice," she said dramatically as we sat staring out at the
shining water, the green trees at its edge, the wheeling gulls,
"I will *die* if we don't move. I will die here," Rose said,
though Bud Ned and I laughed at her.

But Rose meant it. As she grew older, she had to go here,
go there, do this, do that—have this, have that—she hated
being poor and living in the boardinghouse, and could not
wait to grow up and go away.

We both developed a serious taste for distance when our
older brother William and his wife took us motoring across

the country. I was sixteen. I loved that trip, from the first stage of planning our route on the map to finally viewing the great mountains, which sprang straight up from the desert like apparitions. Of course we had never seen such mountains; they took my breath away. I remember how Rose flung her arms out wide to the world as we stood in the cold wind on Pikes Peak. I believe we would have gone on driving and driving forever. But of course we had to return, and I had to resume my duties, letting go the girl William had hired so Mama would permit my absence. William was our sweetest brother, but they are all dead now, all my brothers, and Rose too.

I have outlived everyone.

Yet it seems like only yesterday that Rose and I were little girls playing that game we loved so well, a game that strikes me now as terribly dangerous. This memory is more vivid than any other in my life.

It is late night, summertime. Rose and I have sneaked out of the boardinghouse, down the tiny dark back stair, past the gently sighing widows' rooms; past Mama's room, door open, moonlight ghostly on the mosquito netting draped from the canopy over her bed; past the snoring salesmen's rooms, stepping tiptoe across the wide-plank kitchen floor, wincing at each squeak. Then out the door into moonlight so bright that it leaves shadows. Darting from tree to tree, we cross the yard and attain the sidewalk, moving rapidly past the big sleeping houses with their shutters yawning open to the cool night air, down the sidewalk to the edge of town where the sidewalk ends and the road goes on forever through miles and miles of peanut fields and other towns and other fields, toward Baltimore.

Rose and I lie down flat in the middle of the road, which still retains the heat of the day, and let it warm us head to toe as we dream aloud of what the future holds. At different times Rose planned to be an aviator, a doctor, and a film actress living in California, with an orange tree in her yard. Even her most domestic dreams were grand. "I'll have a big house and lots of servants and a husband who loves me *so much*," Rose would say, "and a yellow convertible touring car and six children, and we will be rich and they will never have to work, and I will put a silk scarf on my head and we will all go out riding on Sunday."

Even then I said I would be a teacher, for I was always good in school, but I would be a missionary teacher, enlightening natives in some far-off corner of the world. Even as I said it, though, I believe I knew it would not come to pass, for I was bound to stay at home, as Rose was bound to go.

But we'd lie there looking up at the sky, and dream our dreams, and wait for the thrill of an oncoming vehicle, which we could hear coming a long time away, and could feel throughout the length of our bodies as it neared us. We would roll off the pavement and into the peanut field just as the car approached, our hearts pounding. Sometimes we nearly dozed on that warm road—and once we were almost killed by a potato truck.

Gradually, as Mama retreated to her room, I took over the running of the boardinghouse, and Mama's care as well. At eighteen, Rose ran away with a fast-talking furniture salesman who had been boarding with us. They settled finally in Ohio, and had three children, and her life was not glamorous in the least, though better than some, and we wrote to each other every week until her death of lung cancer at thirty-nine.

This was as far as I'd gotten.

I quit reading aloud and looked around the room. Joy Richter was ashen, Miss Elena Grier was mumbling to herself, Shirley Lassiter was breathing heavily and fluttering her fingers at her throat. Sam Hofstetter stared fixedly at me with the oddest expression on his face, and Frances Weinberg wept openly, shaking with sobs.

"Alice! Now just look at what you've done!" Martha Louise said to me severely. "Meeting adjourned!"

I HAD TO MISS THE THIRD MEETING OF THE WRITING group because Dr. Culbertson stuck me into the Health Center for treatment and further tests (euphemisms both). In fact, Dr. Culbertson then went so far as to consult with my son Robert, a doctor as well, about what to do with me next. Dr. Culbertson was of the opinion that I ought to move to the Health Center for "better care." Of course I called Robert immediately and gave him a piece of my mind.

That was yesterday.

I know they are discussing me by telephone—Robert, Alex, Will, and Carl. Lines are buzzing up and down the East Coast.

I came here when I had to, because I did not want any of their wives to get stuck with me, as I had gotten stuck with Harold's mother and father. Now I expect some common decency and respect. It is a time when I wish for daughters, who often, I feel, have more compassion and understanding than sons.

Even Carl, the child of my heart, says I had "better listen to the doctor."

Instead, I have been listening to this voice too long silent inside me, the voice of myself, as I write page after page propped up in bed at the Health Center.

It is Wednesday. I have skipped certain of my afternoon medications. At two-fifteen I buzz for Sheila, my favorite, a tall young nurses' aide with the grace of a gazelle. "Sheila," I say, "I need for you to help me dress, dear, and then roll my chair over here, if you will. My own chair, I mean. I have to go to a meeting."

Sheila looks at my chart and then back at me, her eyes wide. "It doesn't say," she begins.

"Dr. Culbertson said it would be perfectly all right," I

assure her. I pull a twenty-dollar bill from my purse, which I keep right beside me in bed, and hand it to her. "I know it's a lot of trouble, but it's very important," I say. "I think I'll just slip on the red sweater and the black wraparound skirt—that's so easy to get on. They're both in the drawer, dear."

"Okay, honey," Sheila says, and she gets me dressed and sets me in my chair. I put on lipstick and have Sheila fluff up my hair in the back, where it's gotten so flat from lying in bed. Sheila hands me my purse and my notebook and then I'm off, waving to the girls at the nurses' station as I purr past them. They wave back. I feel fine now. I take the elevator down to the first floor and then motor through the lobby, speaking to acquaintances. I pass the gift shop, the newspaper stand, and all the waiting rooms.

It's chilly outside. I head up the walkway past the par 3 golf course, where I spy Parker Howard, ludicrous in those bright green pants they sell to old men, putting on the third hole. "Hi, Parker!" I cry.

"Hello, Alice," he calls. "Nice to see you out!" He sinks the putt.

I enter the Multipurpose Building and head for the library, where the writers' group is already in progress. It has taken me longer to drive over from the Health Center than I'd supposed.

Miss Elena is reading, but she stops and looks up when I come in, her mouth a perfect O. Everybody looks at Martha Louise.

"Why, Alice," Martha Louise says. She raises her eyebrows. "We didn't expect that you would be joining us today. We heard that you were in the Health Center."

"I was," I say. "But I'm out now."

"Evidently," Martha Louise says.

I ride up to the circular table, set my brake, get out my notebook, and ask Miss Elena for a copy of whatever she's reading. Wordlessly, she slides one over. But still she does not resume. They're all looking at me.

"What is it?" I ask.

"Well, Alice, last week when you were absent, we laid out some ground rules for this writing group." Martha Louise gains composure as she goes along. "We are all in agreement here, Alice, that if this is to be a pleasant and meaningful club for all of us, we need to restrict our subject matter to what everyone enjoys."

"So?" I don't get it.

"We've also adopted an official name for the group." Now Martha Louise is cheerful as a robin.

"What is it?"

"It's the Happy Memories Club," she announces, and they all nod.

I am beginning to get it.

"You mean to tell me—" I start.

"I mean to tell you that if you wish to be a part of this group, Alice Scully, you will have to calm yourself down, and keep your subject matter in check. We don't come here to be upset," Martha Louise says serenely.

They are all watching me closely now, Sam Hofstetter in particular. I think they expect an outburst.

But I won't give them the satisfaction.

"Fine," I say. This is a lie. "That sounds just fine to me. Good idea!" I smile at everybody.

There is a perceptible relaxation then, an audible settling back into chairs, as Miss Elena resumes her reading. It's a travelogue piece entitled "Shakespeare and His Haunts," about a tour she made in England several years ago. But I find myself unable to listen. I simply can't hear Elena, or Joy, who reads next, or even Sam.

"Well, is that it for today? Anybody else?" Martha Louise raps her knuckles against the table.

"I brought something," I say, "but I don't have copies."

I look at Sam, who shrugs and smiles and says I should go ahead anyway. Everybody else looks at Martha Louise.

"Well, go on, then," she directs tartly, and I begin.

After Rose's disappearance, my mother took to her bed and turned her face to the wall, leaving me in charge of everything. Oh, how I worked! I worked like a dog, long hours, a cruelly unnatural life for a spirited young woman. Yet I persevered. People in the town, including our minister, complimented me; I was discussed and admired. Our boardinghouse stayed full, and somehow I managed, with Ocie's help, to get the meals on the table. I smiled and chattered at mealtime. Yet inside I was starving, starving for love and life.

Thus it is not surprising, I suppose, that I should fall for the first man who showed any interest in me. He was a schoolteacher who had been educated at the University in Charlottesville, a thin, dreamy young man from one of the finest families in Virginia. His grandfather had been the governor. He used to sit out by the sound every day after supper, reading, and one day I joined him there. It was a lovely June evening; the sound was full of sailboats, and the sky above us was as round and blue as a bowl.

"I was reading a poem about a girl with beautiful yellow hair," he said, "and then I look up and what do I see? A real girl with beautiful yellow hair."

For some reason I started to cry, not even caring what my other boarders thought as they sat up on the porch looking out over this landscape in which we figured.

"Come here," he said, and he took my hand and led me behind the old rose-covered boathouse, where he pulled me to him and kissed me curiously, as if it were an experiment.

His name was Carl Redding Armistead. He had the reedy look of the poet, but all the assurance of the privileged class. I was older than he, but he was more experienced. He was well educated, and had been to Europe several times.

"You pretty thing," he said, and kissed me again. The scent of the roses was everywhere.

I went that night to his room, and before the summer was

out, we had lain together in nearly every room at the board-inghouse. We were crazy for each other by then, and I didn't care what might happen, or who knew. On Saturday eve-nings I'd leave a cold supper for the rest, and Carl and I would take the skiff and row out to Sand Island, where the wild ponies were, and take off all our clothes and make love. Sometimes my back would be red and bleeding from the rough black sand and the broken shells on the beach.

"Just a minute! Just a minute here!" Martha Louise is pounding on the table, and Frances Weinberg is crying, as usual. Sam Hofstetter is staring at me in a manner that indi-cates he has heard every word I've said.

"Well, I think that's terrific!" Shirley Lassiter giggles and bats her painted blue eyelids at us all.

Of course this romance did not last. Nothing that intense can be sustained, although the loss of such intensity can scarcely be borne. Quite simply, Carl and I foundered upon the prospect of the future. He had to go on to that world which awaited him; I could not leave Mama. Our final part-ing was bitter—we were spent, exhausted by the force of what had passed between us. He did not even look back as he sped away in his red sports car, nor did I cry.

Nor did I ever tell him about the existence of Carl, my son, whom I bore defiantly out of wedlock eight months later, telling no one who the father was. Oh, those were hard, black days! I was ostracized by the very people who had formerly praised me, and ogled by the men in the boardinghouse, who now considered me a fallen woman. I wore myself down to a frazzle taking care of Mama and the baby at the same time.

One night, I was so tired I felt that I would actually die, yet little Carl would not stop crying. Nothing would quiet him—not rocking, not the breast, not walking the room. He had an unpleasant cry, like a cat mewing. I remember looking out my window at the quiet town, where everyone slept—everyone on this earth, I felt, except for me. I held Carl out at arm's length and looked at him good in the streetlight, at his red, twisted little face. I had an awful urge to throw him out the window—

"That's enough!" several of them say at once. Martha Louise is standing.

But it is Miss Elena who speaks. "I cannot believe," she says severely, "that out of your entire life, Alice Scully, this is all you can find to write about. What of your long marriage to Mr. Scully? Your seven grandchildren? Those of us who have not been blessed with grandchildren would give—"

Of course I loved Harold Scully. Of course I love my grandchildren. I love Solomon, too. I love them all. Miss Elena is like my sons, too terrified to admit to herself how many people we can love, how various we are. She does not want to hear it, any more than they do, any more than you do. You all want us to *never change, never change.*

I did not throw my baby out the window, after all, and

my mother finally died, and I sold the boardinghouse then and was able, at last, to go to school.

Out of the corner of my eye I see Dr. Culbertson appear at the library door, accompanied by a man I do not know. Martha Louise says, "I simply cannot believe that a former *English teacher—*"

This strikes me as very funny. My mind is filled with enormous sentences as I back up my chair and then start forward, out the other door and down the hall and outside into the sweet spring day, where the sunshine falls on my face as it did in those days on the beach, my whole body hot and aching and sticky with sweat and salt and blood, the wild ponies paying us no mind as they ate the tall grass that grew at the edge of the dunes. Sometimes the ponies came so close that we could reach out and touch them. Their coats were shaggy and rough and full of burrs, I remember.

Oh, I remember everything as I cruise forward on the sidewalk that neatly separates the rock garden from the golf course. I turn right at the corner, instead of left toward the Health Center. "Fore!" shouts Parker Howard, waving at me. *A former English teacher*, Martha Louise said. These sidewalks are like diagrams, parallel lines and dividers: oh, I could diagram anything. The semicolon, I used to say, is like a scale; it must separate items of equal rank, I'd warn them. Do not use a semicolon between a clause and a phrase, or between a main clause and a subordinate clause. Do not write, *I loved Carl Redding Armistead; a rich man's son.* Do not write, *If I had really loved Carl Armistead; I would have left with him despite all obstacles.* Do not write, *I still feel his touch; which has thrilled me throughout my life.*

I turn at the top of the hill and motor along the sidewalk toward the Residence Center, hoping to see Solomon. The sun is in my eyes. Do not carelessly link two sentences with only a comma. Do not write, *I want to see Solomon again, he has meant so much to me.* To correct this problem, subordinate one of the parts. *I want to see Solomon, because he has meant so much to me.* Because he has meant. So much. To me. Fragments. Fragments all. I push the button to open the door into the Residence Center, and sure enough, they've brought him out. They've dressed him in his madras plaid shirt and wheeled him in front of the television, which he hates. I cruise right over.

"Solomon," I say, but at first he doesn't respond when he looks at me. I come even closer. "Solomon!" I say sharply, bumping his wheelchair. He notices me then, and a little light comes into his eyes.

I cup my hands. "Solomon," I say, "I'll give you a kiss if you can guess what I've got in my hands."

He looks at me for a while longer.

"Now Mrs. Scully," his nurse starts.

"Come on," I say. "What have I got in here?"

"An elephant," Solomon finally says.

"Close enough!" I cry, and lean right over to kiss his sweet old cheek, being unable to reach his mouth.

"Mrs. Scully," his nurse starts again, but I'm gone, I'm history, I'm out the front door and around the parking circle and up the long entrance drive to the highway. It all connects. Everything connects. The sun is bright, the dogwoods are blooming, the state flower of Virginia is the dogwood, I can still see the sun on the Chickahominy River and my own little sons as they sail their own little boats in a tidal pool by the Chesapeake Bay, they were all blond boys once, though their hair would darken later, Annapolis is the capital of Maryland, the first historic words ever transmitted by telegraph came to Maryland: "What hath God wrought?" The sun is still shining. It glares off the snow on Pikes Peak, it gleams through the milky blue glass of the old apothecary jar in the window of Harold Scully's shop, it warms the asphalt on that road where Rose and I lie waiting, waiting, waiting.

NEWS
of the
SPIRIT

Johnny is having a party.

Driving to the party with her fiancé, Drew, Paula still can't believe it—as far as she knows, as far back as she can remember, Johnny has never had a party. In fact, her brother Johnny's life has been the very opposite of *party*: a long awful jumble and slide of hospitals, group homes, rented rooms. And several periods of time when he was just not here, not anywhere, *missing*, and except for once when their dad flew out to Texas and got him out of jail, they never knew where he'd been. He'd show up again eventually, weeks or months later, grinning that grin, and you'd have to smile back at him no matter what. You couldn't help it. Something inside you, some kind of a seawall that you had built and sandbagged against disaster, would start to seep and give and then collapse, but by then you were so glad to see Johnny that you didn't care, not even when the water came up and swirled around your ankles. You were still smiling when you started to drown.

Paula smiles now, even after everything, just to think of Johnny. She has not been thinking about him, on purpose, for almost three years. Maybe it's time.

Drew reaches across the gearshift of the new Volvo station wagon which he is so proud of, and grabs her hand. "What is it?" he says. "I wish you'd share that thought with me."

Paula stares at him. All her life she has hated people who say the word "share" out loud, she never in her wildest dreams imagined that she might end up with one of them, and certainly not that she could be so much in love with him, which she is. Drew squeezes her hand and smiles at her. His teeth are big and square, white and even, movie-star teeth. But they are real, like everything else about him. Drew is real. Paula has to keep pinching herself to believe it. Drew also has close-cropped, shiny brown hair and big brown eyes, dog eyes, much like the eyes of their Labrador puppy, Muddy Waters, in the very back of the station wagon behind his doggy gate.

Drew and Paula take Muddy Waters everywhere they go. He is in the bonding phase, and they are bonding him for life. This is how their instructor at the obedience class put it, "bonding him for life"; it scares Paula to death. Because, okay, so they bond Muddy Waters to them for life, but what if they die? Or what if one of them dies? What if one of them is in a plane wreck and dies? What if one of them gets spinal meningitis and dies? "You mean, 'What if this doesn't work out,' don't you?" Drew said, right after the dog obedience class Tuesday night when Paula was freaking out in the parking lot. "Yes," she said. "Yes, that's what I mean," and then she cried all the way back to the new house which Drew has bought for them because it was such a steal. Drew is always on the lookout for bargains. He likes to strike while the iron is hot, and maximize his opportunities.

To Paula's surprise, he seems to see Paula herself as an opportunity. Ever since they met when they were seated next to each other at a Leon Redbone concert, Drew has come on like gangbusters. That was six months ago. Already they have a house, they have a dog, they have a station wagon. They have a disposal in the kitchen, which dazzles Paula altogether. Sometimes when she's in the house by herself, she'll feed a whole head of lettuce into it just to watch it work. It's almost soundless. It's amazing. But Paula is amazed by everything these days, by Drew himself, by her gigantic good luck in having been selected by him from among all the women in the world. Just think, she almost didn't go to the Leon Redbone concert, she almost stayed home with a book! Paula feels like a lady in a melodrama who has been saved in the nick of time, snatched back from the cliff in the pouring rain just before she would have slid off the edge and tumbled endlessly into the mist.

But of course this idea is silly, this cliff stuff. Actually Paula was doing just fine before she met Drew; and before she met Drew, it never once occurred to her that she was on a cliff, or in the mist, or in any kind of peril. She can't figure out why she feels so *saved* now. But she does, as she leans back smelling that new-car smell and holding Drew's hand, lacing her fingers through his, while north Raleigh flows past her view in a river of burger stands and car washes and convenience stores.

"I was just thinking about Johnny," she says. "We used to have a lot of fun, too, we really did, before all the bad stuff." Paula takes a deep breath. "We were real close," she says.

"I know you were," Drew says. "I got that. Come here," he says, and she leans over so he can kiss her. He nuzzles his face for a minute into her long curly hair.

She giggles. "We're just like teenagers," she says.

But they are not teenagers, she and Drew, not by a long shot. Paula has been a journalist, a petsitter, a waitress, a kindergarten teacher, lots of things, though she has never been married. Right now she's a proofreader at a printing company. Drew sold real estate for ten years before he went to law school at Carolina. He had a whole other life, and another wife, who left him for her boss at a TV station. Drew's first wife told him he was boring, and Drew thinks maybe this was true, especially while he was in law school.

Now that his practice is well established, he is trying to be less boring, by taking Chinese cooking classes, going to concerts, and jumping out of airplanes. Still, he can't help being a very organized person. He just can't help it. Drew finds Paula stimulating, he says, because of her varied interests, her checkered past. What he's too nice to say is that she's a *flake*, Paula thinks, but she is not, however, as flaky as Corinne, her mother. Maybe Corinne will come to Johnny's party today, maybe Johnny has invited her. Maybe she will drive over from Rocky Mount with her new boyfriend.

Paula cannot imagine what Drew will think of her mother, or of Johnny. Drew has never met anybody in Paula's family except her father the barbecue king and her country-club sister, Elise. Elise thinks Drew is terrific.

Paula has met every single person in Drew's family, which is regular as rain. Drew's parents have lived in the same house in Durham for twenty-five years. Drew's father is a quality control engineer in a textile mill, whatever that means. His mother, nicknamed Boots, says she is a "home engineer." This is her little joke. She has already given Paula some of their family's favorite recipes, all of them involving canned tomato or mushroom soup. Looking at Drew's family gathered around his parents' dining room table last Easter, Paula wondered if the soup was *it*, the secret ingredient always missing from her own family. Drew's father beamed, Drew's grown-up sisters smiled, their husbands ate heartily, their children ran around shrieking like banshees, while Boots blossomed out alarmingly over her apron, a victim of her own good cooking.

Back in the den, framed family photographs were clustered on every available surface like little armies. Weddings, Christmases, vacations. Prom pictures, school pictures, graduation pictures. This was where Drew got it, then, his habit of photographing everything, the only habit he's got that Paula doesn't like, although she hasn't mustered the nerve yet to tell him to quit taking so many pictures, or at least to quit making her stand smack in the middle of every one. Once when she complained gently, Drew told her that the human figure adds perspective. She said, "What's so great about perspective?" and Drew stared at her for a long minute before he hugged her. "You're right," he said. "You're right." But still he takes the pictures and then rushes off with them to One Hour Photo the minute they get home from the weekend. Before Paula has even unpacked her bag, Drew has put the pictures in an album, with captions. One of the captions, under a picture of Paula sticking her foot into the cold ocean on a February trip to Wrightsville Beach, says "Br-r-r-r!"

Right now, Drew has his camera loaded and ready to go. He wears it around his neck. Obviously he plans to take pictures at Johnny's party. Try as she might, Paula cannot imagine a picture of Johnny captured under plastic in Drew's orderly album. Suddenly she can't imagine even introducing Johnny to Drew.

"Listen," she says nervously, "I don't really have any idea what kind of shape Johnny's in, you know. What he'll be like, I mean."

"Oh, come on," Drew says. "He's having a party, isn't he?"

"I just don't know what he's like now," Paula says again. "I haven't seen him for over two years."

"Two years in which he has supported himself and stayed out of trouble, as far as you know. Give the guy a break, Paula. We all make mistakes." Eyes on the road, Drew pats her hand. Drew believes in perfectibility and innate goodness. He believes that enough effort will make things right. He seems never to have considered bad genes, bad luck, or bad timing. If you work hard enough, you will succeed, and all things will come to you. Paula has been drunk on these beliefs for months. But now she's scared, she feels like she's sobering up. It's a big, *big* mistake to take Drew to Johnny's party. She knows it is.

"Have you got the directions?" Drew asks, and she takes them out of her purse. They are printed in Johnny's childish block letters. "Get on 401, heading north toward Rolesville," she says.

"We're already on 401."

"Oh. Okay. Then we start looking out for State Road 1172, going off to the left, just beyond a McDonald's."

In the back, Muddy Waters wakes up and starts moving around.

"I think he needs to get out," Paula says. "Let's pull off and stop for a minute."

"But we're almost there."

"Please let's stop," Paula says. "Please please please."

Drew takes a look at her and pulls over on the shoulder. Before he can say anything, Paula jumps out and runs around to open the back of the Volvo, and Muddy Waters bolts out, wagging himself all over. "Here, honey, here." Paula puts the leash on his collar and pulls him down the bank into the deep summer woods, hot and still.

"Watch out for poison ivy," Drew calls from the car, but now Paula can't see him, he's just a voice somewhere beyond the dusty curtain of green. Muddy Waters pees gratefully. Paula looks around. She likes it in here, it's like a little fort. Nobody can find her, nothing can get in. It's like a little temple. Paula and Johnny had a temple once, in woods like these. They had an altar covered with magic rocks from a magic river, and a fire ceremony. In fact they damn near caused a real forest fire with their fire ceremony, but nobody ever knew. Nobody ever knew they did it. Paula grins, remembering Johnny's dirt-streaked exalted boy's face as they stood together in the red light at the edge of the leaping flames. They had a secret language then, too, and special names: Roger and Darling.

"Paula?" Drew shouts from the road. "Paula! What's taking so long? Come on, we'll be late."

"It doesn't matter," Paula says, but she whispers the

words to herself. Muddy Waters strains at his leash. The leaves are all around her, dark green, fleshy, still. Just before a thunderstorm they will turn their silver sides out, she's seen that, too. It's exciting.

"Paula?" Drew calls.

She lets Muddy Waters pull her out of the circle of trees and up the embankment.

"Tell him to heel," Drew says, but she doesn't. She and the dog charge up the hill together. Drew opens the back door and Muddy Waters hops in, happy as can be. Paula and Drew get in. About three miles down the road, they come to the McDonald's and then to State Road 1172 and turn onto it, slowing down. Paula feels hot and clammy, like she's coming down with a virus. Maybe the party's a joke. State Road 1172 is gravel; dust hangs in the air behind them. *Like a dragon's tail*, she thinks. *Like the train on a wedding gown.*

"Honey?" Drew says. "Honey, this is a test, isn't it?"

"Of course not," Paula says, but of course it is.

MARÍA SITS ON THE BATTERED SOFA WATCHING JOHNNY fly around their half of the cinder-block duplex like a tornado, cleaning up. He grabs old newspapers and pizza boxes and throws them into the closet, opening the door then slamming it fast as a whiz so that everything will not fall out, as in a funny movie. María giggles. He is one wild guy! *Es un gringo loco.* She shakes her head, her long black hair rippling around her shoulders like water. Johnny wears a big red sombrero with mirrors all over it, a hat her brother left here. It is a hat for show, a crazy hat, not a hat to wear. María giggles. She gets up to help him, but Johnny motions her to stay right there, right on the couch. He wants to do everything for her, he will not let her lift a hand. In the mornings he wants her to stay in bed while he brings breakfast to her hot from McDonald's, the Egg McMuffin and the hash-brown potatoes. María loves McDonald's, she loves all the paper boxes. Breakfast in bed. It is American. It was different in María's country, the woman did everything.

Now María must sit on the sofa while Johnny picks up his work clothes and takes them into the bedroom. These clothes he dropped on the floor yesterday after work and then he came to her on the sofa, this sofa, she was watching TV. María loves the TV in the afternoons when all is disaster and chaos, *miseria*, so many unhappy affairs of the heart. And the beautiful clothing of the stars!

Now Johnny pulls the chairs around, wipes off the coffee table, picks up a big empty Fritos bag. Only, whoops! The Fritos bag was not quite empty, the Fritos go everywhere. Now it is a bigger mess than ever! Johnny scrambles around, picking up Fritos. He is so funny. María is laughing. Johnny opens the screen door and throws handfuls of Fritos on the ground; the chickens come running to get them. He bought the chickens at María's request. A house should have chickens, she said. And sunflowers in the yard.

The chickens make María feel better but still it is strange, America. There is so much to understand, and she does not have the language. *No es importante*, Johnny says. We have the language of love. María wonders what her grandmother would say, Abuelita, in her long black dress, what would Abuelita say of Johnny? María wonders when she will see her beloved Abuelita again, but this does not matter too much right now, it seems a distant problem, as on TV. For María is here in America with Johnny, and Johnny fills up the whole world like he fills up this little house. Sometimes it seems to María that he fills it up so much she cannot see another thing.

For Johnny is always laughing, joking, moving around fast. He is cooking. He is playing tapes. He is talking a mile a minute, María cannot follow what he says. He is dancing María around and around the living room until she is dizzy and has to beg him to let her stop for breath. But Johnny never gets tired. He can paint houses all day long and come home and work in the garden or in his workshop or cook a huge dinner, just for the two of them! Leftovers for the dogs. Johnny does everything in a big way. It is American.

One night last week he made the dinner in the middle of the night, a big pot full of spaghetti, María had to laugh at him then! Lucky that he makes *mucho dinero*, more money than María has ever seen, he throws it down on the coffee table on Fridays when he comes home, and lets out a whoop like a rodeo cowboy. "Take it!" Johnny says. "Take it all!"

And then on Saturdays he will bring her shopping at Crab-
tree Valley Mall. María's closet is full of clothes, enough for
a village full of girls. María's pet name for Johnny is Mijo,
the sun. Because his hair is golden like the sun, and because
he has brought her out from the darkness into the light. If
she is sometimes blinded, what is that? She can shield her
eyes, she can wear a big hat. Johnny kisses her all over, even
in the afternoon. He brings her flowers that she does not
know the names of. *Qué importa si María* will not see
Abuelita again, as she is beginning to understand. Old, old
Abuelita, mumbling curses and prayers, sits in the shade of
her hut in Mexico, far away.

Here it is America, and now Bo is at the door with a bag
of ice, which he takes into the kitchen and dumps in the sink.
For the *fiesta*. Bo brings also Coca-Colas and *cervezas*. Bo
is a friend to Johnny for many years, long time. He smiles
and does not talk much. He is nice. Johnny and Bo paint
houses together, they go off in the truck every morning. Bo
used to live here with Johnny. Now he lives over on the other
side with Pete and Lulu and Lulu's brother Dallas. Dallas is
not nice. *Dallas vive aquí poco tiempo,* and María wishes he
will go away. Sometimes he is looking at her from the house
when she hangs the clothes on the line or sits in the chair in
the sun, as she loves to do. He is not a good man, Dallas,
María thinks but does not say. He is just visiting.

Today he is respectful, wet hair slicked back, knocking
on the door, followed by Pete and Lulu. María likes Pete and

Lulu. They are funny. Lulu carries a big pink and white Happy Birthday cake left over from the bakery at Winn Dixie, where she works. "Happy birthday, honey," Lulu says, handing the cake to Johnny. "*Feliz cumpleaños*," Johnny explains to María. María is surprised. "It is your birthday?" she asks.

"No, it is a joke," Johnny says, and takes the cake and María both into the kitchen, where he puts the cake on the counter and kisses her hard. He doesn't stop kissing her until Pete yells, "Hey Johnny, somebody's here," and then María goes to the window with him to see the new station wagon drive up into the red clay yard past Johnny's truck and Pete's truck and the other cars and trucks that Pete keeps scattered around for parts. The station wagon stops in a cloud of dust.

FOR PAULA EVERYTHING GOES INTO SLOW MOTION then, like she's underwater. She's scared. She realizes that sometime—maybe during the past three years, maybe on the way up 401 to Johnny's house, maybe over the past two weeks since she got his letter—sometime, she has begun to hope again, of course she has, this is why she's here. This is why she didn't just crumple up his note and throw it into the trashcan, as she has done so many times in the past with so many of Johnny's demands. Drew's optimism has rubbed off on her. And it *has* been a long time—anything can happen in three years. But now that they're here, Paula is panicking.

It all looks too trashy, this little cinder-block house way out
in the middle of noplace, rusting cars and parts of cars in
the uncut weeds, dogs barking, chickens squawking everywhere. Chickens! Paula cannot imagine. The sun is in her
eyes, she can't really see the man behind the torn screen door.
But it could be Johnny. Oh God, it's been so long, what if
she doesn't recognize him? What if she doesn't recognize
her own brother?

Johnny was always the cute one, the funny one, the brain.
Although he was two years older than Paula, they were insep-
arable. Everybody said they might as well have been twins.
And it was true that they had the special bond that twins are
said to have—an extraordinary kind of understanding. "On
the same wavelength," is how their mother put it. She could
reduce anything to a platitude. It was Johnny who made up
all the games, all the secret codes, all the secret maps, with
Paula his willing sidekick. Years later, in college, Paula would
realize that she was imaginative, too, and smart. But by then
she didn't want to know it, she didn't want to be smart, it
was too late, she did not, not, *not* want to be like Johnny, no
matter what, and she switched her major from English to
education and dropped out of the creative writing program.
Of course she had other problems by then, too.

Can it really be true that everything starts in childhood,
that what we will do and be is inside of us like a seed perfectly formed and growing when we are just little children
like all the other little children in the world? Paula has a

photograph of herself and Johnny taken someplace along the Blue Ridge Parkway: they are blond toddlers, angels both of them, gathered up against their mother's skirts, and their mother is young and beautiful. You can see why she was chosen as Miss Bright Leaf Tobacco and Miss Gastonia. Presumably their daddy took this picture. But where was their older sister, Elise? Maybe she was off at church camp. Elise loved camp, where she always won all the medals. She loved games and sports and organized events.

Johnny and Paula were free spirits, as their mother often said, refusing games and play programs, happiest in their own big backyard outside of town. Happiest in their own world. Here they played Roger and Darling to their hearts' content for years. Roger had many amazing powers, such as the ability to see into anyone's mind. He could also see through clothes. He could see through anything. When Roger and Darling sneaked out at night and walked down the road, Roger would tell her everything that was happening inside every house they passed, everyone's secret thoughts and deepest desires.

When Mrs. Sissy Boone was sent to the hospital for stabbing Mr. Boone in the shoulder with a long-handled fork, Roger and Darling were not surprised. Roger had seen a black cloud full of wasps around her head, he had seen blood seeping out from under her fingernails as she stood on her front porch one day just saying hello.

When young Mrs. Johnson's baby wouldn't grow and

had to go live in a home, Roger and Darling were not surprised then, either. Roger had seen its bones glowing through
its little baby dress when Mrs. Johnson had it out on a blanket in her yard, under a shade tree.

They knew when the big hand closed up on their granddaddy's heart; they were almost bored by the time the phone
rang and their white-faced mother came in the kitchen,
where they were making peanut butter crackers, to tell them
the news.

To this day, Paula has never told anybody these things,
but they are all true. She remembers them in detail, as she
remembers the religion of Oran, and Ungar the Magnificent
and his dog Army and his Queen Orinda of New York City,
and how as Ungar and Orinda she and Johnny wore towels
as capes, safety-pinned to their backs, and jumped off the
shed and out of trees and finally off the Boones' garage, again
and again, and were not hurt. Paula can remember even now
the rush of air under her legs, how it was to fly. They were
magic then. She can still feel Johnny's soft breath in her ear
when he whispers to her in their own language as they sit
on the porch step, knees touching, through all the twilights
of their childhood, and watch the lightning bugs come up
from the grass and listen to the peepers.

How did it happen, when did it happen, when did it all
go wrong? There came a time when Johnny wouldn't stop
playing games, when he wouldn't come in for supper. By
then Daddy had retired from the National Guard and put

in his first barbecue restaurant, so he was often away at mealtime. When he did come home for dinner, it was a command performance. In Paula's memory, Johnny is always late, their father is always yelling, their mother is always on the bright verge of tears.

"Can't you control these children?" Daddy would say in his thunderous, commanding-the-troops voice. "I swear, Corinne, I work all day and I feel like I've got the right to come home to a decent dinner, am I right?" Daddy was a workaholic, though nobody knew that word then.

"Sure, honey." Mama would seem to quiver all over, under her heavy pancake makeup, her winged brows and aqua eyeliner. She was the prettiest mom in the neighborhood.

But the truth was that she did not control them at all, especially not in the summer, when she sat on the porch with her best friend Louise and drank sweet wine in the late afternoons and sewed from Simplicity patterns or looked at magazines and gave Paula and Johnny a dollar apiece to get dinner at the Quickie Mart. Paula's favorite supper was a Dr Pepper and a Baby Ruth, while Johnny favored 7-Up and Cheetos and Red Hots.

In the early days of Daddy's barbecue business, when he was perfecting his recipes, he often brought their dinner home with him. "Whaddaya think, kids? It's got some extra vinegar and a little more sugar this time. Whaddaya think? Corinne? Too much sugar?"

After months of barbecue, Paula found it hard to tell the

difference, but she always made a polite comment. Johnny did not. Johnny became a vegetarian at age eleven, which was the worst thing he could possibly do to his father.

On one especially awful night, Johnny came in late, humming loudly.

"Johnny," Mama said. *"Johnny!"*

Johnny took his seat and put his napkin in his lap and stared straight ahead, and wouldn't stop. "Hmmmm," he went. He didn't look at anybody.

Daddy put a helping of potato salad on Johnny's plate. *"Son,"* he said in that voice.

Mama was giving Daddy looks across the table, looks that begged him to ignore it, which is how Mama handled everything about Johnny. Daddy put baked beans, Jell-O salad, and barbecue on Johnny's plate. Daddy always tried to do what Mama wanted, at least at first. This time it seemed to work. Johnny quit humming and started to eat the Jell-O salad. Elise excused herself and left the table. Mama and Daddy relaxed and began talking about whether or not Daddy should expand his business by buying the little place now available out on the highway (he did), and whether or not they should have those very expensive braces put on Elise's teeth (they did). Johnny didn't say a word. He ate everything on his plate except the barbecue. "Hmmmm," he went.

Daddy stopped talking and stared at him. Daddy looked tired, circles under his black eyes, gray hair peppering his crew cut. "Son, eat your barbecue," Daddy said.

"Now, Luther," Mama said. "Plenty of people in the world are vegetarians. It's a whole religion in India."

"This isn't India," Daddy said, tight-lipped. "This is the U.S. of A."

Johnny was humming.

Daddy looked at him. *"Right now,"* he said.

"Oh Luther," Mama said. Her hand fluttered up to her face.

"Hmmmmm," Johnny went.

Daddy stood up. "Son," he said in a reasonable voice, "let's not have any more of this nonsense. This barbecue is what bought the clothes on your back, it's what paid for that new bike out there in the driveway. Now finish your supper."

Paula held her breath.

Johnny took a big bite of barbecue.

"That's better," Daddy said.

Johnny spit it out all over his plate, all over the table.

Daddy lunged at him across the table, but he was too late, Johnny was already gone, his chair overturned. His high-pitched laughter echoed back at them as he ran out the front door.

"Goddamnit to hell!" Daddy fell forward heavily onto the table, his head hitting the hanging light fixture, his elbow in the potato salad.

"Oh Luther, oh honey," Mama said, pulling him back. She was crying.

"I'll show that little—" Daddy started, but Mama began to cry in earnest, big shuddering boo-hoos that required Daddy's attention.

"I don't know why you're so hard on him," Mama was sobbing.

"Aw, honey, he's spoiled," Daddy said. "You have to keep a boy like that on a shorter rein. He needs to know his limits. When he gets back here tonight, I'll straighten him out."

This made Mama cry harder than ever. "But Luther, remember what that teacher said? Mrs. Logan? What if there's something really wrong—" Then Mama looked up and noticed Paula, who sat petrified in her place at the table, her napkin in her lap. Little black rivers of mascara ran down both of Mama's cheeks. "Well, *go on!*" she snapped at Paula. "Go on, what are you looking at?" As if Johnny were somehow *her* fault, Paula's fault, and so without a word Paula got up and ran out the front door after Johnny, but Johnny was long gone by then and Paula was left by herself in the summer dark, as she has been ever since. She sat on the porch steps for a long time. When she finally went back in the house, there was no sign of Mama or Daddy either one, though they had left everything exactly as it was—all the lights on, the kitchen a mess.

Now, this is Paula's deepest image of her family: the abandoned dinette table with the hanging globe light over it swinging slightly, just quivering; two of the red vinyl chairs overturned, food uneaten. Mama and Daddy were upstairs in their bedroom with the door closed. Oh, there was no question that they adored each other in those days, Mama and Daddy. Big and rough as he was, Daddy worshipped the ground Mama walked on. He watched her in a certain way whenever she came into a room.

Paula knew that he loved them all, but sometimes this was hard to remember. Daddy had trouble expressing himself; he had trouble in particular having a son who did not fit his treasured idea of *son*. Mama explained to them that Daddy felt so strongly about this because his own dad had died when he was three, so he had missed out on all the dad stuff himself. Once Paula heard Mama say to him, "Honest to God, Luther, sometimes I think you just married me so you could get a son!"

Daddy was forever buying presents for the girls, and saying, "Nothing but the best for my ladies!" He would not allow them to work at the barbecue restaurants, though they begged to—first Elise, then Paula when she was old enough. His girls were too good to work at barbecue restaurants. He *wanted* Johnny to work there, on the other hand. He had visions of Johnny going into the business with him: "Luther's Famous Barbecue—A Family Restaurant," the second generation.

Johnny had his own agenda, and after he kicked her out of his club, Paula was not a part of it, either. The original club included Johnny, Paula, Lewis Straus, and Jakey Ramey, who lived down the road. Lewis Straus was a fat boy with hooded eyes who had always made Paula uncomfortable.

One day when she was late for a meeting in the Rameys' garage, she found Lewis whispering intently to Johnny. "No," Johnny was saying, shaking his shaggy blond head. "No way." They all stared at Paula, who sat down cross-legged facing them.

"What?" she asked.

"Nothing," Johnny said. Then he convened the club, but Lewis and Jakey continued to stare at her until she felt funny and sat in a different way.

After that, the club was not the same. The games got to be scary games, bad games, especially when Ken became a member. Nobody except Johnny could really see Ken—at least Paula couldn't see him—but he told them all what to do, and Lewis and Jakey went along with it. Paula did, too, until the day when Ken told her to run home and never come back, and she obeyed. She bought some paper dolls and started playing with Ruthie Jackson instead. Later, after the club got in so much trouble, all the other neighborhood children were told to steer clear of Johnny, and Paula got him back, temporarily; but Johnny seemed preoccupied, even bored. He was always riding off someplace on his bike. School came as a relief for Paula, ordering her days, bringing her friends of her own.

But school was hard for Johnny, though he was "brilliant," according to the guidance counselor, who made him take so many tests. He was constantly in trouble—trouble for talking, trouble for not sitting still, trouble for lying.

Trouble for not turning in his assignments, trouble for talking back. Johnny loved to draw and was said to be talented in art, but he never would draw what the teacher said. He wouldn't follow the assignment.

Since he was two years ahead of Paula, she didn't see him much. Her heart would race whenever she did—from a distance, on the playing field, running faster than anybody else; or across the parking lot at junior high, in the middle of a gang of the roughest boys. His friends in junior high were the worst boys in school, and it seemed he was always out with them, never home. Daddy didn't know this, since he was at the restaurants so much, and it was okay with Mama. It was a lot easier than having Johnny at home.

It was okay with Paula, too. School went well for her. She had three best friends and made junior high cheerleader. Mama sewed all their cheerleader skirts. Paula took band and learned to play the flute.

By the time Johnny was in high school, Paula knew that he was doing a lot of drugs. Later, she could not figure out how she knew this. She never saw him doing any drugs, not even smoking marijuana. By this time Johnny and some other boys had a rock band, the Mystic Cowboys. Johnny played bass. After he flunked junior year, Daddy grounded him for two months. Paula remembers very well those two months, which Johnny, oddly acquiescent, spent lying on his back on the waterbed in his room, listening to music and watching the sun shine blue and red and orange on his walls like a kaleidoscope through the crystal he'd hung in his window. He refused to work at the restaurants. He wouldn't do anything at all. Several times, Paula went to his room because she thought she heard voices, but there was never anybody else there. Nobody but Johnny. At the end of the two months, Daddy kicked him out of the house and Mama started having migraine headaches and bursting into tears at the slightest provocation. Then she got a job at Nails 'N Notions in the mall, and seemed better.

While Paula was in high school, Johnny's band became locally famous. "Oh, your brother is one of the Mystic Cowboys?" her friends would say. "Really? Which one is he?" and Paula would say the cute one with the long blond hair, and she was proud of him and gave him money whenever he came around asking for it. Once she gave him two hundred dollars she had saved up for Christmas.

Sometimes Johnny left elaborate messages with her, for people he said were looking for him, but they never showed up. One time he left an unfinished note tacked on the front door that read

Darling,

I'm in a lot of trouble and

That was all. No explanation, no signature. Paula pulled it down before her mother could see it. She tried to call Johnny, but his phone had been disconnected. She called some of his friends, and nobody knew where he was, but one of his friends said it was cool, for her not to worry about it. When she saw Johnny the next time, she asked him about the note, but he didn't remember. This happened shortly before Paula went away to college.

The first time Johnny flipped out was when he and his band were doing really well—they had a gig at the Granfalloon in Atlanta. The story went that Johnny got on the drums and wouldn't stop. He wouldn't quit drumming. Finally they closed the club and took him away in a straitjacket. That first time, they called it drug psychosis.

JOHNNY WENT TO A STATE HOSPITAL THAT LOOKED LIKE a college campus with its green rolling hills and brick buildings with white columns. If you didn't notice the chain-link fence around the grounds, that is, with the barbed wire at the top. Johnny's room was in a low flat building with a broad concrete stoop in front, where several of the patients sat outside in the October sunshine amid the falling leaves. Other patients walked among the pecan trees, bending to pick up pecans. "That's something, isn't it?" Johnny said. "Nuts for the nuts." But he wouldn't talk much. He looked past Paula and kept his head cocked, as if listening to something. He seemed—how could this be?—*busy*, as if he had a lot going on in his head and Paula's visit was just a distraction. Johnny was skinny and his hands shook and his tongue seemed thick. The nurse said it was the medicine. They had cut off all his beautiful long blond hair.

The nurse said Paula could take him for a walk, but Johnny wouldn't go any farther than the end of the road in front of his own building. "Let's go back now," he said urgently, for no apparent reason, and they did; and when Paula left him sitting on the stoop among the others, she could see that he was comfortable there, that he wanted to stay. This broke her heart.

The next visit was better. Johnny seemed more himself. His eyes were brighter. Now he was in another building, and had the run of the hospital grounds. He was smoking cigarettes nonstop, a habit he'd picked up in the hospital, where everybody smoked. The fingers of his right hand were stained yellow. But he was better, Paula could tell. He talked more. When they got back to his building, a big black woman named Jewel came up to Paula and said, "Me and Johnny's going to get married, did he tell you?" Paula was startled. Jewel must have weighed more than two hundred pounds, and her hair stuck out on one side. She was wearing those fuzzy bedroom shoes.

Johnny grinned, a trace of the old Johnny in spite of his yellow teeth. "That's right, Jewel," he said, "you and me."

"She's going to marry everybody," he told Paula. "She talks about it all the time. Don't pay any attention to her."

They walked to the snack bar for a Coke. When they returned, as Paula was getting ready to leave, Jewel came to the door and yelled out, "Me and Johnny is getting married, honey, just as soon as I gets my divorce."

"Who you married to now, Jewel?" asked a man who sat smoking in a lawn chair under the trees.

"I am presently married to James Brown," Jewel hollered, "and let me tell you, honey, he can *do the deed*!"

Everybody—even the nurse outside on duty with the smokers, even Johnny—was laughing as Paula left.

Johnny stayed in the hospital for a year, which included some of Paula's freshman year and most of her sophomore year in college. As soon as he got out of the hospital, she went home for a weekend to see him. The plan was that Johnny would stay with their parents until he got "squared away," as Dad put it energetically on the phone. Dad seemed to be running Johnny's recovery. Paula thought that was sweet, another chance for Dad; but as soon as she got home, she could see it wasn't working.

It was a cold, bright March day. The big forsythia bushes on either side of the garage were blooming wildly. Paula parked in the driveway and ran to the door, her heart pounding in her throat, her eyes blind with tears. *Johnny Johnny Johnny*, was all she could think, but it was her dad who met her at the door. Usually he was not at home in the daytime.

He looked older and fatter than she remembered, any old man in a short-sleeved white shirt.

"Paula!" He was surprised. "Hi, honey." He peered past her, out the door. She could see in his face that he was looking for Johnny, too, as she had been. He had forgotten that she was coming home. Was this going to be the story of all their lives, then, all of them forever looking for Johnny? *What about me?* she wanted to shout. *Me, Paula? Remember me? I'm home for the weekend, doesn't anybody care? Doesn't anybody want to know how I'm doing?* Obviously not. Her father was gray with worry.

"Honey, is it Johnny?" Corinne's wavery voice came down from the head of the stairs.

"No, it's only me," Paula said. She brushed past her father and went into the downstairs bathroom and washed her face, scrubbing at it furiously with a washcloth until it stung. On the bathroom wall hung a cross-stitched plaque her mother had made: "Love be with you while you stay, peace be with you on your way." Paula was composed by the time she went into the den, where her mother and father sat far apart from each other on the Early American couch, like bookends.

Johnny had been out all night, they didn't know where he was, he hadn't phoned, they didn't know who he was with.

"Don't you think we should call the police?" Corinne asked. It was the first time Paula had seen her without eye makeup.

"Just what would we say?" Dad was sarcastic. "That our twenty-two-year-old son just stayed out all night? Big fucking deal, am I right?"

"Don't curse at me, Luther." Corinne had a squinched-up Kleenex in her hand. She was beating this hand softly against her knee.

"I mean, either he's well, or he's sick, am I right? So which is it? If he's sick, he needs to be in the hospital, and if he's well, he can damn sure act like a decent human being. Is that too much to ask?" Dad's voice rang out in the den. Paula sat in his recliner and stared at the arrangement of artificial flowers in the middle of the coffee table, something else her mother had made. It struck her as pathetic, all Corinne's little crafts, even her sewing, even her job at Nails 'N Notions, just a way to fill the time while Dad was at the restaurants. Paula stood up. "Does anybody want a Coke?" she asked, heading toward the kitchen.

"I've got to go," her father said. "I'll see you ladies in about an hour. Hang tight," he said.

Corinne came to stand in the kitchen door.

"What does he mean, 'Hang tight'?" Paula asked.

"Oh, who knows?" Corinne's pretty face was pale and distracted. "Maybe I *will* have one of those Cokes, honey, with a little sweetener in it." She pulled a bottle of bourbon down from the highest pantry shelf.

"Johnny's not doing drugs again, is he?" Paula watched her mother pour the drink.

"Oh no," Corinne said. "Oh no, that's not it, that's not it at all, that was *never* it, this is what the doctors say. Of course he can't ever do any drugs again, or drink so much as a beer, because of the medicine he has to take. This is what's got me worried right now. I just wish I knew where he was. I mean, he's on so much medicine. You should see all the bottles in the bathroom right now. It's just awful, for a young person to need that much medicine. I don't see how he can keep it straight."

"What kind of medicine?" Paula asked.

"Oh, *I* don't know, but it's very *strong* medicine, Paula, it has all these side effects. . . ." Corinne trailed off, sipping her drink. Her face looked blurry and vague. Then she seemed to pull herself back together; she sat up and straightened her shoulders. "Oh, but you know what I think, honey? You know what I really think?"

"What?" Paula leaned closer.

"I think that's all a lot of hooey," Corinne said. "Young people go through these phases, everybody knows that. Boys will be boys!" She smiled brilliantly at Paula. Corinne drank that drink, and then another, and was asleep on the sofa in front of the TV when Johnny came in later.

"Shhhh!" Johnny said, tiptoeing elaborately past Corinne. "Shhhh!" All his movements were exaggerated, like a mime's.

"Johnny!" Paula stood up. "Where have you been? Everybody's been just frantic." Her magazine slipped to the floor.

"Oh, hi, Paula," Johnny said as if he saw her every day. "What's up?" He wore a blue knit shirt like a golfer, and khaki pants that were too short. Paula had never seen him in clothes like these. She couldn't imagine where he'd gotten them.

"*What's up!*" she repeated. "Where have you been? That's the question."

"Oh," Johnny said airily, "I've just been making a few investments, that's all."

"Investments!" Paula said. "With what?" She followed him into the kitchen. Johnny didn't answer. Instead he opened the breadbox and took out a long loaf of white bread, Rainbo bread, the kind their mother always bought. He unwrapped the bread and got four slices of it and squeezed them together in his hands, forming a ball, and grinned at her.

"Oh, Roger," Paula said before she thought.

He handed the loaf to her, and she took it and squeezed three slices into a ball for herself. When she bit into it, the taste was just like she remembered, yeasty and delicious. A thrill shot through her. They ate handful after handful. Then Roger put what was left of the loaf back in the breadbox and took her hand. "Come on," he said. "I want to show you what I found."

He led her into the hall and down the stairs into their old rec room, now mostly taken over by Corinne's craft materi-als. He switched on the overhead lights. In one corner of the orange linoleum floor was the old record player, surrounded by albums. "Wait," Roger said, placing her in the center of the floor. "Just listen to this, you won't believe it. This is really, really old stuff. It must've been Mom's. It's so funky."

He put on a Percy Faith album, then went back and took her in his arms, ready to slow-dance. The needle dropped. She could feel his shoulder bones like wings beneath the golf shirt. "Unchained Melody" filled the basement. Roger leading, they swooped across the floor. They were perfect, perfect, perfect together—they could have been on TV. Once Roger dipped her back and back and back, nearly to the floor, but Paula was not scared, not a bit, she knew he wouldn't drop her. On and on they danced. It was wonderful. They danced until the door at the top of the stairs opened and Corinne came down, pausing midway.

"Why, what in the world!" she exclaimed.

Roger let go. Paula, winded, bent to switch off the record player and then stood trying to catch her breath.

Behind Corinne, Dad's gray crew-cut head appeared. "Everybody's home, huh?" he called jovially down the stairs. "I didn't think you'd have had time to cook, honey, so I brought some supper home from the restaurant. Now don't worry, son, ha-ha, no barbecue this time, I've got some broiled chicken, an item that's getting very popular these days. . . ."

Paula looked up the stairs at her parents. She could hear Roger breathing hard behind her. "We already ate," she said.

• • •

After that weekend, Paula went back to school, and Johnny went back to the hospital. "Just put it out of your mind, honey," her mother urged her on the telephone. "You can't do a thing about it, nobody can. Johnny is right where he needs to be. They're taking real good care of him. So you just forget about it, and study real hard, and try to have some *fun*, too, okay? These are the happiest years of your life," Corinne said.

"Okay," Paula said. *Sure*. But she was so tired. In the mornings, she couldn't drag herself out of bed in time to get to biology. In the afternoon, she'd nod off during lectures. Her notes were indecipherable. Her grades were falling in every class. Alerted by Paula's roommate, a cheerful perfect girl from Charlotte who was worried to death about her, the dorm counselor paid a visit to their room. *Nothing is wrong,* Paula told Mrs. Abbott. *Nothing. No, nothing has happened. No, I am not pregnant. No. No. I'm just tired, that's all.* They put her in the infirmary and everyone assumed she had mononucleosis, an in thing to have. But the test came back negative. It was not mono. By then it was time for exams, but she was much too tired to study. When they sent her home, her father had one of his famous fits the minute she walked in the door.

"Eight thousand dollars down the drain!" he shouted. "You think I'm made of money? Is that what you think? You and your brother, you'll bleed me to death, between the two of you. I've never seen such kids! Too tired to study, huh? I wish I had had a father to send me to college. I wish I had had these opportunities that you piss away—"

It was clear that he would have gone on forever if Corinne hadn't come in and taken his arm and led him away. Paula climbed upstairs and went to bed. Later, Corinne came to her room and told her not to pay any attention, that Dad was just upset, plus he was a northerner and you know how they are. They just say everything that's on their mind, they always yell but it doesn't mean anything. Plus there was all the stress of Johnny's illness and running the restaurants. Corinne sat on the edge of the bed and stroked Paula's hair. She had the longest, reddest fingernails Paula had ever seen.

Later that summer, Elise married a young surgeon in a big wedding, which set Dad back plenty, as he told every-body. He said he didn't mind, though. "Nothing but the best for my baby," he said. Paula managed to get out of bed long enough to be a bridesmaid, feeling pallid and insignificant among Elise's perky, cool friends. Most of them had been Tri Delts, like Elise. Before the wedding, Paula and Elise had had a fight about whether or not to invite Johnny, who was out of the hospital again—Elise was determined not to, and it was her wedding, after all—but Paula had started cry-ing, and so they did, but when he didn't show up, everybody was relieved, including Paula.

Paula drank too much champagne at the wedding and

ended up sleeping with an oncologist. She dated him for a while after that, but she was finally too weird for him. Though he didn't say so, Paula could tell. She went back to bed when they stopped dating and stayed there until her dad told her to get up, get a job, and that's what she's done ever since—she's had a succession of jobs, a succession of men. She never went back to college.

One of her boyfriends, a graduate student in psychology, suggested that she wouldn't go back because of Johnny. "You can't take the guilt," he said. "You can't afford to be successful." Paula and this boyfriend were having a picnic at the time. Paula put her beer down and stared at him. "You know, that's probably true," she said. Before the picnic, she had thought this graduate student was kind of cute, so earnest; but after that, she didn't think so. She stopped seeing him.

She developed a protective shield around herself, a carapace; this was a word Paula remembered from the days when she used to be an English major, when she used to be smart. When her parents split up, it didn't even bother her that much. She wasn't often home, anyway.

It was Corinne who left Dad. She fell in love with the man who ran the video rental store in the mall where Nails 'N Notions was located. This man's name was Mike Papadopoulos. He was ten years younger than Corinne, and when she was with him, Corinne looked ten years younger herself. They watched movies together on the VCR, and went out to eat a lot.

"Oh, we do everything together," Corinne told Paula. "He talks to me all the time."

"PAPADOPOULOS," DAD SAID GLUMLY. "WHAT KIND OF a name is that?" He sat chain-smoking at a table in his original barbecue restaurant during an off hour, two-thirty, between meals. Waitresses were replenishing the silverware and hot sauce on the checkered tablecloths. Paula sat watching him, a piece of coconut pie before her.

"I loved her so much," Dad said. "I still do, Goddamnit. She could still give it up, all this foolishness, she could come on home. I'd take her back. I told her that on the phone. I said, I'll forget it, forget the whole damn thing. You know what she said? *Nothing doing*, that's what she said. She says there's nothing here for her anymore, it's an empty house as far as she's concerned. An empty house! Can you believe that? That house is full of her crap, that's the God's truth. Everywhere you look, something she bought, something she made. It breaks my heart. I tell you, Paula, it just breaks my heart."

Then he started to cry, Paula's tough old dad, right there in the barbecue restaurant. He cried openly, out loud and with no shame, into a paper napkin. Paula sat watching. She didn't know what to do. Two of the waitresses came running over to hug him and pat his heaving shoulders. Paula could tell they'd done this before. "He's been all tore up," one of them, a big redhead, said confidentially to Paula. After Paula's dad cried for a while, he quit and blew his nose. The waitresses went away. He leaned across the table toward her and asked her point-blank: "So. Paula. Why'd she do it? Whaddaya think?"

"She said he talks to her all the time." Paula couldn't believe she was saying this to her dad.

"Talks to her! What's she got to say, all of a sudden?" He shook his head. He lit another cigarette.

"Eat the pie," he said. "You'll like it."

"I'm not very hungry," Paula said.

"It's good pie," her dad said. "We've got this new woman, she comes in to make them. A very popular item."

Paula got up and walked around the table and hugged him, the way the waitresses had.

"I don't know what happened," he said. "I don't know what to do anymore."

Paula hugged him again and left. About a year after that, the big redheaded waitress, Lena, moved into the house with him.

"He makes me keep everything just like it was," Lena told Paula, who stopped by the restaurant frequently for a sandwich. "He won't let me touch a thing. It's like living in a goddamn museum, I swear." But Lena didn't mind this as much as you'd think, she added. Interior decoration was not her thing. "Besides," she said, "it sure beats the hell out of my former situation." Out of tact, Paula didn't ask Lena what her former situation was. Lena seemed to appreciate her dad, that was the main thing. Lena had a knack for seeing the best in people, the way Drew did.

PAULA GETS OUT OF THE CAR AND SHADES HER EYES, looking toward the screen door. It opens and a man steps out. "Johnny?" Paula says. The sun is still in her eyes. This man is short and wiry, with a brown ponytail and a baseball cap. Not Johnny. The man grins and says, "Hey now." He raises two fingers in a peace sign. Paula is getting confused. Then the door opens again, and this time it's really Johnny, bigger than she remembers, long blond hair bouncing and shining in the sun as he strides through chickens, scattering them across the yard. He picks her up and swings her around and around. "Johnny!" Paula squeals. His mustache tickles her neck. He smells like tobacco and sweat, a workingman's smell. She's dizzy when he lets her go, which is not until Drew says, "Hold it."

"Huh?" Johnny says.

"Hold it right there," Drew says. He stands in front of them with his camera held up to his face. "Got it," he says. Then he steps forward to shake hands.

That picture, when it is printed, will show Paula and Johnny slightly blurred in the foreground, with the aqua-painted cinder-block house and the chickens and the green grass bright and solid behind them, Pete still in the doorway with his hand raised in some strange kind of greeting. Paula and Johnny don't look like brother and sister. Paula looks younger than she is, as if anything could still happen to her. She is pretty in a conventional way, her dark curly hair falling to her shoulders, her face friendly and open. Johnny looks like a lot of things have already happened to him. He looks like he's seen things and been places. Though he grins straight into the camera, his pale blue eyes are serious, ancient, burned clean. Johnny's eyes are the still, dead center of this photograph, despite his strong, healthy-looking body. Muscles bulge under his T-shirt. He has a cocky cowboy stance. He grabs Drew's outstretched hand and shakes it energetically. "Man!" he says. "I'm so glad to see Paula. So who are you, buddy? The boyfriend, am I right?"

Paula can't believe it. Though Johnny has had nothing much to do with their dad for years and years, he still says "Am I right?" just like the old man. The apple never falls far from the tree, as Corinne would say. Johnny hugs Paula with one arm, Drew with the other.

"Actually, your sister and I are engaged to be married," Drew says rather formally, extricating himself.

"No kidding!" Johnny says. "Hey, that's great news!" Now he's clapping Drew hard on the back. "Well then, this here can be your engagement party, how's that? Merry engagement to the happy couple!" He squeezes Paula. "So come on! Come on into my humble abode, honey, I've got somebody I want you to meet."

At Paula's quizzical look, he grins and says, "Hey, don't think you're the only one that can get engaged, baby-cakes. Come on." Paula and Drew stop at the door to be introduced to Pete, the guy in the baseball cap. "Hey now," Pete says. He drains a beer and crushes the can in one hand. Then they're inside, where it's so hot it's stifling and Paula is surprised to see more people. "María!" Johnny yells over the music. But first they have to meet Johnny's partner, Bo, a massive fellow with a blank face and a head too small for his body. Bo wears clean faded jeans and a clean faded work shirt the same color as the jeans. He has a soft sweet look about the eyes. "Paula," Bo says, focusing in on her.

"Low affect, minimal retardation," Drew whispers in Paula's ear. Paula pulls away from him.

"Hello," she says to the man beside Bo, apparently the next person she is supposed to meet, a skinny dangerous-looking guy in a muscle shirt, with tattoos and slicked-back dark hair. He's staring at her. Paula grabs his hand and shakes it. "Hi, I'm Paula," she says, "Johnny's sister."

"Oh yeah?" he says. He's standing too close. He doesn't let go of her hand. For a second, Paula feels like he expects something from her, like she owes him something. Then Johnny is there again, saying, "Uh-oh, you have to watch out for this one, sister, this one's a snake," and the mood is broken. The man smiles and lets go of her hand. The man's name is Dallas.

"Paula, I want you to meet María," Johnny says. He has his arm around a beautiful, giggling Mexican girl, who does a sort of half-bob, half-curtsy to Paula. Paula is embarrassed. The girl's long black hair falls forward over her face. Her jewelry jingles. Her small brown feet are bare.

"*Buenos días*," María says. Johnny whispers something in her ear and she giggles some more, putting her hand up to cover her mouth. Her teeth are terrible, Paula sees when she takes her hand down.

"Say, 'I love Johnny,'" Johnny says to María.

María giggles.

"Come on, say it," Johnny says. "Say, 'I love Johnny.' I'm teaching her English," Johnny tells Paula.

"I love Johnny," María finally says, putting her hand up again.

Then Johnny kisses María, right then and there, in a way that embarrasses Paula even more and makes her feel funny in the pit of her stomach, empty, as if she's lost something. She goes in search of Drew. "*Excuse me*," she says to Dallas, who's blocking the way. Dallas stares at her as he backs up. He raises his beer in a mock salute. The music is very loud, it's old rock, the Eagles.

Paula finds Drew in the kitchen talking to a blond woman who has the biggest breasts Paula has ever seen. Of course she's fat, too, so it doesn't count, or does it? Is Drew attracted to women like this? Is he turned on? The blond woman puffs on a cigarette, leaving a trail of smoke in the air. Paula is surprised. Normally Drew won't accept passive smoke.

He smiles at Paula, looking relieved. "Where've you been?" he asks.

The blond woman turns to Paula. "Honey, I'm Lulu. Pleased to meet you," she says. She has a friendly, worn-looking face with a scar just above her mouth. "How about a drink? I'm having some vodka and tonic myself." There's beer, bourbon, vodka, Cokes, and Hawaiian Punch on the counter, a bag of ice in the sink. The birthday cake on the counter says "Happy Birthday Ann" in neon-pink icing.

"Who's Ann?" Paula asks. "I'm confused. Whose birthday is it?"

Lulu starts laughing. "Honey, it ain't nobody's birthday. It's just a cake."

Drew seems to be sending Paula a signal through the smoke, but she can't figure out what it is.

"I believe I will have some of that vodka," she says, and Lulu pours it over ice in a paper cup.

Now Drew is raising his eyebrows, cocking his head toward the door. Finally he says, "Well, I'd better go out and see how Muddy Waters is doing," but then he hesitates. Maybe he wants Paula to come out with him, too, so they can talk privately. Paula takes a sip of her drink instead. Wow.

"I can tell you how he's doing." Lulu laughs and points out the kitchen window. "He's doing just fine, thank you."

They all look out the window at Muddy Waters, who is humping a skinny mixed-breed bitch with some Irish setter in her.

"Honey, where's the stake-out chain?" Drew is halfway out the door already. He's real particular about who Muddy Waters hangs out with.

"In the floor of the backseat!" Paula yells after him. She takes a cold swallow of vodka and smiles at Lulu. There's a lot to be said for vodka. "It's really okay," Paula says, indicating the dogs. "Muddy Waters has been fixed."

"Fixed," Lulu repeats. She grins. "Honey, you can't fix none of them for good. They don't never get over the *idea* of it, that's the problem."

Lulu and Paula watch Drew chasing Muddy Waters around and around in circles in the yard, raising dust, scattering chickens. "*Come*, Muddy Waters, *come!*" Drew is shouting. But every time Drew gets close enough to grab him, Muddy Waters breaks away. Drew's face grows redder and redder. Then Muddy Waters makes a real break for it, toward the woods, and Drew takes off after him like a man in a cartoon.

"He ought to just leave them be," Lulu says.

Paula sighs. "You don't know Drew."

DREW WAS THE ONE WHO INSISTED ON THE OBEDIENCE classes, not Paula, though Paula was the one who saw Muddy

Waters first in a litter at her friend's house. She brought him home in a cardboard box. Drew was reading the paper. Paula put the box on the carpet in front of him, with the top closed. *Thump! Thump! Thump!* All you could hear was Muddy Waters wagging his tail, banging it against the sides of the cardboard box. Drew folded his paper. "Okay," he said. "I'm game," and then, when she opened the box and Muddy Waters came wagging out, peeing with joy, he was just as smitten as Paula.

"But do you realize what a responsibility a dog is?" Drew asked her later, when it had become clear they could never take him back to his litter. Muddy Waters was noisily asleep in Paula's lap.

"I guess so," Paula said.

Drew shook his head. "I doubt it," he said, "but I love your enthusiasm."

Paula had had several dogs before, including a notoriously screwed-up mutt named Elvis, but Drew had never had one. He went out immediately and bought several dog books, intending to raise Muddy Waters right. He had a chain-link fence built around the backyard, got a doghouse at Lowe's, and ordered a special cedar-chip bed from L. L. Bean. He got a high-tech leash that worked like a tape measure; you could make it any length you wanted to. Muddy Waters had his shots at the vet's, and now he has big heartworm pills to take each month. Drew has put heart-shaped stickers on the calendar so they won't forget. Muddy Waters eats only Science Diet, no scraps. Paula had no idea there was so much to it, having a dog, but she's just as crazy about Muddy Waters as Drew is. Muddy Waters is totally adorable, the way he comes over and puts his head in your lap to be patted, the way he jumps up and down when they get home from work. He's so glad to see them!

Actually, Paula has enjoyed the obedience classes, too, although she hates the teacher's voice, which is very shrill, like Julia Child's. Maybe dogs respond well to it, though, it's like those high-pitched dog whistles. In any case, the teacher's own dog, a border collie named Burt, is amazing: at an inspiring demonstration during the first class, Burt came, sat, lay down, rolled over, barked, heeled, played dead, and fetched. Then the teacher shrieked, "Kennel!" and Burt trotted over and went into a big wire cage, which he appeared to like just fine. All the dog owners in the class applauded Burt's performance, but the puppies were not impressed, lunging back and forth, barking at each other, entangling their owners in their leashes. It seemed obvious to Paula that many of these dogs would *never* be trained, especially a mixed-breed hound named Rocky II, owned by a very thin older couple who couldn't control him at all. They looked hopeless and sad.

The first lesson was Making Eye Contact. "You can't teach your dog anything unless he will make eye contact with you!" the teacher shrilled. To make eye contact, the owners were to hold a dog biscuit up between their eyes and say, "Look! Look!" Drew did this. Paula collapsed in hysterics.

"Come on now, shape up," Drew muttered, with the biscuit between his eyes. It was not clear who he was talking to. But the trick worked. Muddy Waters loved making eye contact. He was great at eye contact. Paula tried it next, and it worked again. To their right, the thin couple's hound would not even glance at his owners but slunk abjectly around on the floor. It was certain he would come to no good end. Muddy Waters made eye contact better than any other dog in the class, and was brought forward as an example to the rest.

"I'm so proud," Drew whispered to Paula as they watched Muddy Waters on the platform with the instructor. "I know this is ridiculous."

But she thought it was sweet. She thought Drew was sweet. She had brought Muddy Waters home from her friend's house not only because he was so cute but also because Drew kept talking about children. Drew wants children. He's almost pathetically interested in all his little nieces and nephews. Paula recognizes this as a good trait in a man, but it scares her. There's a way in which she cannot stand to think about having a child or doing anything else irrevocable, such as grow up. If you have a child, you have to grow up.

Muddy Waters is enough. Training him took up all their extra time and energy for several months. But it was rewarding—Muddy Waters was a model student. The only thing they really had trouble with was his chewing. If they didn't watch him every minute while he was inside, he'd chew something up. Anything—electrical cords, chair legs, dish towels. He was most fond of personal items such as slippers, jockey shorts, and socks. He even chewed up the leather briefcase that Paula gave Drew for his birthday. Reprimanded for this ("No!" in a deep stern voice, "No! No! No!"), Muddy Waters appeared sorrowful at first but then seemed to grin back over his shoulder as he walked away. He was not sincerely repentant. He kept right on eating their things. He also chewed their hands and feet—as if, Paula told Drew, in this way he could get closer and closer to them, as if he could somehow *be* them. He wouldn't quit. He just loved them too much, it seemed.

But then Drew hit upon a method of discipline that appeared to be at least halfway effective, or maybe Muddy Waters was growing out of the chewing stage by then anyway. Drew would grab him by the muzzle and squeeze, shaking his head back and forth. "We don't love with our teeth!" he'd say sternly, maintaining significant eye contact all the while. "*No!* We don't love with our teeth!" Muddy Waters hated to have his head shaken back and forth. He'd sidle away downcast, not grinning. It always worked for a while.

Now Drew finally gets Muddy Waters staked out in the yard, but the other dog, who is free, won't leave him alone. Paula and Lulu, drinking vodka, watch all this through the kitchen window. They are not surprised when Drew, red-faced and sweaty, appears at the door and says, "Whose dog is that?" to Lulu.

"Pete's," Lulu says. "Her name is Raquel Welch."

"Well, let's find Pete, then, and tell him to do something about Raquel." Drew is trying to control himself, Paula can see, but there's a note in his voice he can't help. Behind him, the dogs are humping in the yard.

Lulu takes a swallow of her drink and smiles at him. "Sure," she says. "Pete!" she yells, and then disappears. A minute or so later, there's Pete out in the yard, dragging Raquel away by the collar to a pen where two other dogs are barking.

"Why don't you have a beer?" Paula asks Drew.

"I guess I'd better," he says. He decides to move the stake-out chain into the shade so Muddy Waters won't get too hot. While he's outside, Pete comes back into the kitchen.

"Thanks," Paula tells him. Pete has that same look around the eyes that Johnny does, she notices. She wonders what his story is. Drew comes back in and grabs his beer. "Are those hunting dogs?" he asks Pete.

Pete nods. "Yep," he says. "That little Raquel, she's the best I ever had." Then he tells a long hunting story starring Raquel. Drew listens carefully, nodding. Paula knows he won't say he's opposed to hunting, which he is. Drew is sensible as well as sensitive, a good combination. Johnny comes into the tiny kitchen, still with his arm around María.

"Mom's coming," he tells Paula. "She just called to get more directions."

"With that guy?" Paula asks. "The new one?"

"Yeah." Johnny grins at Paula and the years fall away and *Here's Johnny!* all over again, *Here's Johnny!* just like Ed McMahon used to say, Johnny big as life and twice as handsome as ever, Johnny who stole money and cars and went on credit card sprees across the country, Johnny who wore them all out finally, his whole family . . . *Here's Johnny!* having a party as if he never did any of it, or as if it didn't matter. Maybe it doesn't. Water under the bridge, that's what Corinne would say. Spilled milk. Paula's heart rises up in her chest like a bird.

Johnny smiles at her. "So how've you been?" he asks.

"Pretty good," Paula says. "The same. You know."

"Nice guy," Johnny says, meaning Drew, meaning it. "Are you living with him, or what?"

"Yes," Paula says, and they both laugh. "Or what, I mean. It's mostly or what. He wants to . . . oh, I don't know. You know."

"Yeah," Johnny says.

María looks back and forth between them, smiling, trying to follow the conversation.

"And you?" Paula says. "You look, I don't know, different. *Happy*," she adds.

"Things are good," Johnny says. "They're real good. Hey, watch out now," he says, letting go of María, grabbing three saucers from the stack where Lulu has put them beside the untouched cake. "Watch out, now!" Johnny sends the saucers into the air one by one, juggling them perfectly. María claps her hands.

"You can still do that," Paula says.

"I can still do it." Johnny catches them deftly and puts them back on the counter. "Hey, what's going on? I bet Mom's here." Outside, all the dogs are barking, including Muddy Waters. Johnny pulls María out of the kitchen with him. Maybe they're joined at the hip, Paula thinks.

"How old is María?" Drew asks Pete, after they've gone.

"Sixteen, seventeen maybe. Maybe even eighteen, we can always hope." Pete smiles. "They grow up real fast down there in Mexico."

"How did he meet her?" Paula says.

"It ain't the prettiest story in the world," Pete says, and pauses. Drew and Paula look at him.

"It's okay," Paula says.

Pete leans back against the counter and pops another beer. "Well, me and Johnny was together, actually, the day it happened, so I was right there. I seen it all. I had got a call to go out to this farmer's place outside of Benson to put in some electrical wiring, and it sounded like right much of a project, so I got Johnny to ride out there with me. Him and Bo was between things at the time. So Johnny, he went out there with me, and come to find out this was one of them big-time tobacco operations that hires a lot of migrants. You know how that works?"

Paula shook her head no.

"Well, a farmer like that will hire him a certain number of contractors, they call them, and each contractor will be responsible for hiring a certain number of workers—twenty, say, or even thirty or forty in the camps. Each one of them contractors will have him a camp to run, see, that the farmer gives him. So the contractor is the one that's in charge of getting so many head of workers to the field ever day, see, and running the camp. The farmer pays the contractor, and the contractor pays the workers. Pays them what he feels like, anyway," Pete adds darkly.

"You mean sometimes they don't pay them what they're supposed to," Paula says.

"That's exactly what I mean, little sister. And these damn Mexicans, they're so ignorant, they don't know no better. Or these Negroes that they pick up in the homeless shelters in Miami and bring up there, hell, I've seen them get paid in liquor, in crack, every kind of damn thing. You name it. It's awful what goes on in the world." Pete shakes his head.

"You mean that's the kind of place you went to?" Paula can't believe it. María looks so sweet and so, well, *clean* now.

"It wasn't the worst I've been to, but it wasn't the best, neither. Not by a long shot. It was Mexicans, okay, which is better than Negroes, but it was some sorry setup, let me tell you. They didn't have no bathrooms, no running water, nothing. Nothing but a cookhouse and a row of jerry-built rooms sitting out in the sun in the middle of a field, and it about a hundred degrees in the shade. We was out there to replace this generator that run the whole place. It looked like it had been broke for a while, too, so I don't know what in the hell they had been doing for light or cooking. Anyway, it was the middle of the afternoon, and it was real deserted, everybody out in the fields, or so we think at the time. *So we think*." Pete raises his eyebrows. "The generator is in this hot-as-hell shed by the cookhouse. So we're in there working, and all of a sudden we hear this scream, it made the hair on your arms stand right up. Then there's all this yelling in Mexican, then there's more screams, then there's more yelling. By then Johnny was on his way out there. I tried to stop him. 'Johnny,' I said, 'it ain't none of our business, and besides, it's Mexican.' Johnny just kept on going."

"He always was kind of a cowboy," Paula says.

"No kidding," Pete says. "So I follow him out there, what else can I do? and it's the biggest goddamn mess you ever saw. There's these two guys down in the dirt hollering and going at it, and finally one of them gets on top of the other and bangs his head on the ground for a while. Guy had the hardest damn head in the world. So this goes on. And María, she's standing over there against this ripped-up screen door crying, all wrapped up in a sheet or something. Her nose is bleeding all down the sheet. Finally this guy on the ground starts hollering something over and over in Mexican, I forget what it was, and the guy on top lets him go. The guy on top is a big fat Mexican, and the one he's on is real little, it's a wonder he's still alive but he's a tough little fucker. He gets right up and finishes buttoning his pants and shakes his fist in the air. Then he starts limping off, yelling all the time. The big one stands there breathing heavy and watches him go. 'Well, thank God,' I says to myself, 'that's over.' This shows you how much I know about Mexicans. Because it ain't over by a long shot. Hell, no. The minute the little Mexican gets on down the road a ways, the big one turns around and starts hollering at the girl. Now this confused me, you know. Up to that point, I figured the big one was protecting her. Shit, no. He hauls off and slams her in the stomach, her hollering *mi ayuda* and shit all the time. So she slumps over and kind of falls back through the screen door, and he looks like he's going to hit her again." Pete stops to light a cigarette.

Drew is staring at him. "So what happened then?"

"Johnny was there, of course. Johnny got over there in about a second and cold-cocked him. Big Mexican goes out like a fucking light, big cut on the side of his head. 'Shit,' I says to Johnny, 'you've killed him.' 'I hope to God I have,' Johnny says. Then he's picking the girl up, real gentle-like. 'Johnny,' I tell him, 'you'd better leave that alone.' 'Damn if I will,' he says. So Johnny steps right through the busted screen door and carries her into the room, her crying all the

time, and me following. The big Mexican, he don't say nothing. He just lays on the ground. We get in the room, and it's
hot as an oven in there, no windows, no nothing. Nothing
but a mattress on the floor and cardboard boxes and junk
and clothes strewed all around and a mirror on the wall and
a washbowl on a little table. Johnny looks around as good as
he can, still carrying her. Then he says to me, 'Get her
clothes.' I'm still standing in the doorway. 'Huh?' I say. I
can't believe it. 'Get her clothes,' Johnny says. So I grab a
thing or two, some jeans maybe, but it makes me real nervous to be fooling around in there. You don't want to get
mixed up in nothing Mexican. I said as much to Johnny, but
he was already out the door by then, still carrying her. Her
hair was hanging down over his arm, and he was sort of
patting her and saying little things to her like you would say
to a puppy or something. 'Now Johnny,' I says, 'I have still
got to fix this generator.' 'Fuck the generator,' he says, and
puts her in the truck. Well, I walked over and took a real
close look at the Mexican laying there and I come right on
around to Johnny's way of thinking that maybe we ought
to get on back to the house after all. So we did."

"When did this happen?" Drew asked.

"End of May," Pete says.

Drew shakes his head. It's early September now. "No
legal problems?" he asks.

"None," Pete says. "It turns out that the contractor comes
back with the crew at the end of the day, hauls the big guy

off to the hospital, where they have to operate on his head, and during the course of all this, they come to find out he's wanted in Florida, in the worst kind of way. So he gets his ass extradited, and Johnny gets María. Bingo."

"Bingo," Drew says. Drew and Pete look at each other, and Pete smiles. "I told Johnny, I said, 'The last thing you need, my man, is this little girl out here. This ain't no fucking Montessori school,' I told him, but hey, what can you do? So we got us a day-care situation, after all."

Paula doesn't get it. "Wait a minute," she says. "Who was the big guy? The one Johnny hit?"

"Her brother," Pete says. "He brought her along to do tricks. That happens, with the harvest. There's a lot of that."

"Jesus." The vodka is getting to Paula's brain. But she can recognize her mother's voice now in the other room, that laugh just like a girl's.

And Corinne still looks like a girl, too, or at least she's trying real hard to—but it's a girl of another era, with flame-red lipstick and nails, her blond hair pulled up in back and held by a red bow. She wears white Bermuda shorts and a frilly red blouse with white polka dots on it. Red flats.

"Hi, sweetie," Corinne says, coming in the kitchen to wrap Paula in a cloud of perfume. Paula breathes in deeply, hugging her mother tight, surprised by how glad she is to see her.

Corinne holds Paula out at arm's length and scrutinizes her professionally. "Honey, you look like a million bucks!" she says. "Now where is he?"

"Right here." Paula introduces Corinne to Drew, Drew
to Corinne. Corinne herself does not look like a million
bucks, close up; she's got deep lines around her eyes, and a
scrawny wrinkled chicken neck. Paula wishes Corinne
wouldn't wear so much makeup, but then she's wished this
all her life. She remembers how her mother used to pinch
her cheeks, hard, in the morning as she went out the door
to school. "Let's get some color in those cheeks!" Corinne
would say. It really hurt. But Paula never doubted, not once,
that her mother loved her. Now Corinne is talking to Drew,
very animated. Paula pours some more vodka into her cup
and gets a piece of melting ice from the bag in the sink.
Across her mother's frosted, frizzy hair, Drew makes eye
contact with Paula and shakes his head slightly: *No.* Paula
puts another ice cube into her drink and smiles at him. "Hi,"
she says to the large florid man who has come to stand awkwardly in the door.

"Paula, this is my friend Norell Hubbard," her mother
says. "Everybody, this is Norell." Norell has a wide country
smile; Paula likes him immediately. She has liked all her
mother's boyfriends, even Mike Papadopoulos, the inappropriate young one with the gold chain. Norell looks about
right, to Paula. He wears a short-sleeved blue shirt and a tie
with leaping fish on it.

Corinne drifts over to whisper in Paula's ear, "He can do
anything with his hands. *Anything!* Just wait till you see the
patio!" Paula squeezes Corinne's hand, and they are just

girls together after all, talking about boyfriends. Johnny and
María come in the kitchen then, where Lulu is handing out
cake. Drew looks at Paula in a funny way but she can't be
sure, the vodka is hitting her brain. Whammo! María is giggling, she's very cute. Then Paula and Drew are in the other
room, where the music is very loud, they are talking to Lulu.
Bo is there, too, but he's not talking. Paula isn't sure he can,
come to think of it. Paula starts giggling.

"You know she's pregnant," Lulu says.

"Who?" Paula says.

"*María*," Lulu says. Drew goes grim, like a lawyer in a
soap opera. They all talk some more, and then Drew leads
Paula outside to check on Muddy Waters, who turns out to
be asleep in the shade. Drew pulls Paula to him and hugs her
tight. "Don't drink any more," he says. "You don't have to.
It's all right." Drew is good, good. He understands everything. Paula can feel the beat of his heart through his Izod
shirt. "Okay," she promises.

But then Drew spoils everything by saying, "Of course
she shouldn't be allowed to have that child. Social services
ought to step in, or something. Abortion ought to be man-
datory in a case like this one. It might have anything in the
world wrong with it, diseases, anything. It's probably not
even your brother's child—who knows? Somebody ought
to make her get rid of it."

Paula draws back to look at him. "I can't believe you
really think that," she says.

"Are you kidding? I'm a lawyer. And what chance does that baby have, anyway? I ask you. The child of a mental patient and a retarded Mexican teenager?"

"How do you know she's retarded? I don't think she's retarded. I think she just doesn't know any English, that's all."

"Come on, Paula. Grow up. Do you think these people could take care of a child?"

Paula looks at him. He's so attractive, Drew, those Labrador eyes, that strong chin. He's so perfect. Paula looks at him and her eyes fill with tears. At their feet, Muddy Waters is having a running dream; he makes snuffly noises and jerks his feet in his sleep.

"Let's go now," Drew says. "Let's go home."

But Paula says, "No. I want to go back to the party. Come on, just for a while. Mama just got here."

"Your mama is a piece of work," Drew says, and Paula laughs. "I told you," she says, and they walk back through the weeds to the cinder-block duplex, hand in hand.

But Paula is thinking about the little dark-skinned baby in María's stomach. Why shouldn't Johnny get to have a girlfriend? Why shouldn't Johnny get to have a baby? Why shouldn't Johnny get to have something of his own for once? Inside, the party is getting wild. Lulu is dancing with Dallas, Corinne is dancing with Bo, although Bo mostly just stands there while Corinne dances around him. He looks like he's in a trance. Norell looms in the doorway smiling, watching

Corinne. He adores her, Paula can tell. Then that song is finished and Corinne sails over to hug Norell and say in a stage whisper to everybody, "Well, Norell is *not* perfect. He needs a penis reduction." This joke cracks Drew up.

"Mama!" Paula says. She goes in the kitchen and pours a paper cup full of vodka and drinks it straight down while Drew isn't there to see. Dallas comes in and pushes her against the kitchen wall. "You're hot, aren't you?" he says. "You hot little thing." But Paula ducks under his arm and goes back into the other room, where it's a slow dance and Lulu is dancing with Pete, Johnny with María. Actually, Johnny and María aren't dancing much, they are all wrapped up around each other, it's like the whole rest of the world has fallen away from them. Johnny's eyes are closed and his mouth is pressed into María's thick black hair. You can't see her face.

Corinne comes over and hugs Paula. Corinne's crying. "Look at that," she says. "Just look at that. Aren't they sweet? Isn't it wonderful?"

As soon as her mother says this, Paula is not so sure.

"You know, I always believed Johnny would turn over a new leaf one day," Corinne goes on. "It all goes to show you, if you just keep believing and hoping and praying, everything will come out all right in the end." Paula turns to look at her. Corinne's red bottom lip is quivering. She is utterly sincere. Paula remembers that Corinne has become a churchgoer, that Corinne and Norell go to church. *His church*, Paula guesses, looking at him. Some old church he's attended for thirty years, probably Baptist. Norell stands just outside the door now, talking to Drew about cars. Paula watches Johnny dancing with María, the two of them like a single being, they move to the music in time. Suddenly Paula is filled with an old awful longing, that emptiness she can't name.

"You know what I believe?" Corinne says brightly at her elbow. "Whatever *should* happen, *will* happen!" Corinne goes over to stand beside Norell.

Paula goes back in the kitchen for another drink. But after this one, things get too confusing, and she wouldn't remember much at all about the rest of the party if Drew hadn't taken those pictures.

There will be one of her and Corinne hugging each other around the waist, all smiles. Corinne looks like a Kewpie doll. Paula looks drunk.

There will be one of Corinne and Norell, looking like solid senior citizens, waving good-bye from Norell's big white Lincoln Town Car as they leave. There will be one of Pete passed out in a lawn chair. There will be one of Johnny and María standing close together on the front stoop holding hands and staring solemnly into the camera, both of them wide-eyed, as if they are looking straight into the unimaginable future. There will be one of Johnny by himself with his hands clasped behind his back, like he's in a police lineup. There will be one of Lulu, Paula, and Lena standing in the kitchen, deep in conversation.

Lena! When she comes in the front door carrying a foil-covered tray of barbecue, Paula can't quite place her. She's a big redheaded woman wearing a white uniform. Is she a nurse? Then Lena says, "Hey, sugar," to Paula, and then Paula recognizes her. Nobody else calls Paula "sugar." Paula kind of likes it.

"Hi, Corinne," Lena says to Paula's mother, then introduces herself to Lulu. "Luther couldn't make it, we're catering a Kiwanis cookout in Cary, five hundred people, you can imagine. But he wanted me to bring this over for him. He sends his best," Lena says. "Now where the hell can I put this down?" She's still holding the heavy platter.

Lulu and Corinne spring into action, clearing a space on the tiny counter, Lulu with her cigarette hanging out the side of her mouth. Paula is enjoying the passive smoke, in fact she's enjoying this whole party. This is a terrific party! Lena pulls the tinfoil off the top of the tray, and Paula almost faints, it smells so good. Of course it does, it's famous: Luther's Famous Barbecue. Paula picks up a chunk of barbecue and eats it ravenously. It's delicious. She glances out the window and is surprised to see that it's getting dark. They've been here all afternoon. *Time flies when you're having fun.* Mama used to say this.

But Paula shouldn't make fun of Corinne, not even in her mind. Corinne means well, always did. And Corinne does love Paula, always has, Paula knows this. Of course a mother worries more over the one who's the weakest, the one who has the most trouble. But of course Corinne didn't "spoil" Johnny, as their dad used to accuse her of doing. Paula eats more barbecue. Dad just couldn't understand. He always thought Johnny should "shape up." Dad blamed himself as well as Corinne for Johnny's failure to do this. Dad just had to believe in blame, in fault. Now Paula wonders which is worse, which is more awful to believe in, fault or chance? Which is scarier to consider? Finally, Corinne has refused to believe in either one. She likes to look on the bright side, as she says. Tears come to Paula's eyes. She loves her mother's dumb little red shoes.

"Plates!" Lena calls, and Lulu says wait a minute, she'll go get some. Lulu disappears out the back door. Paula wishes she lived here, too, with Johnny and María and Pete and Lulu and Bo, it's like a big happy family. Everybody taking care of everybody else. Lulu comes back with some paper plates with Santa Claus on them.

"Come and get it!" she yells.

Paula moves away from the barbecue as everybody else crowds into the kitchen. She's already stuffed. Norell and Pete and Bo and Drew pile up heaping plates—barbecue, hush puppies, slaw. They eat standing up.

"I get so sick of barbecue!" Lena says. "I mean, it gets old, you know what I mean? No thanks, hon. Thanks anyway," Lena says as Lulu hands her a plate. "I got a chick filet at McDonald's on the way out here." Lena lights a cigarette.

Paula finishes off somebody's abandoned drink. Bourbon. There's a lot to be said for bourbon. Drew and Pete are having a serious conversation about the plight of migrant workers. Johnny and María are feeding each other bits of food with their fingers, off a single plate. Corinne and Lena are talking about issues of health in the friendliest manner you can think of. Paula finds this amazing, considering the circumstances. Or maybe it's not, considering her mother. "I may have to have an operation," her mother is saying. "I have these very close veins? See right here, on the inside of my thigh?" Lena bends down to look.

Paula goes back through the house to the bathroom, walking carefully. You have to watch out how you put your feet. The bathroom sobers her up, though. It's a mess, looks like it hasn't been cleaned in weeks. María really *is* a child, Paula realizes. Paula looks under the sink and finds an old can of Comet, which has solidified. She bangs it against the sink to loosen it, then sprinkles some in the sink. With a ragged gray washcloth, she scrubs the sink, then the tub, then finally the toilet. Then the bathroom door opens and Dallas comes in, his dark eyes wide.

"Hey, hey, *hey*!" he says, in the act of unzipping his fly.

Before Paula can think, he closes the door behind him and comes toward her, all in one motion. He takes the can of Comet from her and sets it on the sink and kisses her, hard but somehow slow, as if this kiss is inevitable and perfectly natural, as if they've got all the time in the world. Paula kisses him back. His mouth tastes like tobacco, like bourbon—wild and sweet.

"Paula? Paula, are you in there?" Drew is banging on the door, but Paula doesn't do a thing. She *wants* Dallas to put his hand on her breast, she wants to feel him get hard against her leg.

Drew pushes the door open. He looks at them and grabs her arm. "Paula, we're leaving now," he says.

"Let go of me!" Paula can hardly breathe.

Drew speaks very carefully, as if to a child. "We have to go now," he says. "I'm going now to put the dog in the car. Then we'll go," he says, pulling her along.

"Okay," Paula says.

"Later," Dallas says, pinching her butt. But it's just friendly, it doesn't mean anything, just as the kiss didn't mean anything to him, either. Dallas will come on to anybody, Paula realizes. It's what he does.

"Later," Paula throws back over her shoulder.

In the living room, Johnny is dancing alone, eyes closed. María sits on the couch beside Corinne, who is trying to tell her something. Corinne apparently feels that the way to communicate with somebody who speaks only Spanish when you don't speak Spanish is to use plenty of gestures and move your mouth a lot. "When eez the baby due?" Corinne asks María, who smiles and shrugs. Paula starts laughing. Johnny turns in the middle of the floor. Paula goes over to him and taps him on the shoulder.

"Roger," she says, "can I have this dance?" He opens his eyes and grins at her. He takes her in his arms and guides her across the floor. Out of the corner of her eye, Paula sees Drew in the doorway, holding Muddy Waters on a tight leash. Johnny dips her. "Have you got a minute?" Johnny says into her ear. "I want to show you something."

"Where is it?" Paula looks back at the door, but now Drew is engaged in conversation with Norell, who is patting Muddy Waters.

"Out back in my workshop," Johnny says. "It'll only take a minute."

"He can't have that!" Drew is saying to Norell, who is feeding Muddy Waters some barbecue. "He's not allowed to eat that!" Muddy Waters loves the barbecue.

"Come on." Johnny pulls on Paula's arm.

But Paula hesitates, nervous about Drew. It occurs to her that he might really leave her, that nobody could blame him if he did. Johnny twirls her around and around and Paula closes her eyes and loses herself in the dance and when she opens her eyes she sees Drew looking at her hard in a new way, as if they have just met. "In a minute," she tells Johnny, still watching Drew, and then she just can't believe it when Drew winks at her and puts his own plate down on the floor to give Muddy Waters some more barbecue. "Okay," Paula says. She and Johnny go through the kitchen and out the back door. Pete has passed out on the lawn chair. The dogs in the pen start barking. "How far is it?" Paula asks.

"It's not far. It's here." Johnny opens a door, pulls a hanging light cord, and leads her inside the shed.

"Oh, Johnny." This is all she can say. The slanted roof of the shed slopes up to a height well above Johnny's head on the far wall, where plywood has been painted white and then entirely covered by tiny, tiny writing and drawings. Paula steps closer. She sees clocks, lots of clocks, but the numbers are all different from those on real clocks. Beautiful little birds fly through the sentences. Paula squints to read. One little sentence says, *The sons of the spirit wear rainbow armor.* Paula closes her eyes. "Well?" Johnny says at her elbow. "Whaddaya think?" Paula thinks he has stopped taking his medicine. She thinks it is happening again. "See, this is a new kind of book," Johnny says. Paula opens her eyes and reads, *They ride the horses of dawn.* "I think it's beautiful," she says.

Then Lulu is at the door. "Honey, your boyfriend wants you in the worst possible way," she says to Paula. "Far out, huh?" Lulu indicates the shed wall. Paula notices the blank space at the lower right. Johnny hasn't finished it yet. He's still working on it.

"Far out," Paula repeats.

Paula and Johnny walk back through the weeds arm in arm. The party is breaking up. Corinne and Norell have already left—the big white car is gone. Bo stands silhouetted in the yellow light of the doorway, motionless as a tree. "Honey?" Lulu says, poking Pete. Dallas rides his motorcycle off down the driveway in a red roar, going God knows where. Paula can still taste his kiss. Drew is already in the Volvo, she sees, and Muddy Waters is already in the back. In a few minutes Drew will drive her away from here, and in a few months they will get married, and sometime after that they will have a baby. Paula sees all this written out in tiny sentences on a big wall in her mind. A little wind comes up and the trees blow and the weeds swirl around her feet. It's going to storm. It will be nice to ride home in the rain with Drew, Paula likes how the windshield wipers go in the rain, she'll hold his hand all the way. Maybe she'll fix him some scrambled eggs when they get home. Johnny hugs her. "Thanks for coming to my party," he says. "I wanted you to come." They are old, old souls, Roger and Darling. They know each other. "Listen," Paula says sincerely, "it was a great party. I wouldn't have missed it for the world." Then the first big drops of rain hit her face, and she runs for the car just as the thunder cracks and lightning pierces the sky like an arrow.

ABOUT THE AUTHOR

LEE SMITH is the author of fifteen works of fiction, including *Oral History, Fair and Tender Ladies,* and her recent *Mrs. Darcy and the Blue-Eyed Stranger.* She has received many awards, including the North Carolina Award for Literature and an Academy Award in Literature from the American Academy of Arts and Letters; her novel *The Last Girls* was a *New York Times* bestseller as well as winner of the Southern Book Critics Circle Award. She lives in North Carolina.